The Measure of Katie Calloway

∽ A NOVEL ∾

SERENA MILLER

Revell

a division of Baker Publishing Group
Grand Rapids, Michigan

© 2011 by Serena Miller

Published by Revell
a division of Baker Publishing Group
P.O. Box 6287, Grand Rapids, MI 49516-6287
www.revellbooks.com

Printed in the United States of America

Library of Congress Cataloging-in-Publication Data
Miller, Serena, 1950–
    The measure of Katie Calloway : a novel / Serena Miller.
      p. cm.
    ISBN 978-0-8007-1998-2 (pbk.)
    1. Title.
  PS3613.I55295M43 2011
  813'.6—dc23
                                             2011020354

11   12   13   14   15   16   17   7   6   5   4   3   2   1

To Lyle Edgar Bonzo—sawyer and woodsman.

God hath not given us the spirit of fear; but of power, and of love, and of a sound mind.

2 Timothy 1:7

1

September 18, 1867

A drop of rain seeped through the sodden roof of the Georgia cabin where Katie Calloway lay. The raindrop fell on her bare foot—a small, welcome kiss on her bruised and battered body.

She had survived another night.

Maybe there was a God in heaven after all.

Katie eased her head to one side, hoping not to awaken her husband, but her caution was unnecessary. Harlan was gone. Thank God.

And yet, this struck her as odd—it was rare for him to leave without first demanding breakfast. But she didn't dwell on the fact. She was too grateful that he was no longer lying next to her. Limp with relief, she inched her body off the ancient feather-tick mattress, grimacing from the pain. Harlan had been roaring drunk when he staggered home last night. With all her heart, she hoped that her eight-year-old brother, Ned, had not heard the blows she had silently endured.

A note lay on the rickety bedside table. She reached for it, stifling a groan at the pain. Her eyes squinted as she tried to read the note in the dark cabin. There had been a time in her life when she would have lit a candle without a second thought, but candles were scarce these days. She seldom used one unless

Harlan demanded it. In semi-darkness, she carried the scrap of paper outside the cabin into the faint, early morning light.

To her surprise, it said that Harlan would be spending the day in an adjoining county visiting relatives. The note was written in careful, well-penned words. This, too, was strange. It was not Harlan's habit to be so thoughtful as to give her a hint where he was going, let alone to leave her a message.

As she pondered this, she traced the spiky penmanship with her finger. There was a light mist falling. The paper had grown damp, and the homemade pokeberry ink smeared when she touched it. In a sudden fit of anger, she rubbed at the words until they were a purple blur. With all her heart, she wished that she could erase her bond to Harlan as easily.

Ever since he had returned from what he called the War of Yankee Aggression, he had treated her—born and reared in the North—as though she were the enemy. He even enjoyed taunting her about the fact that her father and brother, both valiant Union soldiers, were lying in the ground.

Tears welled in her eyes, and she roughly dashed them away. Grieving would not bring her loved ones back, nor would it make her life any easier. It was wiser to focus on caring for the brother she had left.

Her mother, a world away in Pennsylvania, had taken to her bed over the loss of her husband and oldest son and had never again arisen. A courageous member of her parents' church had made the trip South, bringing Katie's precious little brother to her after her mother willed her soul to flee this earth.

Harlan was furious over this small addition to their household. He had not been pleased with having another Yankee under his roof, even if that Yankee was only a child.

In the distance, she heard her two Jersey milk cows bawling for relief from swollen udders. She threw the crumpled note into the ashes of the fireplace, donned her old choring dress, grabbed her tin milk pails, and limped through the autumn drizzle to the barn. She would use the fresh milk to make a thick mush of cornmeal for Ned's breakfast. It was a luxury to have a full bag of cornmeal—a luxury she would never again take for granted.

If nothing else, Mr. Lincoln's war had taught her that hunger burns and gnaws until even she, a gently reared minister's daughter, could wring a stray chicken's neck and gut the carcass with as much gleeful anticipation as she had once opened a box of chocolates.

Unfortunately, Harlan had also learned things during the war. Things he enjoyed describing in bone-chilling whispers in her ear at night. A large, powerful man, he had fought in hand-to-hand combat and often boasted that he had enjoyed it.

Now, with only the three of them living in the cramped overseer's cabin and with no servants as witnesses, Harlan's anger toward her seemed to know no bounds. She had hoped and prayed things would change, but Harlan possessed a streak of brutality so broad and deep she marveled at the fact that he had ever managed to sweep her off her feet.

Frequently, she thought of the many choices once open to her. There was a time, a weary lifetime ago, when she had been extraordinarily pretty—at least that was what she had been told. Many sweet boys in her home county had come courting. None had interested her. Instead, she had caught the attention of her brother's dashing friend from West Point—the sole heir of Fallen Oaks Plantation.

Her head had been filled with romantic notions about the life of a plantation mistress. Harlan, at six foot two, with golden hair and a perfect physique, had been stunning in his West Point uniform. At seventeen—fool that she was—she had been incapable of seeing past that uniform. Dazzled by his veneer of well-born Southern gentility, she had not seen the cruelty buried within.

"I'm coming. I'm coming," she mumbled as she hurried along the path to the ramshackle barn.

Although their plantation house lay in ruins, this barn, the small overseer's cabin, and a few slave shacks had been overlooked during General Sherman's slash-and-burn march to the sea. She had hidden away, deep within the forest along with the pitiful remnants of their livestock, watching her home go up in flames while Sherman and his men stormed through Georgia, ruthlessly cutting a wide swath of destruction, breaking the back of the Southern rebellion.

Surviving the devastation had almost broken her back as well. By the time Lee surrendered at Appomattox, she was so sick of war and deprivation that she no longer cared how things ended—just as long as they did.

And yet the end of Mr. Lincoln's war had brought no cessation of struggle to her life. Within one week of her husband's return, the beatings had begun. Discovering that his ancestral home had been burned to the ground had pushed Harlan into a dark fury that never left except on those nights when he passed out, benumbed by alcohol.

For reasons she could not comprehend, he equated the fact that she had been born a Yankee with having everything to do with his losses. Harlan couldn't be convinced, no matter how hard she tried, that there had been no more chance of deflecting Sherman's men from their grim purpose than one could have of holding back the ocean. He threw at her apocryphal accounts of brave Southern women facing down Union soldiers, shaming the invaders into leaving their precious homes alone.

From what she could tell, he also held her accountable for failing to stem the tide of slaves who had melted away—abandoning Fallen Oaks in the days after he rode off to fight a war to keep them enslaved.

For a while, she had been pleased that she had managed to save two cows and a few bedraggled chickens by hiding in the forest as Sherman's men rampaged through the countryside. With little to work with, she had tried hard to make the overseer's cabin habitable, but Harlan had been disgusted with her pitiful attempts to have a home waiting for him when he returned from war.

As she squatted on a stool, resting her forehead against the Jersey's warm belly, a fateful slant of light drew her attention to a thin wire she had never seen before. It was attached to the end of a loose board on the bench where she always set the heavy buckets after finishing the milking. Following that wire upwards, she saw that it was attached to a massive oak beam balanced ever-so-carefully directly above where she always stood while straining the milk.

The hair on the back of her neck prickled. So *that* was why Harlan had left before dawn—to have the privacy to set up the final blow to her body. Her knees grew weak as her mind tried to wrap itself around the realization that her husband intended to kill her.

Once her breathing returned to normal, she chided herself for her shock. After the way he had treated her, why should she be surprised? No doubt he had hoped to discover her body here today, the barely discernible wire easily removed and himself a handsome widower.

Harlan frequently informed her while spewing venom about her failure to produce an heir for the crumbled Calloway throne that lonely war widows now filled the countryside—women who would be happy to welcome him into their homes and beds. If it weren't for her.

He was right, of course. The war had wiped out an entire generation of Southern men. She often caught local women casting envious glances at her virile, living husband. Two were still mistresses of intact, if moldering, mansions—homes that had somehow escaped Sherman's notice.

They would be welcome to him.

She found herself almost envious of her own former slaves. *They* were now free, but there would be no war fought to emancipate her.

It was futile to even think about petitioning the courts for a divorce. Locals considered Harlan a war hero. Judges would laugh at any accusations that she, a Yankee, might make against her husband.

Deep down she knew, without accepting the fact until this moment, that the only way she would ever get out of this miserable marriage was if one of them died. Obviously, Harlan had decided it would be her.

He would get by with it too. The Calloway name alone would protect him in this county. It always had.

Her father's words came to mind—the ones with which he had tried to dissuade her from the headstrong decision to marry her brother's fascinating friend. Marriage, her father had advised her, wasn't like choosing a dress pattern that could be discarded when she tired of it. Marriage was forever. Marriage was for life.

"That's what I'm afraid of, Papa," she spoke into the chilly autumn air. "I'm afraid I won't *have* a life if I stay with Harlan."

Hurriedly, she stripped milk from the cows' udders while frantically casting about for a plan. She knew that Harlan would never think to take care of their animals—something he considered a slave's job—or, barring slaves, *her* job. Carefully stepping around the wire, she drove the cows into the larger pasture beside the river, dumped the milk into the lone hog's trough, and left the gate open so the poor thing could get out and root for itself.

Then she remembered her flock of chickens shut up for the night in the weasel-tight chicken coop. They wouldn't survive if she didn't release them. She wrenched open the door and pounded on the roof, frightening the biddies and startling the rooster, who strutted, slightly befuddled, out into the morning drizzle.

Bruises and aches forgotten, she ran to the house.

"Ned!" she yelled as she burst through the door.

Her brother's tousled brown hair and dark eyes peered over the loft. "Yes, ma'am?"

"Get dressed. We're leaving."

"But . . ." His eyes went wide with fear.

"Harlan is gone. We have to go."

The look of hope and relief on his freckled face made her want to weep. Although she tried to protect her little brother, Ned had also experienced the sting of Harlan's hand.

She began stuffing her few clothes into a sack and stopped. What was she doing? There was no time to pack. In spite of the note, there was no telling when Harlan would be home. Releasing the animals had taken time she didn't have. They had to move fast.

She pulled on her "good" black dress, now worn and rusty. Then she jerked on a pair of Harlan's britches beneath her dress, rolled up the pant legs, and cinched the waist with a piece of twine. She tied on a black bonnet and dug her threadbare cape out of the closet.

Now, all they needed was food. And money.

She swallowed hard. There *was* money in the cabin. Harlan's money. Funds he had received for selling two hundred acres on the back side of the plantation. If she took it, he would follow her to the ends of the earth to punish her.

If she didn't take it, he would follow her anyway.

Visions of that heavy oak beam swam before her eyes as she pulled a box from beneath the bed and took out a pouch of silver coins.

This was the money he planned to use to get Fallen Oaks back on a paying basis again—land he had once ridden over like a young prince. His boasts were empty, of course. Without slaves, Fallen Oaks would never thrive. It would never again be the well-manicured Eden into which she had ridden as a young bride. She knew these coins would be used to buy strong drink until the money was gone.

She secreted the coin pouch, along with a hastily wrapped chunk of cheese and two small loaves of bread, in her cape pockets without the slightest pinprick of conscience. She had earned the money many times over, and she had made the bread and cheese with her own hands. She could buy or scavenge what she needed later. With any luck, Harlan wouldn't be home until after dark. Hopefully, she had hours ahead of her in which to escape.

And she wasn't going on foot.

Harlan had made the mistake of leaving behind Rebel's Pride, the horse that had safely carried him through four years of war. Rebel was fast, well-rested, and had the endurance of an ox. It was she who fed and curried him, she whom he nuzzled for windfall apples.

Ned's weight combined with hers was half of Harlan's, and she and her brother rode well. Her father, who had loved horses almost as much as he had loved his church and children, had made certain of that. This fine horse would carry them far.

"Harlan will kill us for this," Ned said as she saddled up.

"He'll have to catch us first." She gave the saddle an extra cinch and swung her leg over Rebel's back. There was no way she was going to ride sidesaddle on this trip. Wearing Harlan's britches beneath her clothing had been a decision calculated for endurance, not style. She had lost all vanity long ago.

From on top of the powerful gelding, with an autumn rain now pelting her, she surveyed the home she was leaving. The mansion was a pile of burnt timber. Every treasured material possession she ever had was gone. The cabin in which they now lived was a sagging wreck.

The only thing she regretted abandoning was her meager livestock and the crops planted with her own hands. The yams would be ready to dig soon. The winter squash needed to be put in the root cellar.

But she would not be the one doing it. She was sick of the South. Sick of Georgia. Sick of rationalizing the slavery that had supported her husband's family. She was especially sick of enduring her husband's anger. Like the slaves who had left Fallen Oaks before her, she was headed North—and God help the man or woman who tried to stop her.

She reached a hand down to Ned and hoisted him up. "Let's ride, little brother."

2

Come all young men, and you attend,
and listen to the counsel of a friend.
If you ever seek another land,
don't ever come to Michigan.

"Don't Come to Michigan"
—1800s shanty song

Bay City, Michigan
October 5, 1867

The massive locomotive moaned as the brakeman slowed the iron monster to a reluctant, huffing crawl. As the train came to a full, shuddering stop, Katie peered past her brother through the soot-filmed window at the street scene beside them. Buggies, horses, and pedestrians vied with street vendors. Women with fluffy plumage attached to brightly colored hats walked about in small gossipy groups. Ferocious-looking men bearing axes, with sacks slung across their backs, strode across the sawdust-covered roads. She saw what appeared to be an Indian wearing buckskin and entering a general store.

This bustling city was a different world from the war-ravaged country from which Ned and she had fled, hiding in haystacks and empty barns until they could access a railroad. Determined to put as many miles as possible between Harlan and herself, she rode the train as far north as the tracks went. This was, in every way, the end of the line for her.

"That horse reminds me of Rebel's Pride." Ned pointed at a sturdy gray gelding. "Do you suppose Rebel is all right?"

"The man we sold him to seemed kind," Katie said.

"Rebel was a good horse."

"He saved our lives."

Parting with that valiant animal had just about killed her, but she had sold him the minute she could access a train going north. A locomotive was so much faster than a horse, and there couldn't be enough speed to take her away from Harlan.

The travel-weary occupants of the train came to life around her, collecting their bundles while Katie gathered her courage to face the grim reality of her decision to flee to this raw town.

She knew no one here. There would be no support from any quarter.

It was exactly as she had planned.

During those long hours on the back of Rebel's Pride, she had come to the conclusion that the best way to escape her husband's vengeance was to do the exact opposite of what he might expect—even if it meant cutting herself off from the remnants of her own blood relatives. Her cousins' modest homes in Pennsylvania would be the first place Harlan would look, and there was always the possibility that, seduced by the façade of his practiced charm, they would turn her over to him. It had certainly blinded *her* at one time.

No—it would be dangerous to rely on anyone except herself. Survival rested entirely in her own two hands.

She glanced down at those hands. Unlike the other women on the train, she wore no gloves. Once elegant, her hands were now calloused and rough. Her knuckles wore permanent scars from scrubbing Harlan's lye soap–soaked clothes. She closed her eyes, remembering how he had stood over her, making her wash those clothes over and over again until her hands had bled. Harlan liked to look good.

She brushed at the skirt of her dress. Cinders from the engine had scorched small holes in it.

"We'll be all right." Ned looked up at her—already trying to be a man. "I'll take good care of you."

"Of course you will." Her heart melted with love for the boy. "We'll take good care of each other."

Once again, she looked out the window at the unfamiliar scene. What had she done? This was such an alien place. For a moment, her heart failed her.

"We're the only ones who are still on the train," Ned pointed out.

"You're right." She squared her shoulders. "It's time to begin our new life."

She had prayed long hours as the train swayed over hills and valleys, begging God to show her the way to provide for their needs when her remaining coins were gone. She had prayed so many times before, when Harlan had been hurting her, that her faith was quite low, but a smidgen had begun to return with each mile that took her farther from her husband. With all her heart she prayed that God would lead her to honest work and make it possible for her to care for her brother. Nothing would be too hard. Nothing would be beneath her. At twenty-eight she was as strong as she would ever be. She would do whatever it took.

In spite of all she had endured, she felt a lifting of spirits as they stepped off the train into this bustling city. She was no longer the shy, innocent girl who had said yes the moment Harlan Calloway had proposed marriage. Her struggle with shyness had faded along with the bruises. Whatever it took, no matter how hard she had to work—she would survive.

"I want a beefsteak. Rare," Robert Foster instructed. "And vegetables that aren't boiled to a pulp. I'd like them sometime this week if you can manage it."

"Yes, sir." The waiter scurried off. From what Robert could tell, the man was both waiter and proprietor. As the restaurant filled up, he noticed other patrons becoming impatient as well. He wondered if there was anyone in the kitchen besides the unkempt woman he had glimpsed. From the way the two bickered, he assumed they were husband and wife. He had some sympathy for the couple. With Michigan turning into the lumber capital of the world, Bay City was a busy town, and it was difficult to find good help.

He picked up a fork and absentmindedly drew numbers onto the white tablecloth. The spring river drive had been a nightmare. Logjams had backed up the Saginaw River and its tributaries for miles. Many peaveys, one of the most expensive tools a lumber boss provided, had been jerked out of the drivers' hands into the swirling waters. Valuable logs had been lost as the river sprawled out into the surrounding areas, dumping precious timber far from the stream when the waters subsided. He had needed to put down two of the camp's mules because of hoof rot.

Even though the price for lumber was holding high, he had managed to do little more than break even. If his luck didn't change this coming season, everything he had invested to establish an independent lumber company would be lost. He would be cutting timber for someone else for a living.

His father, who had run lumber camps in Maine, had made it look easy. It wasn't. Owning a lumber camp involved one worrisome detail after another. Still, it was better than the years he had spent in the Union army.

He had been at Gettysburg.

He shoved the memory of that nightmare away. Much better

the clean, frozen forests of Michigan, where he owned the rights to 680 acres of the finest timber he had ever seen.

A young woman entering the restaurant with what appeared to be a son caught his attention. Her shabby dress was plain black like her bonnet, and there were a few holes burned into the skirt—he suspected from train cinders. Her cape was threadbare, and a corner of it was torn, but the unfashionable clothing didn't mask the graceful lines of the woman's figure. He wondered if she was yet another war widow. There were so many these days, eking out starvation livings on backwoods farms.

The woman and boy stopped as they entered, as though unsure of what to do next. In spite of the obvious poverty, there was a simple dignity about them.

The pair distracted him for only a moment before the endless march of numbers began to once again crawl across his brain. Board feet, payroll, tonnage of fodder, teamsters carrying flour, salt pork, and dozens of other supplies. Making the numbers balance out was like a vicious game of chance playing in his head day and night.

The biggest headache he had right now was the loss of his camp cook. Old Jigger, a scrawny, scrappy man, had challenged the biggest woodsman in the saloon to a brawl. A busted nose and broken right arm later, Jigger had learned his lesson, and the lumber camp was in need of a new cook—at least until Jigger could once again heft fifty-pound sacks of flour and thirty-pound cast-iron Dutch ovens.

Without a decent cook, Robert didn't have a prayer of attracting the skilled woodsmen who made life so much easier for a camp owner. These knights of the woods could choose any lumber company they wanted—and the ones they wanted to work for were those with the best food. Unfortunately, good camp cooks were as scarce as hens' teeth. Finding someone willing to live in a damp log shanty in the middle of the deep woods seven months out of the year while shoveling out food for thirty or more hungry men was not an easy task.

Without a good cook, he would be ruined.

The woman and boy seated themselves at the table next to him, once again distracting him from his worries. He noticed that they were carrying only two small bundles.

"Just water, if you don't mind . . ." the woman said when the waiter came for their order.

He could tell she had intended to say more, but the waiter hurried off before she could finish. The boy looked around the room with open curiosity. "Have we enough money for a sandwich, sister?"

"We do," she answered, "but I don't want to spend it here. We'll find a store soon and get some crackers and cheese. Best to fill your belly with water while I try to talk to the owner. It appears they are understaffed. I'm feeling hopeful."

"Tell him I'm a hard worker too," the boy said.

"Yes, you are." She smiled at the boy, and Robert was taken aback. The woman, in spite of her unattractive garb, was exquisite. A heart-shaped face and dark blue eyes fringed with long, dark lashes. A tendril of copper-colored hair peeped out from beneath her nondescript bonnet. He glanced at her work-roughened hands. She was wearing no wedding ring, but of course, many farm wives couldn't afford one.

His meal arrived and was shoved beneath his nose. The beefsteak was overcooked. His potatoes and carrots boiled to a near mush. It was futile to send the food back to the kitchen. Considering the way the restaurant was filling up, there was a good chance it would be another hour before he would see anything edible again. Resigned, he toyed with the food, trying to force himself to eat it. He reminded himself that he had endured much worse in the war.

The waiter put glasses of water on the table in front of the woman and boy. "I'll be needing this table soon," he said pointedly. "For paying customers."

The woman flinched at his words. "I didn't come here to eat or drink. I wanted to see if you might be in need of some hired help." She swallowed hard. "I'm—I'm handy in the kitchen."

Robert laid his knife down and folded his arms. This was getting interesting. He expected the man to jump at the offer.

"Sorry." The waiter glanced at the kitchen door apprehensively. "My wife doesn't like anyone else in her kitchen. We prefer to take care of things by ourselves."

"I understand." The woman lowered her gaze. "Thank you anyway."

The waiter hurried back to the kitchen.

"Let's leave, Ned," she whispered. "I'll look for work somewhere else."

"Excuse me." Robert's curiosity got the better of him. "Where are you good folks from?"

A look passed between the woman and boy.

"Ohio." The woman's astonishing blue eyes narrowed with suspicion.

"Are you going to be in Bay City long?"

Again the look passed between the woman and the boy.

"If I can find work."

"What sort of work are you looking for?"

"Anything respectable." The tone of her voice informed him that her morals would not be compromised. "I can clean. I can do laundry, and"—her chin, which he noticed had a tiny cleft, lifted a quarter inch—"I'm a good cook."

He knew he couldn't be so lucky. Even if she was telling the truth, there was little chance she would want to work in a lumber camp. The few women who did were usually wives of the owner or foreman. Still, those work-roughened hands told him that the woman wasn't allergic to hard labor. And he was desperate enough to take a chance on a complete stranger.

Robert turned to the boy. "Is she a good cook?"

"The best." The boy's eyes were innocent and without guile. "Just like our mother."

"Are you married, ma'am?"

She gave a small shake of her head.

"Widowed?"

She hesitated then nodded.

A widow, just as he suspected. It explained a lot. The woman probably had a farm she couldn't keep up, and the hope of something better in town had drawn them here. It happened.

In spite of his earlier gloom, his mood lifted at the possibilities. If this woman truly was a good cook, and if she was willing to live in the deep woods for a few months—that *plus* the novelty of a beautiful young widow living in camp would attract some of the finest woodsmen in the business. Women were scarce in the north woods. Beautiful young women were even scarcer. The men would travel miles on foot just to get a glimpse of her. The fortunes of his camp might hinge on this one woman.

Of course, he had no intention of firing Jigger. The old, seasoned cook would stay. Even with a broken arm, Jigger could teach her plenty about lumber camp cooking. The boy was not a problem. Many camps employed "chore boys" to fetch and carry, and this one seemed sturdy enough to at least tote a bucket of water.

"I'm curious, ma'am," he said. "What is your specialty? As a cook, I mean."

She pursed her lips while she thought. He noticed they were full and well-formed.

"I make an excellent apple pie, sir."

Apple pie. He hadn't had a decent apple pie in months.

Suddenly, he was ravenous for one. He waved the owner over. "Do you have any fresh apples in your kitchen?"

"Yes."

"Flour? Lard?"

"Of course."

"If the lady is willing, I'll pay you the equivalent of ten meals if you can talk your wife into allowing this woman access to your kitchen for the next two hours to make one apple pie. If she makes it to my satisfaction"—he glanced her way—"I'm going to offer her a job."

"Ten meals?"

"Yes."

"For one apple pie and the use of an oven?"

"That's my offer."

"Come along with me," the waiter said to the woman. "I'll talk to my wife."

She stood, her forehead creased in puzzlement. "You have a job for me?"

"Yes," Robert said. "If you're as good a cook as you say."

He saw desperation warring with integrity in her eyes.

"Is this a respectable job?"

"Very respectable, but very hard work."

Again the small lift of her chin. "I am not afraid of hard work." She turned to her brother. "You be a good boy while I'm gone."

"Yes, ma'am."

The boy drained his water glass and then looked around the room, eyeing the various diners and their food.

"Do you want this?" Robert pushed the plate of overcooked food away from him. "Bring your bags over to this table. You can eat while we wait, if you want. It'll make the owner happy if we leave that table to other customers."

The boy obediently moved their belongings. Robert noticed

that his homemade britches were several inches too short. Even though the meal was unappetizing, the boy bowed his head and silently gave thanks, then methodically polished off the food.

"Is your sister truly a good cook, or were you just saying that because she was here?"

"She's very good." The boy laid the knife across his empty plate. "When she has something to cook with." His clear-eyed gaze spoke volumes.

This boy and his sister had known hunger. Perhaps, if things worked out, they would not have to experience it again. At least they wouldn't if he could stay in business.

3

She's tall and slim, her hair is red,
her face is plump and pretty.
She's my daisy Sunday best-day girl,
and her front name stands for Kitty.
          "Bung Yer Eye, Boy"
          —1800s shanty song

It was not easy preparing food in another woman's kitchen while that other woman scowled, but Katie managed to find the necessary ingredients and a clear space to lay out her supplies.

It felt good after all she had been through to fall into the comforting rhythm of slicing apples and rolling out pie dough. Unlike Harlan, she had not come from a wealthy family. Her father had ministered to a church outside of Pittsburgh while running a small horse farm. Her mother had been a gifted gardener and an intuitive cook.

Although there had never been an abundance of money, there had always been plenty of food in their home. Her mother had managed to fill her family's bellies with tasty meals, and as a minister's wife, she hosted frequent guests at their table. She had taken care to teach Katie everything she knew.

For the first time since she had run for her life, Katie felt a measure of peace just being inside this heat-filled kitchen. She reached for the tin of cinnamon and sprinkled it over the tart apples. Then she added just enough sugar to offset the tartness, yet not enough to make the pie sticky sweet. Several pats of good butter to melt over the apples. She was delighted to find two lemons in a bowl and scored a few strips of zest into the mixture as a small surprise to the tongue. After contemplating the height of the pie, she decided to create a fancy latticework for the crust. If this man truly had a job for her, she wanted to do everything possible to impress him.

Fortunately, the oven was already heated. In slightly over one hour from the time she entered the kitchen, she pulled a golden-brown apple pie out of the stove.

"Thank you," she said to the woman as she folded two dish-cloths into heat-resisting pads and carried the still-sizzling pie through the customers to the table where her brother now sat. The waiter brought a dessert dish and a serving knife to the table.

"It looks delicious." The man eyed the pie hungrily. His dark brown hair was cut short, and unlike most of the men she saw here in the restaurant, he was clean-shaven.

"It should cool first," she said.

"I don't care." He cut a large wedge and slipped it onto his plate.

She stood, waiting, as he blew on a forkful of pie, still so hot it was dripping butter. He put it into his mouth and chewed. He closed his eyes, and a low moan escaped his lips. Then he ate another bite, rolling it around in his mouth. He swallowed and sighed with pleasure.

She felt a thrill shoot through her body at his obvious enjoyment. It had been a long time since Harlan had acknowledged her cooking with anything more than a grunt.

In the meantime, she saw the harassed waiter fending off orders from other patrons for apple pie—which he didn't have.

She waited for the man to compliment her on the pie. Instead, he cut a thick piece and laid it in front of her brother, saying, "Eat."

Then he tipped back in his chair and gave her a calculating look.

"I'll give you two dollars a day to cook at my lumber camp. The boy will get a nickel a day to keep the wood box filled and do any other chores you might have for him. You'll have a private room inside the cook shanty. It won't be fancy, but I'll have one of the men build you a private privy."

He let her absorb all this while he wolfed down another piece of pie. Her mind struggled to grasp the fact that the man was offering her two dollars a day! That was more than a good male laborer made back home—those few who could find work.

"You might go months without seeing another woman." He wiped his mouth with a napkin. "There is no town nearer than a hard day's ride on horseback. My camp is well run. I'll make certain you're safe and that the men treat you with respect. If you think you can abide those conditions, I'll pay you two weeks' salary in advance. You'll need it to purchase enough warm clothing for you and the boy to survive the next seven months."

His speech finished, the man tucked back into his pie.

Shocked, she plumped down into the seat beside him, her mind whirling. If the good Lord had picked her up and set her down on the other side of the moon, she couldn't have been more surprised. This was so much better than she had dared hope. Even the isolation of the camp would be a gift from God—a perfect place to hide from Harlan.

"What is your name, sir?" she asked.

The man glanced up from his pie, which he seemed intent on consuming in one sitting. "Robert Foster at your service."

His eyes, she noticed, were a light hazel rimmed with black. His lashes were thick and dark. They were handsome eyes, but she didn't give a fig about the man's looks. Harlan had been the

26

most handsome man she had ever known. No, it was kindness that she was looking for, and it was kindness she saw there.

"And your name, ma'am?"

It occurred to her that it would be a mistake to give her real name. She cast about for a made-up name. Unfortunately, she wasn't good at lying, and her mind went blank. Then her eyes caught on a Smith Brothers Cough Drop advertisement on the wall.

"Smith," she said. "My name is Katie Smith. And this is my brother, Ned."

"It's good to meet you."

She felt so guilty about lying that she expected Mr. Foster to see straight through her—ferreting out the lie she had told about her name, seeing the still-living husband looming in the background. She held her breath, waiting for him to withdraw his offer.

Instead, he seemed impatient to be finished with their conversation. He plucked his bowler hat from a vacant chair. "Do we have a deal, Katie Smith?"

She released her breath. The job was hers. She had no idea if she could trust the man or not, but she needed a job and she *was* a good cook.

Two dollars a day! She made some quick calculations. For seven months of work, she would receive nearly four hundred dollars! It was a staggering amount of money.

"Yes, sir. We have a deal."

"My men call me Robert, and you will too." He laid thirty Union greenbacks on the table in front of her. "The hotel across from here is clean and safe. You should be able to do the shopping you need to do this afternoon. I'll come for you with the supply wagon tomorrow morning at dawn."

"But tomorrow is the Sabbath."

"The men will start showing up by Monday evening. Some

may already be there. I'm already behind schedule. It will take us the bigger part of two days to get there. If we start early tomorrow, we might be at the camp in time to feed them. I hope you won't change your mind. I'm depending on you."

"I won't change my mind," she said. "You have my word."

He stared hard at her, as though evaluating her.

"Your word is good enough for me." He paid up, set his bowler hat firmly on his head, and departed, leaving one slice of pie untouched. She wondered if he had known she was hungry and had deliberately left it behind for her. She doubted that Robert or any other man would be so thoughtful. In spite of the kindness she had read in his eyes, her faith in men was not high.

It occurred to her that she had just agreed to live in the middle of the woods with a camp full of them. Goodness.

She picked up her brother's fork and took a bite straight from the pie plate. Yes, the pie had turned out very well.

"Do you trust that man?" her brother asked.

"No. I don't trust anyone except you and me." She laid her hand over his. "But we will work hard for Mr. Foster. I don't want him to regret his decision to hire us."

Ned toyed with his napkin, avoiding her gaze. "Will you ever marry again?"

"No." The question shook her. "I'm still legally bound to Harlan."

"But what if he dies?"

The idea of Harlan dying had never crossed her mind. He had made it unscathed through four years of war. He seemed immortal. But even if he did, she would never remarry. Never again would she give another man control over her mind and body. Never again would she put herself through seeing the disgust on a man's face each month when he found out she was not with child.

"No." She shook her head. "Never."

28

Her brother released a sigh. "I'm glad." He captured a stray crumb and licked it off his finger. "You lied to Mr. Foster. More than once."

"I know." She folded up the money he had given her and tucked it deep into a pocket of her cape. "I'm sorry I had to do that."

"Aren't you afraid of going to hell?"

She gave his question the weight it deserved. "I think that is where I have been for a very long time."

⁓

Harlan stared at the massive beam balanced above where Katherine set her milk pails every morning and evening. The beam—balanced just so—was heavy enough to crush her. The death he had arranged would have appeared to be an accident. Now that she was gone, he was in legal purgatory. No wife, but no legal right to remarry.

This was highly inconvenient. There was only one way out of the heinous poverty in which he found himself. Carrie Sherwood, a local widow, had managed to hang on to a few loyal servants and was reported to be quite wealthy. Her elderly husband had possessed the foresight to invest in Northern textile mills before the war. That woman's money, which would be under his control were they to marry—would help him turn Fallen Oaks back into the paradise it had been before Sherman destroyed it.

The problem he had was that he knew absolutely that Carrie would never consent to marry him until he was, in truth, a grieving widower.

It was imperative that he find Katherine, bring her back here, make his terrible "grief" a reality, and accept the rich woman's condolences very soon.

He had not fought a war only to come home and live like a pauper.

4

Then he took me to cook camp
and rigged me out neat:
an old stove and two kettles,
a full rig complete.

> *"Budd Lake Plains"*
> —*1800s shanty song*

"We're staying in a hotel?" Ned asked as they left the restaurant. "Isn't that expensive?"

Katie fingered the greenbacks folded into her pocket and wondered if Robert Foster would truly come for them tomorrow morning. Or would he change his mind and ask for his money back?

As she hesitated on the crowded wooden sidewalk, someone accidentally bumped into her. She found herself thrust against a bejeweled and heavily powdered woman whom she almost knocked down.

"I'm so sorry!" She grabbed the woman's arm to steady her.

"Oh, that's all right, honey." The woman winked, and Katie saw that she was older than she had first thought. "This isn't the first time I've been knocked around."

Katie caught her breath. Although she was certain the woman

didn't mean anything by what she said, the words still cut to the core of her own experience.

"You all right?" The woman peered at her. "You look kinda pale."

It was strange, Katie thought, to hear such common words coming from such a well-dressed personage. The bustled dress was watered purple silk, the gloves immaculate white, the large diamond earrings dazzling in the bright sun.

The woman looked as though she could have presided over one of the finest pre-war mansions in the South—except that the colors of her clothing were a mite loud, and the sound of her voice a bit coarse, and her décolleté a little too revealing.

"I—I'm all right," Katie said.

"Are you new in town, honey?"

"We just got off the train."

The woman's eyes swept her up and down. "You looking for work?"

"I was."

"I got a place over on Water Street. Real nice. Classy joint. I can always use another good worker. I pay good too. We could find a place for the boy—maybe helping out in the kitchen."

"Really?" Katie was stunned. Her gamble in coming to this busy town had been inspired. Two job offers in one day! Things were certainly different in the North.

"Some of my clients would pay big money for a pretty little redhead like you." She glanced down at the bundle Katie held. "Of course we'd have to do something with those hands of yours. Our clientele don't fancy rough hands."

Katie gaped as the woman's meaning became clear. She ran a bordello and was offering her a job as a—a . . .

"Oh, honey." The woman smiled. "Now I've gone and shocked you. I'm sorry. There was just something in your eyes that made me think you've been through some rough times

31

your own self. A lot of girls who come to work for me have that beaten-down look. My mistake." She shrugged, but her eyes were calculating. "Of course, if you'd like to come on over to Water Street, you could rest your feet and we could discuss things over a nice cup of tea."

The words, spoken in a grandmotherly voice, felt like a slap.

"Hello, Delia," a cool, masculine voice spoke up. "You aren't trying to hire Mrs. Smith away from me, now are you?"

Katie whipped around and saw Robert Foster standing beside her. A cigar was clenched between his teeth.

"Long time no see, Foster. Where you been keeping yourself?" Delia rocked back on her heels and smiled up at him as though she were an old friend. "This girl is working for you?" She gave a great belly laugh. "I can't see *her* bucksawing logs."

He glanced at Katie and removed his hat. "Mrs. Smith, let me introduce you to Miss Delia Flowers. She runs one of Bay City's better known houses of . . ." He looked at Ned and scratched his head as he searched for a proper word. "Ill repute."

"Ill repute?" Delia scowled. "I resent that. My place is classy."

"And I resent you lifting a year's worth of paid labor off my men each time the spring river drive comes in."

"They get their money's worth."

Robert took the half-chewed cigar from his mouth. "No, Delia. They don't. Half of them end up drugged and rolled for every nickel they've got."

Delia's face turned red. "Not at my place." Her fists clenched.

It was an odd thing, Katie thought, to see such lovely clothes on a woman who appeared willing and able to engage in fisticuffs with Robert right on the spot.

Again Robert glanced down at Ned, who was watching the scene with rapt attention.

"A truce for now, Delia. Please." He dropped his cigar and ground it out with the heel of his boot. "Mrs. Smith is my new camp cook. A respectable widow from Ohio who, no doubt, has just been shocked right down to her toes by your offer."

"Not as shocked as you might think." Delia looked at her, assessing her like a prime side of beef. "But Mrs. Smith might have to get a lot hungrier before she accepts my offer."

Katie was mortified and concerned for Ned. She considered putting her hands over his ears. And eyes.

"Come along, Mrs. Smith." Robert took her elbow and firmly steered her away from the angry prostitute.

Delia fired one final shot as they walked away. "You'll work like a slave in that camp, honey. You'll get up at two in the morning to make breakfast for a bunch of stinking shanty boys. You'll put in sixteen hours of hard labor before you fall into bed each night. Then you'll do it all over again. Day after day. For two measly dollars a day. At my house you'd sleep till noon and other people would cook for *you*!"

"I think I'd better accompany you to the hotel before someone else tries to hire you away from me," Robert said as Delia's voice faded.

"Was that woman . . . serious?"

"Yes. Being a camp cook is hard work."

"No, I mean about . . ." She swallowed hard. "About . . . that other thing."

"She was dead serious. Michigan is the lumber capital of the world. Loggers are arriving from all over."

"But I would never, ever . . ."

"I know."

"But . . ."

"Don't let Delia get to you." He gripped her elbow more tightly. "Let's just get you safely settled in the hotel. It might be best if I made you a list of things you'll need. It'll make your shopping go faster. You only have a few hours before the stores close, and as I said, we leave at dawn."

33

⁓

"You hired a dad-blamed *woman*?" The wiry old man was so furious he was shaking. His sparse gray beard trembled in indignation.

Robert hadn't seen this coming. He had forgotten just how territorial Jigger could be about the cook shanty, which he ruled with an iron fist. It had been foolish to hire another cook without factoring in the old man's pride.

"I had no choice. You aren't fit." He glanced around the tiny room that was situated above one of Bay City's many saloons. Jigger had once again managed to spend an entire season's pay in one glorious and ill-conceived splurge after finishing the spring log drive. Even though he was past seventy, he had fought and sung his way through all the dives of Bay City, challenging men twice his size to battle. Now, he was broke both physically and financially and had been living on Robert's generosity ever since May, waiting for October when he could go back and preside over the cook shanty again.

It was a feast or famine mentality that most loggers possessed and which Robert understood only too well. The work was hard, the dangers great, the pleasures few. Most of the shanty boys, the term with which loggers referred to themselves, spent every dime they made within two or three weeks after the spring river drive—mainly, in Robert's opinion, from sheer relief that they were still alive.

Robert didn't indulge in the shanty boys' three "B's"—bars, brawls, and brothels—something Bay City was entirely too quick to provide. He had responsibilities, a business to run, and two children to support.

"I don't need a stupid woman cluttering up my kitchen." Jigger spit a stream of tobacco juice at a clay spittoon sitting in the corner—and missed. "I still got me one good arm." He wiped his mouth with the back of his hand.

"Which you will *use* to help Mrs. Smith learn the ropes of cooking for thirty men."

"I ain't gonna to teach her nothin', except . . ." Jigger wriggled his bushy eyebrows.

Robert bristled. "She's a decent woman. A widow. You'll treat her with respect or you will be working in some haywire camp so quick it'll make your head swim—if you can find one to hire you."

The leer on Jigger's face was replaced by sober reflection. No one wanted to work at a haywire camp. The term had been coined because of the wire teamsters saved from the bundles of hay they shook out for their horses and oxen. Too much haywire holding things together meant a badly run camp and probably a dangerous one. Owners of haywire camps were so desperate that they sometimes kidnapped shanty boys and forced them to work at gunpoint.

"I could find work somewhere else besides a haywire camp."

"Not with a broken arm, and you're not getting any younger."

Jigger scowled. "I've *forgotten* more about feeding hungry men than most camp cooks learn in a lifetime."

"You were one of the best."

"Were?" Jigger's voice rose in indignation. "Were?" He rose to his full height, which came to Robert's chin. "I'll have you know that I can still run faster, spit farther, jump higher, and belch louder than any sorry-eyed shanty boy in the business!"

Robert smiled inwardly. He had hoped to rile Jigger enough to keep him sober until they got back to camp.

"Pull yourself together, Jigger. I need you. The woman I hired will make your work easier—that's all."

"She won't be boss cook?"

Robert considered. "Not unless you want her to be."

"I'll still be the boss?"

"You'll rule the roost—as long as you treat her with respect."

35

"I'd never lay a hand on a respectable woman, you know that. Neither would any of the rest of the boys."

"I'm counting on it. Now help me check over the provisions I've ordered. We're leaving tomorrow morning."

The old cook drew himself up with dignity, a broken-down racehorse anxious to get back to the track. Jigger knew the lumber business inside and out, and he knew how to cook for a crew of hungry men. It was about all he knew, but he knew it well.

"I'll pack up my turkey." The old man dredged a worn feed sack from beneath the sagging bed. "You're gonna need me real bad if all you got is a dad-blamed woman workin' in the kitchen."

—◦◦—

With some trepidation, Katie perused the list Robert had written out for her. She had not bought so many things since she had gathered her bridal trousseau, and that had taken her months. Now, she had exactly five hours.

"You're growing so fast," she said as Ned and she walked down the plank sidewalk. "We'll need to purchase two pairs of boots to get you through the winter. Longer pants and a heavy coat as well."

"Mr. Foster said he'll be paying me too," Ned boasted. "Can I buy a pocketknife?"

"A boy with his own job definitely deserves a pocketknife." Katie glanced at her list again.

Ned opened his mouth to thank her, but she threw her arm across his chest and shoved him flat against the nearest building. Someone she had hoped never to lay eyes on again was just ahead. It was Harlan, walking with that distinctive walk, that strut that told everyone he was king of all he surveyed. His shoulders were broad, and he had strong, muscular arms that could send a woman or child flying against a wall.

She shrank against the side of the building, melting into the shadows. She and Ned could still run, could still get away.

"What's wrong?" Ned asked.

"It's Harlan." Her finger at her lips, she motioned for him to be quiet. Her heart thudded against her chest so hard she could hear it drumming in her ears. She nodded toward the man she knew to be her husband—the husband from whom she had stolen money.

The man stopped to look at something in a display window. His profile was strong and pronounced.

Except it wasn't Harlan.

Harlan's nose had been chiseled and perfectly formed. This man's nose was hooked and bulbous. Where Harlan's jaw had been strong, this man's was ordinary.

"Thank you, Jesus," she whispered.

"That's not Harlan," Ned pointed out, "if that's who you were thinking."

"I know." Her knees felt weak. "It did look like him, though, didn't it?" She had to ask: "Didn't you think it looked like him?"

She feared the stress of the past two years had made her start seeing things. Was she going to mistake every other man she saw for her husband?

"Maybe a little." Ned didn't sound convinced.

A high-pitched wail split the air. The eerie sound, following so closely upon the heels of seeing "Harlan," startled her. The wail was followed by another and then another.

"What *is* that?" Ned grasped her hand. "It sounds like someone screaming."

"I believe it's a sawmill. While he was making out our shopping list, Mr. Foster informed me that there are over a hundred operating near here."

"Oh," Ned said as they began to walk again. "It smells different here too, don't you think?"

Katie breathed in a lungful of the lake-fresh air. The air did smell different here. Spicy, clean, invigorating. So different from the humid, heavy scent of rotting vegetation that had hung over her decaying home in Georgia.

"That's newly cut pine," she said. "You're too young to remember, but Father once had some pine trees cut off our farm. I recognize the smell."

Ned's upturned nose sniffed the air with appreciation. "I like it."

"I do too." She had noticed that the same clean, piney scent had also clung to Robert.

"Is this one of the stores we're supposed to go in?" Ned asked.

She stopped and stood back a few feet to read the lettering on the giant building. "Jennison Mercantile. Yes, I believe it is."

As they entered the store, she once again checked the long list Robert had given her. It was quite overwhelming. Woolen gloves, boots, woolen stockings, three woolen blankets apiece, woolen underwear, heavy woolen coat . . . heavens! How cold did it get in Michigan, anyway? It appeared that she was going to be spending the next seven months swathed in wool. Her skin itched at the mere thought.

"Can I help you?" The pretty clerk appeared to be about Katie's age and had a smile that immediately put her at ease.

"Yes. I will be cooking for a lumber camp this winter." Katie felt a measure of pride just saying the words. "It will take me a while to gather everything together."

"I'm in no hurry." The girl gestured toward the well-stocked shelves. "I'll help you with anything I can."

It had been years since Katie had seen so much merchandise in one place. In the front of the store there were bolts of lovely calico in several different patterns. She checked the price—three cents per yard. Very reasonable. It had been so long since she had owned a new dress that she was tempted to buy yards and yards of each color. Outing flannel in many different colors sat beside a wealth of percales. She fingered the material, loving the feel and smell of new cloth.

This riot of colors after the grayness of the past few years was a salve to her soul.

Embroidery threads, different kinds of laces, multicolored silk and taffeta ribbons, all displayed like jewels on wooden spools. She stared at them, in awe that there were still so many colors in the world.

"Were you looking for embroidery supplies?" the clerk asked. "We have some new designs in the back."

"No, no," Katie said. "I was just admiring your stock. I'm afraid I won't have time for embroidery."

She noticed heavy black hosiery for only ten cents a pair. It would be wise, she decided, to purchase several. She could double up for warmth.

"We have children's shoes with copper toes to keep them from wearing out," the clerk said. "And we have a nice selection of handkerchiefs—only five cents each, not to mention these lovely calf-skin women's gloves."

Katie ran a finger over the gloves. They were as soft as butter. But perhaps not practical for someone who would be cooking for a lumber camp.

There were ready-made flannel nightgowns for sale as well as underwear in red and white flannel. Fleece-lined men's coats, suspenders, and hats. Trunks of different sizes and shapes.

The choices dazzled Katie. She was looking through some woolen blankets when Ned tugged on her sleeve.

"Can I look at the knives now?"

Katie motioned to the clerk. "My brother would like to see your pocketknife selection. Do you mind?"

The girl brought out a display case, which captured Ned's rapt attention.

As Katie sorted through the blankets, the bell over the door rang. She looked up to see Delia entering. The clerk glanced in Delia's direction, frowned, turned her back, and began discussing the knife display with Ned with much more interest than she had previously shown.

Delia sauntered over to Katie. "Are you really going out to the pineries?"

Katie had hoped never to see this woman again, but her mother had taught her to be polite under all circumstances, regardless of people's occupations. She supposed her mother's training still applied—even with someone like Delia.

"I am."

The fancy woman winked. "Not going to take me up on my offer, then?"

"Th-thanks." Katie didn't want to have this conversation with Delia. "But no."

"I understand." Delia shrugged and then ran a hand over the woolen blankets. "Would you mind some advice?"

"What kind?" It came out sounding more suspicious than she intended.

"Oh, honey. Don't worry. I know lots of things that won't offend your delicate ears. For instance, all this wool will itch a tender-skinned redhead like you half to death. You'd better purchase some thick cotton long johns to protect your skin, or you'll never make it through the winter."

That made sense.

"And don't forget to take plenty of flannel . . ." Delia glanced at Ned and lowered her voice. "Red might be your best choice. You know . . . for pads."

"Pads?"

"There's no privacy in a camp. The men will be seeing your most private laundry. If you take enough cloth, you can just burn it in your stove each month. Or if you need, you can hang it on the line with the rest of the laundry without announcing to the camp that it's your time of the month. I'd take enough to last for all winter, if I were you."

"I will." Katie was struck by the sheer common sense of Delia's suggestion. "Thank you so much."

Katie glanced over at Ned. He appeared to have narrowed his choices down to two favorites and was now chewing his lower lip trying to decide.

"And don't forget a chamber pot," Delia said. "As cold as it gets, you'll definitely need that."

"Mr. Foster said I would have my own private privy."

"That's nice of him," Delia purred. "But you'll freeze your tail off going to the outhouse at night in the middle of January."

"Of course." Katie was again grateful for Delia's suggestion. "You're absolutely right."

"You really are a lamb, aren't you?" Delia looked at her with pity. "You have no idea what you're getting yourself into."

"Not really." Katie was already intimidated enough by the need to outfit Ned and herself on such short notice. She didn't need someone pointing out her ignorance. She lifted her chin in defiance. "But I do know how to cook."

"Oh, you'll cook, all right." Delia laughed. "You'll cook until you can't stand up. You'll cook until you wish you had never seen a skillet or a stove." She glanced over her shoulder at the salesclerk. "Won't she, Julia?"

The clerk turned away without speaking and began to vigorously dust shelves. Delia glanced at the clerk's rigid back. Her smile faltered, and her face fell into world-weary creases. In spite of the expensive jewelry glinting at her ears and throat, Katie caught a glimpse of the desperate life the older woman had lived.

"Julia here used to work for me, you know," Delia said, a little too loudly. "I took her in when she was sick. Nursed her back to health." She straightened her spine, as though sloughing off the deliberate slight. "Now she acts like she don't know me."

"I appreciate your help." Katie was uncomfortable with the animosity filling the room. "Thank you."

"Robert Foster is one of the better operators to work for." Delia turned her attention back to Katie. "He runs a clean camp. But if you find out that you can't make it out in the woods, come to my place on Water Street and I'll give you a job. There's another girl at my place who looks a lot like you. Same coloring. She does real well for herself."

"I won't be working for you, Delia."

"There's not many options for a woman who's alone." Delia patted her on the cheek. "You might be real glad to know old Delia before it's all over."

She shot a venomous glance at the salesclerk before swishing out. The door jangled, and then a strained silence descended upon the store.

"I wish we could keep her from coming in here," the salesclerk said. "I don't care how desperate you get, take my advice and don't you go near that place of hers."

Katie cast a glance at Ned, who was looking at some small axes over in a corner of the hardware section. She hoped the little boy hadn't picked up on their conversation.

"Is it true you worked for her?"

"Not like she means." The salesclerk blushed. "I helped out by cooking and cleaning until I could get on my feet. That section of Water Street is called 'Hell's Half Mile' and with good reason—sometimes loggers go in there and they don't come out alive. They have secret tunnels beneath the place where Delia and her girls work. It's called the Catacombs, and those tunnels lead down to the lake."

"What on earth for?"

"For one thing—the better to dispose of a body."

"You're not serious!"

"Those loggers come in from the woods with a nice fat payroll in their pocket. Sometimes the bartender will put something in a shanty boy's drink to make him pass out. Then the girls steal his money and he wakes up back out on the street—if he's lucky."

"Delia does this?"

"She's not as bad as the others, but she's definitely no saint."

"Why doesn't anyone do anything about it?"

"I can't prove it"—the girl looked over her shoulder—"but I think even the sheriff is in on it. No one is ever arrested for anything that goes on in the Catacombs."

Katie shook her head in dismay. There was nothing she could do about the situation, and time was rushing by. She still had much shopping to do, or she would be going into the woods even more unprepared than she already was.

"I guess I'll be needing a bolt of red flannel," Katie said, "and a chamber pot. And some cotton blankets and long johns." She paused for a moment, considering the display of items. "I'd better go ahead and buy one of those trunks too."

"Of course." The girl was suddenly all business, as though nothing of importance had been said between them. "I'll start writing things up."

Ned had been so preoccupied with his pocketknife that he had missed the entire conversation, for which Katie was grateful. He clicked the selected knife open and shut. "See?" he asked. "It's like the one Papa used to have."

"Yes, it is. Good choice."

She hoped that her own choice in coming to this wild town was as good.

5

We have big swamps covered with brakes
and they're alive with rattlesnakes.
They lie awake, do all they can
to bite the folks of Michigan.
> *"Don't Come to Michigan"*
> *—1800s shanty song*

October 7, 1867

The wagon lurched over the rough road, nearly unseating Robert's new cook. She held onto the seat with one hand and grasped her brother's shirt with the other as though to protect Ned from falling overboard.

But she didn't complain.

In fact, she hadn't complained about anything—not the rough road, nor the beans and hardtack from which they had made their few meals. She hadn't even complained about the fact that all Jigger had done so far was scowl, stare at her, and spit tobacco juice.

Robert had half a mind to fire the old man, except Jigger had been feeding shanty boys ever since the Maine woods—when all the camps consisted of were a primitive shanty in which the men slept, cooked, and ate. Jigger's only "stove" for most of his working life had been nothing more than a huge fire pit of sand placed in the middle of the sleeping shanty upon which he had roasted meat on spits and baked everything from biscuits to pies to gallons of baked beans in giant cast-iron Dutch ovens that he buried in the hot sand.

Things were much more modern now. Jigger complained that younger camp cooks had gone soft because of all the modern conveniences. He mourned the fact that no one knew how to "cook in the sand" anymore. But it was 1867, the Civil War was over, and times were changing. The country—at least the North—was experiencing some prosperity. With amusement, Robert noticed that Jigger didn't refuse to use the wood cook-stove they had lugged into camp last spring. In fact, it seemed to have become Jigger's pride and joy.

Unfortunately, Jigger had gotten to an age when Robert doubted the man's arm would ever heal enough to be a force in the cookhouse. And he feared that Jigger was getting slack in the cleanliness department too. It would take only one partially chewed wad of tobacco discovered in a pot of stew to send some of the men scurrying off to a better camp. Of course, there were others who would probably dredge it out and not care.

A woman cook would be a nice change. She would bring her own standards to the cook shanty and keep Jigger on his toes. The fact that she was pleasant to look at didn't hurt one bit.

The shanty boys were a breed all to themselves and they had their own strict code of ethics. Hellions when they descended upon a town after the river drive was over, they managed to be gentlemen to the women whom they deemed respectable. He predicted that they would treat Katie Smith like a lady, and if the rest of her cooking was as tasty as the pie he had sampled, she would be downright revered.

If they didn't treat her with respect, they wouldn't have a job.

It had been a rough trip, but nothing Robert hadn't expected. He made a mental note to have a few swampers, men with axes

45

and grub hoes, level some of the worst places on the tote road. With all the food the men put down, he would need several more wagonloads of supplies before winter.

His lumberman's eye expertly surveyed the forest through which they were traveling. Old growth oak and hickory lifted lofty branches high above their heads. Most of the multicolored leaves had fallen, providing a damp, variegated carpet over which the hooves of Robert's horse trampled.

The hardwood forests were beautiful but useless except as firewood for the camps. The gold that he and other lumbermen craved was pine—the ancient white pine that soared as high as two hundred feet and were often as thick as six feet in diameter at the base. The finest pine the world had ever seen had been recently discovered right here in Saginaw Valley.

It was only the white pine logs that floated down the rivers as buoyant as corks. It was only the beautiful, knotless white pine that cut like butter when fed to the hungry saws waiting at the mouth of the Saginaw River. It was white pine that was rebuilding the nation as Civil War veterans returned to jobs and homes and reconstructed their lives.

With limitless white pine forests spreading across hundreds of thousands of acres of Michigan—no one wanted to take the time to cut and drag out the hardwoods. The oaks, maples, and hickory trees were too heavy to float down the rivers. The dense logs dragged along the bottom, created logjams, and caused problems at the mills.

White pine was king.

The 680-acre section he owned would keep his camp occupied for the rest of this winter if he could keep the men fed, healthy, and content enough to stay with him. Hopefully, he would have enough profit left at the end of this coming spring's log drive to purchase logging rights to another section or two. The government charged $1.25 per acre for the land upon which the magnificent pines stood. It was hard to lose money at rates like that—but when you were a small operator with a lot of overhead, it was more of a struggle.

Again he glanced at Katie. Her back was rigid as she rode on the hard bench beside the teamster. He hoped she wouldn't take one look at his primitive camp and demand to be taken straight back to town. He didn't think she would. That rod-straight spine impressed him. Had she been a soldier under his command, he would have judged her to be one upon whom he could depend.

His plan when they reached camp was to have Jigger stay in the bunkhouse with the men and give up his room at the back of the cook's shanty to Katie and her brother. Robert had been waiting for the right moment to break this news. It would not sit well with the old cook.

"I'm sorry," Katie called out. "But could we please stop for a moment?"

They were the first words she had spoken for the past three hours.

"Stop the mules," Robert commanded as he reined back his horse.

Sam, the teamster, silently managed to make his mules come to a full stop, but Robert knew it was a struggle for the man. Like most teamsters, Sam could cuss out a team for a solid half hour without using the same four-letter word twice.

Jigger, sitting in the back of the wagon atop a box of supplies, shook his head as Katie clambered out of the wagon and hurried into the woods.

"That woman has to go every five minutes," Jigger said. He emphasized his contempt by aiming a stream of tobacco juice at a tree.

"We've been on the road three hours, Jigger. It's time to rest the mules anyway."

"You don't see *me* needing to go every three hours."

47

"Leave it alone, Jigger." Robert was not interested in continuing this conversation and tried to cut it off. "Women are just different."

"That's my point. A lumber camp ain't no place for 'em."

The mules snatched at a few blades of the sparse grass while Sam took the opportunity to light a short, stubby pipe the loggers called a "nose warmer." The smell of strong pipe tobacco filled the air.

Sam was, to Robert's best recollection, not usually so quiet. Robert was guessing that Sam, unsure of his ability to converse without cussing, had chosen the better route of keeping his mouth shut while Katie rode beside him.

If that was the effect Katie would have on the men, so be it. He wouldn't mind the men cleaning up their language. Besides, the less a shanty boy talked, the harder he worked.

He couldn't help but wonder what thoughts were going through Katie's head as she rode into the wilds with three men who were strangers to her—the oldest of whom was making his resentment of her quite obvious.

While Katie was in the woods, Ned climbed off the wagon and occupied himself throwing twigs against a tree. He, too, had not complained about the trip. Robert couldn't help compare Ned's stalwart attitude with that of his own daughter, who would have been pitching a fit by now.

Not for the first time, he found himself wishing things had turned out differently. Had his wife lived, he wouldn't have had to leave his children with his sister—a woman who, no matter how hard he tried, he had never particularly liked. He was afraid her attitude was rubbing off on both of his children, but he didn't know what to do about it. They were fed, clothed, safe, and had access to school in town. It would not be wise to bring them into the woods with him.

As Katie came out of the forest, he noticed that she looked

longingly at his black mare—as though she wished she could ride it instead of sitting in the wagon.

"Thank you, gentlemen," she said with dignity as she returned to her seat. Sam clucked his tongue at the mules to get them to move. Robert hid a smile at the teamster's obvious discomfort.

"At this rate, we'll *never* get to camp," Jigger grouched.

Katie did not respond to Jigger's remark, but she held her head a bit higher as the wagon rattled down the rough trail.

Watching the old man and the young woman, Robert hoped his impetuous move in hiring her hadn't been a mistake. Every dime he owned was riding on this venture. If Katie and Jigger couldn't establish a working relationship and start turning out good food, the crew would shoulder their axes and walk through the woods to a smoother-operating camp. It was that simple.

With all his heart, Robert hoped his two cooks would smooth out the friction between them. Failure was something he could not afford. Failure was something none of them could afford.

—ᏋᎾ—

Katie hoped they would get to the camp soon. It was embarrassing having to have these three men wait on her while she hid herself behind a tree. She hoped that Robert would make good on his promise to make sure she had her own private privy. Hopefully, it would be tucked away behind another outbuilding where the men wouldn't be able to see her trotting back and forth. Bodily functions were best kept private.

She looked around at the hardwood forest pressing in on her. Never in her life had she imagined there could be so many trees. They had traveled for hours without a break in the dense woods. Pennsylvania, where she had grown up, was fairly settled. There were woods, but nowhere a person could ride for a day without seeing a farm or village. Georgia was much the same. But Michigan was a wilderness. There was a primeval feel that increased with every mile they traveled—an ancient darkness that felt like a brooding presence.

Practically every woman she knew would be appalled by this trip. And yet she was grateful. Every step into the dense forest took her one more step away from Harlan's temper. Every step made her feel less weighed down with worry. Harlan would never, ever think to look for her in this out-of-the-way place.

"We're here." Robert nodded toward a clearing.

As the camp came into view she saw a handful of primitive log structures that were larger but not much better than the slave quarters back at the plantation. Although she glimpsed a dense pine forest in the distance, the immediate camp was a barren place, with tree stumps clustered in between the buildings. There was no color, nothing of beauty, nothing but raw shelters built to facilitate the cutting of trees and nothing else.

Robert silently rode beside her, as though waiting for her to comment. Her mother's training for social situations rose to the occasion. One always complimented one's host.

"It's—uh, very nice."

Robert barked out a laugh. "No—it isn't. But it will do."

As they drew closer, he pointed. "That long building to the left is the bunkhouse." He pointed to a smaller structure. "That's the blacksmith's shop, and that place built into the hillside is the barn. The building over there is a combination office and store. Beside it is my cabin. The largest building is the cook shanty. The cook's quarters are built onto the back. That's where you and Ned will be living."

A sound of spluttering erupted from the back of the wagon as Jigger strangled on a wad of tobacco. She heard him spit and cough until he was breathless.

"What did you just say, boy?" the old man demanded.

Robert's voice was stern. "Katie and Ned will be living in the cookhouse."

"Over my dead body! That's *my* home!"

"It's not your home, Jigger. You can stay in the bunkhouse with the other men."

"It ain't fair!"

"It's more than fair."

Katie felt sick. She was taking the old man's living quarters? Had she known that was part of the deal, she would never have agreed. Or—at one time in her life, she would never have agreed. At the moment, she didn't have a choice. They were all at the mercy of Robert's decisions. She wanted to protest but knew she had little choice. She and Ned couldn't exactly move into the bunkhouse with the men, or sleep in the barn, or live in the woods.

Sam pulled the wagon up to the door of the cook shanty, and she and Ned set foot on the springy, pine-needle-covered soil where they would be living and working for the next few months.

Robert and Jigger appeared to be involved in a silent test of wills. They were staring at each other, motionless. Jigger's jaw jutted out like he was ready to fight.

"It won't hurt you to bunk with the men," Robert finally said.

"I'm the cook, son," Jigger complained. "How can I keep order at mealtimes if you demote me to bunking with the men? They won't respect me, and you don't think they're going to pay attention to *her*, do you? They'll be too busy cutting up and making moon eyes at her. Besides, I gotta get up at two in the morning just to get breakfast ready. You don't want this old man stumbling around in a dark bunkhouse waking up all the loggers, do you? Them men need their rest."

Two in the morning? Katie remembered Delia's warnings about how hard she would work. No one got up that early—not even the dairy farmers she had known.

Jigger's injured arm was cradled against his chest, his sparse hair combed straight back over a liver-spotted scalp. To her astonishment, tears trickled down his wrinkled cheeks. Jigger dashed them away and glared at Robert.

A muscle in Robert's jaw twitched. He fidgeted, obviously uncomfortable with Jigger's despair.

"Oh, all right. You win—you ornery old coot. She can have my cabin. I'll bunk with the shanty boys."

She started to protest, but Robert cut her off with a look.

"You need to get supper on. We have men to feed." With that he strode toward the small cabin he had pointed out as his own.

"Come on, woman." Jigger, rejuvenated by winning the argument, headed toward the cook shanty. "Time to earn your pay."

———✦———

Robert surveyed his living quarters from last year. So *he* would be the one living in the louse-infested, crowded bunkhouse. If it was anyone but Jigger, he would never have given in—but he figured he owed the old man. It had been Jigger who had kept him out of trouble when he was a boy poking his nose into every inch of his father's lumber camps. Then later, when he had crawled back home, a grown man so broken by war and the loss of his wife that he despaired of ever being able to support his own children—it was Jigger who had reminded him about this section of timber his father had invested in back when the rest of the world was still under the impression that Michigan was nothing more than a swamp.

His small savings and this section of timber had been enough to put him back on his feet. If this season went well, there should be enough in this year's harvest to support his sister and two children for another year.

"Name's Ernie." A sturdy young woodsman stood in his open cabin door. "Heard you was hiring."

"I might be." Robert took in the young man's appearance. He was dressed in the uniform of a Michigan lumberman: gray britches cut off several inches above the ankle, heavy boots, suspenders, knit cap covering longish black hair, and a bright red flannel shirt—the better to be seen in the woods. An old flour sack, tied with thin rope and filled with his few possessions, hung over one shoulder. A double-bit axe with a straight hickory handle was held loosely in his right hand.

"Cletus and me are a good axe team, or we can swamp if you want," Ernie said. "This here's my twin brother." He stood aside, and another young man, dressed identically but with sandy-colored hair and gentle blue eyes, appeared. "We can ride the logs good too," Ernie announced.

"Where else have you worked?" Robert asked.

"Dempsey's camp over on the Tittibiwassee last year," Ernie said. "And the year before that."

"Why aren't you going back?" Robert asked. "Dempsey runs a good camp."

Ernie looked at him as though the answer ought to be obvious. "We heard you'd hired a redheaded girl camp cook who makes a good apple pie."

"Ah." The word was getting out. Loggers, like Napoleon's army, marched on their stomachs, and most had an uncanny ability to ferret out the best cooks. "Put your turkeys in the bunkhouse and grab a bed. Then head on over to the cook shanty and help the new cook with whatever she asks you to do."

Both men looked as though he had just given them a Christmas present.

"Thanks, boss!" They hurried away.

Robert stood in the doorway of his cabin, looking out at the receding forest. The clean air of the pine woods filled his lungs, and he breathed deeply, grateful that he had this work to turn to. It was going to be a good year—he could just feel it.

Other men would hear about Katie. Hopefully they were already walking through the woods, down the various tote roads, with their turkeys and axes slung across their shoulders. A ten-to twenty-mile hike was nothing to true woodsmen. Soon, they would begin to arrive.

Some, like him, would still be recuperating from the nightmares of battle. Some would be raw farm boys supplementing income wrestled from thin-soiled farms springing up in clearings that the timbermen left behind. Some would be true axe men following the lumber industry as it worked its way across the country. Some would be immigrants struggling to understand English. Some would be scoundrels. Few would be saints. If he was lucky, at least one would own a fiddle and know how to play it. A lumber camp needed a fiddler and a storyteller to keep the men's spirits up.

He refocused his attention on his cabin, making note of the things he would need to take to the bunkhouse with him. He had tried to keep the vermin out of his own living space, so at least he wouldn't be putting that woman and her brother into a nest of lice and bedbugs.

He yanked up the straw-tick mattress and gave it a shake. It smelled moldy and felt damp. He was grateful he already had commissioned plenty of fresh straw and hay to be delivered to the barn.

The last thing he had expected to do when he awoke today was to ready his cabin for a woman—but it was now his first order of business. Her life would be hard enough the next few months—but he would help her as much as he could.

─⟨⟩⟨⟩─

The sight of the hen's egg hidden in a nest beside the barn made Harlan's mouth water. It had been a long time since he had eaten an egg.

Then he remembered that he hadn't seen a chicken on the place since the day Katherine had abandoned him. There was no telling how long the egg had been there. He picked it up and flung it against the trunk of an ancient magnolia tree. It burst open, filling the air with a sulfurous smell. The stench caused his eyes to water, which soon turned into self-pitying tears. Everything was rotten these days—ruined. His beautiful home had been destroyed. Fallen Oaks was a wasteland of brambles. He had become less and less welcome at the table of old friends.

The hunger in his belly added fuel to his fury at the Yankee wife who had scurried away. Without even one slave to rely on anymore—who was going to cook for him now?

6

*'Twas all the fault of Old Joe, our dirty greasy
  cook,
for fixing up the grub for us no pains at all he took.
Hot biscuits were nothing but raw dough and
  heavy as stone;
and often times we had to make a meal of them
  alone.*

"Driving Logs on the Cass"
—1800s shanty song

The silent, burly teamster unloaded boxes as Katie and Jigger entered the cook shanty. It smelled of pine, stale men, and hundreds of meals of beans and bacon. A long table made of rough pine split the room down the middle, with benches on either side. Looming at the far end was the kitchen, which held a giant woodstove. Wires ran the length of the cooking area, hung with cobweb-covered dishcloths. Rough shelves were filled with bowls, plates, and cooking pots. The whole place was covered with a thick layer of dust. A dead bird lay on the floor.

Ned pressed close to her side as they surveyed the workplace that would be their home for the next several months. She instinctively put her arm around his thin shoulders.

"Where do you want this?" The teamster appeared in the doorway with a case of canned tomatoes balanced on his shoulder.

"On the floor, over there." Jigger gestured toward a far corner of the cook shanty.

Katie approached the cast-iron stove. It was the biggest she had ever seen and must have taken enormous effort to get here. Robert obviously took feeding his men very seriously if he dragged a monster like this into the woods. Nearby, a huge square table created a work surface large enough to roll out any number of piecrusts.

In spite of her exhaustion from the trip and being fairly overwhelmed by all the changes that had taken place in her life, she felt a small thrill of excitement. The cook shanty had a bare bones utilitarian simplicity that would make cooking for a crew of men quite possible and in some ways even enjoyable.

"Are you just gonna stand there?" Jigger asked.

"What do you want me to do?" They had been inside for less than a minute.

"You're the new cook." He spat a stream of tobacco juice directly onto the wooden floor. "And none of us et since morning. Cook us something, woman."

"What is there to fix?"

Jigger sat down on a bench and shrugged his scrawny shoulders, abdicating responsibility for anything to do with food.

Sam brought in a fifty-pound sack of flour. "Where do you want this?"

"Over against the wall with the canned 'maters," Jigger said.

"Put it on the cook's worktable," Katie ordered. "I don't want the flour sitting on that dirty floor."

Sam looked back and forth between them. He chose to compromise and set the sack down in the middle of the long dining table—between the two locations—and returned for another load.

"You must have a better place to store food than against the wall," Katie said.

Jigger spit on the floor in answer. The contempt in his action got on Katie's last nerve. She was tired and hungry too.

"Quit doing that!"

"You ain't gonna last long around here, girlie, if you can't stand a little tobacco juice," Jigger said with satisfaction.

Sam carried in two buckets of lard, set them beside the sack of flour, and returned for another load.

"I'm hungry," Ned whispered, tugging on her sleeve.

"You heard the boy," Jigger sneered. "He's *hungry*."

If there was one thing she hated, especially after living with Harlan, it was a bully. And Jigger, although probably incapable of physically hurting her, was definitely a bully. She tried to decide what to do about him as she watched Sam carry in two cases of corned beef and return with sacks of onions and potatoes.

As though disinterested in the entire proceeding, Jigger sat on the bench, staring out of one of the fly-specked windows.

"I saw a stream in back." Katie grabbed a bucket from a shelf and handed it to Ned. "Bring me as much water as you can carry. I'll fix us all something to eat soon."

"Yes, ma'am." Ned scurried away with the bucket.

Katie approached the huge stove. She had cooked plenty of meals on her mother's stove before her marriage, and many more at Fallen Oaks after their cook disappeared. The principle was the same, regardless of the size. Wood went into the stove's firebox and heated the oven and the smooth cast-iron top. The temperature was regulated by the type and quantity of firewood. Fortunately, a pile of split hardwood lay beside the stove. A box of dry wood shavings to use for tinder sat nearby.

"Where are the lucifers?" she asked.

Jigger nodded toward a jar on a shelf, within which were stored the wooden matches she needed to strike a flame. Soon, she had a crackling fire started in the belly of the stove, and the oven was warming up.

Sam brought in boxes of sugar and tea. Ned struggled in from outdoors, sloshing a bucket of cold, clear creek water against his pants leg. Still, Jigger did not move from his seat.

"Thank you, Ned." She set a dishpan on top of the stove and poured the water into it. "Could you bring me another?"

"Sure." Her little brother ran off.

On a hook, there was a large, white apron that appeared relatively clean. She shook the dust out of it, tied it on, and rolled up the sleeves of her dress. Dipping a rag into the pan of water, she began wiping off the worktable. She had expected at least a few minutes to pull herself together before her work began, a few moments to get her bearings in this new environment—but that was not how things were working out.

She could deal with it. She had dealt with worse.

Even with Jigger glaring at her from across the room, the familiarity of being back inside a kitchen was comforting. The growing mountain of foodstuffs seemed miraculous to her after the privations of the past few years.

"Is this enough?" Ned carried in another bucket.

"For now." Grasping the ice-cold pail of water, she grabbed a broom and marched toward Jigger. There was something she needed to tend to before she could stomach fixing dinner.

"Excuse me." She sloshed water across the floor directly in front of him, soaking his pants legs and saturating the tobacco-stained floor.

"Hey! Watch it!" Jigger leapt to his feet and sidestepped out of her way.

"More water, please." She handed the bucket back to Ned, grabbed the broom, and began to sweep the water and tobacco debris out the door.

She was so intent on her job she almost swept it right into the face of Sam, who, startled, danced out of the way while holding two fifty-pound bags of dried beans, one on each shoulder.

"What the . . ." He opened his mouth to say more, thought better of it, shut it tightly, and grimly stepped over the threshold. "Where would you like these, ma'am?" he asked meekly.

"Put them on the table. In fact, would you mind putting everything you've brought in on the table for now? I want to give this floor a good scrubbing."

"Can't I put things in the kitchen storage shed or down in the cellar?" It was the longest sentence he had uttered in the past two days.

Storage shed? Cellar? What kind of game was Jigger playing with her, anyway?

"Yes, please," she said. "That would be lovely."

He tracked over her wet floor, straight toward the back of the cook shanty and out the back door. She leaned the broom against the wall and started to follow him.

"Where you going?" Jigger asked.

"Apparently, the storage shed." She turned to look at him, her hands on her hips. "When were you going to tell me?"

"I was fixin' to." Jigger held up his drenched pants leg with his good hand, his pinky stuck up like a finicky lady. "Afore you started dumpin' water on me."

Her pique of anger evaporated. Sloshing the old man with water was extreme, and she regretted doing it. But really! Spitting tobacco juice on the floor! Even Harlan hadn't had that filthy habit.

"I apologize for getting you wet, but from what I can see, there's too much work for us to be fussing with each other. Could we just call a truce and get on with it?"

"Sure thing, missy." The old man grinned evilly and held out his gnarled hand. "We'll just have ourselves a little truce."

She had watched that same hand dig a plug of tobacco out of

his cheek not fifteen minutes earlier. Steeling herself, she shook it, determined to wash her hands the minute his back was turned.

Sam, his previous load stashed in the storage shed, returned with two wooden barrels of sorghum. "Storage shed or cellar?"

"Storage shed," Jigger said at the same moment Katie said, "Cellar."

Yet again, the teamster stood with his burden, undecided whose instructions to obey.

"Put it in the cellar," Robert said, coming in the door. His eyes swept around the cook shanty, taking stock of the wet floor, the teamster's pained expression, and Jigger's bedraggled pants.

"This isn't going well," Robert observed.

"No, it ain't," Jigger said.

Katie held her peace.

"Obviously, we need a line of command here. Jigger, until you get your strength back and your arm heals, Katie is head cook. She makes all the decisions. You can keep your room here in the cook shanty, but you'll take your directions from her."

"But you said—"

"I know what I said, Jigger, but this isn't working. Katie, this man, in spite of what you might think from his recent behavior, is a seasoned lumber camp cook. You can learn some things from him."

"Yeah." Jigger scowled at her. "You can learn some things from me."

"That's enough." Robert slammed his fist down on the table, and both Katie and Jigger jumped. "I don't want to hear another word out of you, Jigger!"

The anger in his voice, the impatience on his face, were all too familiar. She felt an old, familiar panic. She backed away, until she bumped against the rough-sawn wood wall.

"You know what's at stake here, man." Robert's voice was raised as he shook a finger under Jigger's nose. "It was your idea for me to come out here in the first place. Everything I have is invested in this venture. You said you would help me."

"I have helped you."

"Yes—right up until you picked that crazy fight in the saloon. The rest of my crew will be arriving soon. Two are already over at the bunkhouse. They'll need to be fed. How exactly do you plan to cook for them with a broken arm?"

Jigger stared down at the damp floor.

"Don't make our lives any harder, old friend. I hired Katie because she was our best chance at making this camp turn a profit." As though Robert suddenly realized she was watching, he turned and saw her pressed against the wall. He frowned as though trying to puzzle out what she was doing, but he didn't apologize.

"The new men's names are Ernie and Cletus." His voice softened, but she didn't trust it. "They'll help you get this place ready. In the meantime, I would appreciate it if you could start getting something together for supper."

She nodded, afraid to say anything that might set him off again. The best way she had found to placate Harlan was to do everything he asked without question.

Once again, she had misjudged a man. Robert had a temper that she was going to have to be careful not to ignite, but at least she was getting paid for her work this time—and he hadn't tried to hit her.

At least not yet.

⁓

"Are you going to cook or are you going to just stand there and gawk, woman?" Jigger said.

"I'll cook."

Katie found a large wooden bowl, opened the sack of flour, dipped out several ladles full of creamy white lard, worked it into the flour, and began to roll out piecrusts. There wasn't enough time to set yeast bread to rising, so her plan was to make dozens of meat-filled pastries. It was the quickest meal she could think of on the spur of the moment. Canned corned beef, potatoes, onions, and carrots were minced and mounded in a large bowl, ready for the filling. By the time the meat pastries were finished, the oven should be heated enough for baking.

She cut circles into the piecrust with a large, empty tin can, spooned the vegetable and meat mixture into the middle, and pressed the edges together to create crescents. Soon, she had several trays laden with the savory pies. Each would be a meal, all by itself.

That chore finished, she cast about for some sort of dessert. It would have to be simple. No time for anything more. Her eyes lit on a case of canned peaches. She still had some piecrust left over. She dumped four large cans of peaches into an enormous baking tin and added cornstarch, sugar, and vanilla extract.

There wasn't quite enough crust to cover the top of the baking dish, so she made another latticework. Then she sprinkled sugar over the whole thing and shoved the cobbler into the oven the minute the pies came out. A pot of green tea that Jigger had told her to make simmered on the back of the stove.

She checked the firebox. As she had suspected, it had died down. She placed three pieces of hickory inside to keep the temperature even.

Jigger ignored her. Instead, he took on the job of bossing the two men Robert sent over. As she worked, Cletus and Ernie swept out everything from cobwebs to dead birds. They helped Ned with his job, carrying in bucket after bucket of fresh water, scrubbing the floor until the heat of the stove made the steam rise from its damp surface. The long table was cleared of supplies and freshly scrubbed. After it dried, a red-checked oilcloth was rolled out and tacked on. Under Jigger's supervision, the table was set with freshly washed tin plates and cups. Bowls of sugar and salt shakers were placed in the middle. Last, the two men washed and shined the filthy windows. She could see the whisper of a pink sunset reflected in them.

It had been three hours since they had pulled into camp, and she hadn't had a chance to sit down, unpack, or even see where she would be sleeping. She was already exhausted, and tonight she was cooking for only a fraction of the men who would be coming. If today was any indication of how things would be over the next seven months, she would be earning her wages, indeed.

7

Potatoes, apples, turnips, beans,
and syrup, pure and sweet.
Although we have no appetite
we cannot help but eat.

> *"Johnny Carrol's Camp"—*
> *1800s shanty song*

"Supper's ready." Katie blew a tendril of hair out of her eyes and placed the cobbler on the table.

"It's about time," Jigger complained.

Although Katie thought it was overkill with so few people in the camp, Jigger pulled a giant tin horn off the wall and marched outside. The horn was about two feet taller than he was. He rested it on a stump and proceeded to blow it like a bugle, trilling a few notes, flubbing a few more.

She wiped her hands on her apron and checked the table one more time. For so little notice, the food didn't look too skimpy. She had unearthed some pickles from the cellar to add to the makeshift supper.

Ernie and Cletus were already inside where they had been working and commenting on the delicious aromas for the past hour. Sam and Ned stomped through the door as Jigger put away the horn. Ned was red-cheeked and breathless, having earlier been given permission to explore the rest of the camp.

Robert was the last in. He stopped and stared at the tray of cobbler and the mound of golden meat pies heaped upon the table. Then he took stock of the dining room, which was now as clean and shining as it was possible for bare wood to be. A look of relief settled on his face.

While Jigger assigned the others their permanent seats, Robert walked over to her.

"How in the world did you manage to do so much so fast?" he asked in a quiet voice. "I wasn't expecting anything more than some canned beans and hardtack soaked in tea—maybe some cheese to go with it if we were lucky. That's all Jigger fixes the first night. Instead, you've made us a real meal!"

His kind words took her breath away. She couldn't remember the last time she had been complimented for her cooking—or for anything else.

"Jigger helped," she said modestly. "He got the place into shape."

"He's a competent man when he wants to be. I apologize for the way he's been acting."

"I've dealt with worse."

"Hello the camp!" A burly woodsman wearing a bright blue shirt and brown pants cut several inches above the ankles walked through the door with an axe in his hand and a sack slung over one shoulder. "Was that Gabriel's trumpet I heard blowing? Or was it just the dinner horn?"

"Skypilot!" Ernie jumped up and pumped the man's hand. "It's good to see you. Are you working here this winter?"

"If your boss has a job for me." Skypilot rested his axe on the floor. His eyes, a mild blue above a dark, bushy beard, were filled with good humor. "I've heard there's a new cook in this neck of the woods."

"Skypilot is one of the best axe men in Michigan," Ernie told Robert. "We worked with him last winter."

"I've always room on my crew for someone good with an axe, and welcome," Robert said. "My name is Robert Foster. This is my camp. Come take supper with us."

"I appreciate it." The big woodsman leaned his axe against a wall and dropped his pack beside it.

As soon as Skypilot had seated himself, to Katie's surprise, all hands grabbed a meat pie.

"Pass the pickles," Ernie said.

Robert scooted the bowl down the table to him. The only sound was that of the stove making clicking noises as it cooled and men wolfing down food. Teeth crunched into crisp, hot pastry, and gravy dripped onto tin plates.

This didn't seem right. At her mother's table, there had always been polite conversation. Evidently, none of the men had been taught better manners than to eat in total silence. She decided it might break the ice if she initiated some polite dinner conversation.

"How did you get the name of Skypilot?" she asked.

The big logger stopped in mid-bite, acting surprised at the interruption. His eyes slid over to Robert, and he swallowed before he spoke.

"That's camp lingo for preacher—which I used to be before the war."

Jigger, standing near the head of the table, frowned. "No talking at the table!"

"Excuse me?" She had never heard of anything so ridiculous. "Why?"

"We got rules, girlie. Loggers don't need to be wasting time jawing at each other while they eat. What do you think this is? Some sort of ladies' tea party?"

"There are only a handful of us," Robert intervened, glancing at her as she felt herself turning red. "Surely we can relax that rule a bit for tonight."

"Humph!" Jigger set his mouth in a hard line of disapproval. "You're the boss. If you want to start changing things just because a woman's got fancy ideas, I guess that's your right."

"Why don't you sit down, Jigger," Robert urged. "You've had a long day and you must be tired and hungry. I'm sure your arm hurts. Let Katie handle things while you eat."

Reluctantly, Jigger sat down, and Robert plopped a meat pie onto his plate. Jigger stared at it for a full minute before picking it up. Katie watched closely—afraid he would find fault with it. He nibbled an edge, looked at it, took a full bite, and gobbled the rest, reaching for a second.

"Not the best I ever et," the old man mumbled. "Not the worst, either."

She figured that was as close to a compliment as she could hope for from the old cook. She retrieved the kettle from the stove and walked around the table, pouring the scalding hot tea into mugs.

"Have you ever cooked for a lumber camp before, ma'am?" Skypilot asked, holding his cup out for her to fill.

"I'm afraid not."

"Then I guess you don't know the way us shanty boys like our tea brewed."

"How's that?" She had merely dropped a large fistful of green tea leaves into a kettle filled with boiling water. How else could it be made?

"Well, first, you need to find an old axe head," he explained. "You got one of them things lying around that she could borrow, Foster?"

Robert solemnly agreed to loan her an axe head.

She couldn't imagine how it could improve the flavor of tea, but she was eager to try. "Then what?"

"After you boil up the tea, you put the axe head in the water." Skypilot paused.

"Please go on." She had always been fascinated with new ways of preparing food. Could there be some sort of reaction between the iron in the axe and an ingredient in the tea that made it taste better?

"If the axe head falls to the bottom of the pot," Skypilot said, "the tea is too weak."

Katie noticed that several of the men were grinning.

Skypilot's eyes were dancing, but his expression was sober. "And if it floats on the top, it's pretty good."

"Uh-huh." She crossed her arms over her chest, realizing that Skypilot was joshing her.

"And if the axe head dissolves—it's just right."

Cletus snickered, and Katie smiled. She glanced around the table and saw that even Jigger was enjoying the joke—at her expense, of course.

Skypilot took a long slurp from his cup. "I believe an axe head would dissolve pretty fast in this brew, ma'am. It's near perfect."

"Thank you." Strong tea it was, then. One large fistful per two-quart kettle. "I apologize that there's no coffee. I couldn't find any in the supplies."

"Shanty boys drink green tea." Jigger made a disgusted sound. "Everybody knows that. Keeps 'em from gettin' sick—that and plenty of chaw tobacco."

"I wouldn't mind some coffee now and then," Sam offered. "Got kind of used to it when I was a mule skinner in the army."

"We drink tea in my camp!" Jigger glared at Sam. "Always have. Always will." He reached for another meat pie as he warmed to his subject. "Next thing you know, you'll be sucking on those fancy sticks called cigarettes. Real men drink green tea and chaw their tobacco." He pointed the meat pie at everyone in turn. "I ever catch any of you smoking those little sissy sticks, I'll kick you outta my camp!"

Katie noticed an amused smile playing around Robert's lips

at the old man's belief in his ability to control the lumber camp, but he didn't correct him.

Jigger, having voiced his opinion to his own satisfaction, resumed his meal.

The mound of meat pies was disappearing, and most of the cobbler. She had hoped there would be something left over for her, but at the rate the men were inhaling their supper, it didn't appear likely. At least Ned was getting his belly filled. He sat beside Robert, concentrating on shoveling in as much food as possible. It did her heart good to see him getting plenty to eat.

All but the last pie was gone. Ernie reached for it, but Robert grabbed his wrist in midair. "The lady hasn't eaten yet."

"Oh." Ernie blushed through the peach fuzz on his face. "I'm sorry, ma'am. I wasn't thinking."

To her surprise, Robert arose from the table, grabbed a clean plate, placed the meat pie on it, dished up what was left of the cobbler, and added a spoonful of sweet pickles. "Here. You're dead on your feet, Katie. You eat and then I want you and Ned to go to your cabin. You need to get some rest before tomorrow. Ernie and Cletus will clean up. Jigger can supervise."

It had been a long, long time since Katie had been treated with such civility. She sank down onto the far end of the bench, away from the knot of men, and gratefully tucked into her meal.

"Sam already unloaded your things into the cabin," Robert said when she was finished. "Are you ready to go?"

"Yes."

"I'll take you over there before I turn in."

As they made their way to Robert's cabin, she wondered if she should apologize. She and Ned were taking the man's private quarters and there was not a thing she could do about it.

He opened the heavy door and she stepped into a room filled with the soft glow of a kerosene lamp covered with a golden shade. A fire snapped and crackled inside of a small airtight stove. Short, neat lengths of firewood were piled in one corner.

A double bed covered with what appeared to be a fresh sheet sat in another corner. A table with two chairs was pushed beneath the single window. A dresser stood against the opposite wall. In the middle of the room, near the stove, was quite a treasure—a large rocking chair. In one corner sat the trunk she had purchased in Bay City, ready to be unpacked. A strong woodsy scent pervaded the cabin.

"I like this place!" Ned said.

"It's very nice," she said. "But why does it smell like Christmas in here?"

Robert stuck his hands into his pockets. "It's the spruce."

"Spruce?"

"It's a shanty boy trick. Sometimes they cut the tips off of spruce trees and layer them beneath a blanket. It makes it a little easier to sleep. I thought it would make things more comfortable for you if there were fresh boughs beneath that straw-tick mattress."

"When did Ernie and Cletus have time to gather spruce boughs?" she asked. "I watched them cleaning the cook shanty the entire time."

"They didn't," Robert said. "I did."

She found it hard to imagine the lumber camp boss going to that much effort just for her comfort. Then the thought struck that Robert might have less chivalrous reasons for making her bed comfortable. They were, after all, going to be isolated together in this camp for an entire winter. A cold chill ran down her spine. What had she let herself in for? She glanced at the door. There was no lock or bolt. Feeling a jolt of panic, she grabbed for Ned's hand.

Robert saw her looking for the reassurance of a lock, and realized why. He berated himself for his thoughtlessness. It had

71

been stupid of him to fuss over her sleeping arrangements. Of course she would take it the wrong way.

While wondering what to do about the situation, he reached up to scratch his head.

Her reaction to his raised hand was startling. She flinched and ducked. Ned backed away and worriedly glanced back and forth between them.

Her terrified reaction stunned Robert. This woman and child acted as though he intended on hitting her! He had never struck a woman in his life. Never had. Never would. He despised men who did.

He had no idea what to say, so he simply stalked out of the cabin, went to the blacksmith's shop, and came back with a hammer, a large nail, and a short length of oak board.

Without a word of explanation, he pounded the board into the heavy wooden door and then loosened it just enough that it could be moved in a circular fashion. It would make a sturdy makeshift lock for the night.

"I'll have the blacksmith make you a proper sliding bolt when he gets here tomorrow."

"Thank you." Tears trembled on the lashes of her pretty blue eyes.

He could hardly believe what he was seeing. It was only a piece of wood, for pity's sake.

"I hate to bring it up." She wiped tears away with the back of her hand. "But you said I could have my own private privy?"

He had already forgotten about that. There was just too much to keep track of. Having a woman around was going to be one thing after another. On the other hand, eating meat pies that melted in his mouth made it worth it. Having a woodsman like Skypilot show up out of the blue was proof that his gamble in hiring Katie was going to pay off.

"Bill Spicer should here tomorrow. We call him Tinker, which is camp slang for carpenter. I'll put him on it first thing," he promised.

"Thank you. I can make . . . other arrangements until then."

He wasn't certain what she meant by "other arrangements," but he had no intention of asking. Taking the trouble to put those spruce tips beneath her mattress had spooked her enough. She'd have to take care of . . . well . . . other things the best she could.

———⌒⌒———

The bed looked inviting, but there was still work to do. She opened her trunk and pulled out two woolen blankets along with a heavy cotton one for lining. It wasn't cool enough for her to face donning cotton long johns.

"Are we going to bed?" Ned asked.

"Soon." She rummaged in the trunk. "Here's your new night-shirt."

"Mr. Foster said I would make a good logger," the boy boasted.

"I'm sure he's right." She appreciated Robert telling Ned that. After his sojourn with Harlan, the child could use all the encouragement he could get.

While Ned dressed for bed, the lamp cast shadows on the rough logs and she made small, domestic plans for the cabin. She noticed a corner table holding a plain, white pitcher and washbasin near the door. There was just enough space on it to hold her combs and hairbrush. She decided she would hang a small mirror she had purchased at the mercantile on the wall above it.

Inside the trunk was a bolt of blue calico that had caught her eye. She had entertained visions of sewing an extra dress out of it in her spare time. After today, she doubted she would have enough spare time to sew a dress, but she *could* fashion a makeshift curtain for this corner. That would give her some privacy to wash and change clothes.

As her brother got into bed, she stuffed more logs into the stove. In Georgia, she had rarely needed a fire except to cook. This far north, it appeared that keeping fires going was going to absorb a great deal of her time.

"I like it here," Ned said as he wriggled into the straw-tick mattress.

"I do too."

Based on Robert's behavior tonight, she realized that she meant it. He had many responsibilities weighing on him, and he might be frustrated and worried enough to bark at Jigger from time to time, but she was beginning to entertain hopes that at heart he was a good and chivalrous man.

With Ned tucked in, she blew out the light and slipped one of her soft, new flannel nightgowns over her head. She removed her hairpins, shook out her hair, and threw it into a long, loose braid. The rope webbing creaked beneath her weight as she climbed in and snuggled down.

In the darkness, she heard the bone-chilling sound of a chorus of wild howls that went on and on. It was one of the most eerie and yet one of the most beautiful sounds she had ever heard in her life. Unless she missed her guess, it was a choir of timber wolves. She decided that she and Ned would not be walking around the camp after dark any more than absolutely necessary.

"Are you afraid, sister?"

"A little."

"Me too."

"The wolves can't get in here," she assured him. "The walls of this cabin are thick."

"Are you afraid of Mr. Foster?"

"I think I'm a little afraid of all men right now, Ned."

"I know." Ned patted her shoulder to comfort her. "Do you remember Papa's favorite Scripture?"

"He had so many."

"I liked the one about not being afraid, but I can't remember all the words."

"God hath not given us the spirit of fear; but of power, and of love, and of a sound mind." She kissed his hand. "Is that the one you were looking for, little brother?"

"Yes." Ned curled into a ball and yawned. "I like that one best." He was asleep beside her in an instant. She drew her baby brother's skinny little body close to her, curled herself around him, and silently gave thanks.

In the middle of the Michigan wilderness, serenaded by howling wolves, inside a borrowed cabin, she closed her eyes with a combination of exhaustion and relief. She would *not* be afraid. She would *not* give in to the spirit of fear. God *had* been faithful. He had miraculously brought her to this strange, good place. For the first time since they had fled on the back of Rebel's Pride, she allowed herself to relax and fall into a deep sleep.

8

You ought to see them jump and run
when the cook his horn does blow,
for it ain't like any of the boys
to miss their hash, you know.

"Shanty Boys in the Pine"
—1800s shanty song

October 8, 1867

Katie awoke with a start and glanced around in confusion at the dark, unfamiliar walls. The only light was that which spilled from a crack in the stove.

Where was she? What had awakened her? Her heart pounded with fear.

She had been dreaming of their flight from Georgia. She and Ned were in that abandoned, derelict barn in which they had sheltered in southern Tennessee. It had rained for two solid days while they had hidden Rebel's Pride and themselves, counting themselves lucky that the rain would wash away Rebel's hoof-prints. The barn had been so old, she had feared it would collapse from the weight of the rain, but it had held, and they had stayed fairly dry, albeit so hungry they gnawed on a few ears of sodden field corn overlooked by harvesters.

What *was* that sound? She instinctively reached for Ned and found him still asleep beside her. This reassured her.

As she fought her way to full consciousness, she realized that the sound she was hearing was nothing more than rain on the roof, which must be why she was dreaming about those rainy nights in that barn.

Her heartbeat returned to normal as she remembered where she was and what she was doing here. She was in Michigan, inside Robert Foster's cabin. She had a job as a cook. Her brother was beside her.

Smiling at her irrational fear, she climbed out of bed, lit the lamp, and walked barefoot over to the stove to add more firewood. Just as she bent over to pick up a length of firewood, the doorknob jiggled.

She leaped away from the door. Who could be trying to open her door at this time of night!

Grasping the length of firewood in both hands, she stood ready to protect Ned and herself from whoever was trying to get in. She blessed Robert for having put that barrier on the door. If it weren't for that nail and piece of wood, anyone could have walked right in.

Now, something pecked at the window behind her. She whirled and stared straight into the face of Jigger, pressed close to the glass, peering in. Rain was pouring off of his hat.

"Open up!" he shouted through the glass.

Ned bolted awake, his eyes wide with fear. "Who is it?"

"Shhh. Go back to sleep. It's just Jigger."

Ned snuggled back under the covers.

Thinking there must be some sort of emergency but still grasping the sturdy piece of firewood just in case, she shifted the makeshift lock and opened the door. A sodden and extremely unhappy Jigger stepped in.

"Why ain't you in the kitchen yet, woman?" he spluttered. "You're supposed to be cooking!"

"What time is it?" It felt as though she had barely closed her eyes. It couldn't be time to start breakfast yet.

"Half past three! You're late. The men'll be up and ready to eat in an hour. I kept waitin' for you to get your lazy self up and into the kitchen, but you never came."

"Why didn't you knock instead of trying to open the door? I could have brained you."

"I did knock. And I yelled. Never saw someone sleep so sound."

The old man looked so sodden and miserable, she felt bad, but grateful to him. How long would she have slept had he not awakened her? She could have lost her job!

"I'll be right there," she said. "Just let me get dressed."

Jigger suddenly seemed to be aware that she was standing there in her bare feet and nightgown. The gown was high-necked and modest and covered everything that needed to be covered, but he quickly backed out of the cabin.

"You better hurry," he said over his shoulder as the rain enveloped him. "More of the crew came in during the night. They need a decent breakfast if they're gonna do a full day's work. The boss won't be happy if they don't get it."

―⟡―

Robert awoke to the sound of that infernal horn and Jigger yelling, "Get up, you lazy shanty boys! Daylight in the swamp!"

That traditional wake-up call would be echoing right now in lumber camps all over Michigan. It came from the fact that the state had once been described as an "impenetrable swamp" by a disenchanted government surveyor.

Of course, the word "daylight" was a joke. It was 4:30 a.m. and as black as India ink outside. If Katie did her job well this morning, his men would be fed and out in the timber long before morning light.

Torrential rain pounded against the roof, driving water into the ceiling vent hole and sending water down onto the stove, where it sizzled. The men were used to working in wet weather but not when the rain was falling with the force of a waterfall. The rest of the crew he had expected today probably wouldn't materialize until it was over.

Much like farming, the timber business depended upon the weather. He needed a dry autumn to get the roads and the camp readied and a below-freezing winter to keep the tote roads solid. The roads would be iced down by a giant watering wagon, providing a slick surface for sliding logs to the river, where they would be stacked in huge piles.

When spring came, the snows needed to melt at a consistent rate, causing the rivers to rise just enough to carry the logs off to the mills at the mouth of the Saginaw—but not enough to flood their banks and float the logs out to heaven-knows-where like last spring. Finding and dragging those logs back to the river while the mosquitoes and black flies swarmed was nearly impossible.

A few bunks down, Ernie groaned as he got out of bed, still dressed in his logging clothes. Cletus, in the bunk above him, was sound asleep.

"Wake up," Ernie said in a friendly tone.

Cletus didn't move.

"I said"—Ernie slapped his brother on the shoulder—"get up!"

With his eyes closed tight, Cletus punched Ernie in the chest.

Ernie laughed, stepped back, and lit a lamp hanging from the ceiling. "That redheaded widow woman is cooking breakfast, Cletus."

Cletus sat straight up in bed, wide awake. "Wonder what she's fixing!"

Both of them began jerking on socks and boots. Ernie yanked on a hat and headed out the door. Cletus hopped on one foot, got his other boot on, then followed his brother out into the pouring rain.

Tinker and the blacksmith they all simply referred to as Blackie, both of whom had arrived long after supper, headed out the door as well.

Robert stared at the wet, pitch black morning, trying to work up enthusiasm for the day. Thinking of pretty Katie presiding over a pot of scalding hot tea was a pretty good motivator.

"Interesting weather," Skypilot observed from a top bunk.

"It's raining cats and dogs."

"I wish I had me a good cat right now to catch whatever the critter was that was gnawing on the bottom of my bed all night."

"We got traps over in the storage shed," Robert said. "I'll set a couple tonight."

"I'd be much obliged." Skypilot arose from his bunk, pulled on his boots, stretched upward until his fingers touched the rafters, then donned a worn, black, rubberized raincoat. He stood with one hand on the doorjamb, looking out at the darkness.

"This is the day that the Lord has made," Skypilot spoke aloud into the downpour. "Let us rejoice and be glad in it!" Then he plunged into the pouring rain and jogged to the cook shanty. Sam, unhappy about having to go out in the downpour, added a few choice *non*-biblical words of his own before following.

Robert added more logs to the stove and straightened his bedroll. It had been a rough night. Both Ernie and Cletus snored like thunder. Sam made a sound like a steam locomotive huffing into a station. The sawdust-filled bed he lay in was hard. The mouse, or rat, that Skypilot had mentioned had kept him awake most of the night as well.

He hoped Katie Smith and her brother had enjoyed their slumber. Maybe it would translate into a good breakfast. Those meat pies and cobbler last night had been amazing, but his stomach was already starting to growl again. Being in camp gave him an appetite he never enjoyed in town.

He laced up his boots, threw on the same well-worn mackintosh that had seen him through the war, and went outside. He gasped as the rain, with no trees to break its force, hit him full in the face.

A few steps later he entered the cook shanty. It was like entering a different world. Katie and Jigger had lit every lamp in the place, and the dining room was alive with light. Good smells wafted from the kitchen area. Stacks of flapjacks filled the middle of the table. Sorghum, known to the men as "long sweetening," sat in pitchers ready to be poured. Pork gravy had been made for the men who preferred it to sorghum.

Ernie and Cletus were already at the table, forks in hands, looking longingly toward the flapjacks. Ned carried over a large bowl heaped with fried potatoes. Katie was behind him holding what appeared to be a bowl of stewed dried apples.

Robert noticed that she seemed a little frazzled this morning. Her hair was especially unkempt. Instead of the tight bun she had worn for the past two days, it now hung to her waist in a loose braid. Much of it had escaped the braid and had frizzed up in the dampness of the morning.

"Good morning," he said.

She blew a strand of hair out of her eyes as she carried the dish past him. "Morning," she mumbled.

Her face was damp with perspiration, and her skin pink from exertion. She had obviously been rushed in getting the breakfast ready. And there were only ten of them this morning.

Would she be able to keep up when he had a full crew?

He went over to the kitchen area where Jigger stood with a fork in his good hand, frying ham.

"Is everything all right?" Robert asked.

Jigger's mouth was tight. "Silly woman wouldn't get out of bed this morning."

Robert's stomach plummeted.

"And she almost brained me with a piece of firewood when I tried to wake her up," Jigger added sourly.

Well *that* was wonderful news to add to an already bleak morning.

"Is the ham ready?" Katie came around the worktable with an empty platter.

Jigger stacked the ham onto the platter, and she rushed with it to the table. Robert noticed that her petticoat draggled on the floor. His spirits plunged even further.

"You need to give me a couple of good shanty boys to train to cook, and fire that girl," Jigger said as he slid more sliced ham into the skillet. "She's gonna be more trouble than she's worth."

After his sleepless night, Robert felt quite tempted by the idea. If she left, he could have his cabin back. But, a deal was a deal, and he shouldn't judge her on the strength of one day. The poor woman had been exhausted last night. He could understand the depth of her slumber this morning, but he could not tolerate it long. A cook who wouldn't get up early enough to fix breakfast was worse than having no cook at all. As the old saying in lumber camps went, "Roll out of bed and get to work or roll up your stuff and hit the road."

On the other hand, Jigger had been known to exaggerate—especially when it was to his own advantage.

Again, Katie flew past to grab the pot of tea, practically panting from going back and forth getting the food on the table.

"Where's Ned?" Robert asked.

Katie wrapped a rag around the handle of the boiling liquid. "I left him asleep in the cabin."

"I'm paying him a nickel a day to help you, not to sleep."

She stopped in her tracks, registering his words, and her face looked as though he had slapped her. Too late, he realized that his morning voice had come out much gruffer than he had intended.

"He's so little." She lowered her eyes. "I didn't realize you intended for him to get up in the middle of the night too. It won't happen again."

She went to the table and began to fill the men's mugs while avoiding his gaze.

This morning was not going well. Now, he felt like a beast for having said anything at all. He would never expect one of his own children to get up before dawn to wait on a group of coarse men. Of course Ned was too little to get up in the middle of the night. Robert had simply been reacting out of his frustration over the weather and Jigger's complaints.

Disgruntled, he sat down at the table where the men had already begun to eat. Katie poured his tea as he helped himself to the flapjacks.

His first bite lightened his mood considerably. It was as light as a feather, and had a rich, yeasty flavor that was delicious. Definitely an improvement over Jigger's flapjacks, which the men had started calling "stove lids" last winter because of their heaviness. Somehow she had managed to do this with exactly the same supplies that Jigger had used.

When he sampled the stewed dried apples, he found they had been seasoned with cinnamon, and they made a nice complement to the flapjacks. He saw Skypilot pile them on top of his stack of flapjacks, drizzle sorghum over the whole, and dig in. The ham was good, but then Jigger had always been expert at cooking meat. The diced potatoes had been fried to a delicate crispness. A light dusting of salt and pepper, along with some flecks of onion, made a dish he would have been happy to have eaten as a meal all by itself.

Katie Smith, draggling petticoat or not, was most definitely a good cook—even if she did have trouble getting out of bed in the morning.

"Breakfast is delicious," he said, hoping to bridge the gap he had caused by his comment about Ned.

83

She stopped pouring tea long enough to give him a long look. This time, it was he who looked away. He would, he told himself, have to be more careful about what he said to her in the future. Regardless of Jigger's comments earlier, he was willing to keep this woman around just for her fried potatoes and flapjacks alone.

—☙❧—

Katie fell, panting, into the rocking chair. It had been close, but she had managed to get those men fed. As they ate, she had put four dozen biscuits into the oven, with which she intended to make ham sandwiches for their noon meal. She had set a day's worth of bread rising and a pot of beans simmering for supper before coming out here to catch her breath.

Ned had eaten and was now busily refilling all the firewood boxes and carrying more water into the kitchen from the river. The rain had stopped.

She drew a deep breath, her first since Jigger awakened her this morning. She thanked God that she had arrived when the number of men in camp was still small enough for her to get her bearings. This morning would have been a disaster had she been cooking for any more.

She did not consider herself a late riser. Most of her life, she had awakened at first light. But she had no idea how to go about getting herself up in the middle of the night. How did Jigger do it? A lifetime of cooking for lumber camps?

Relying on Jigger to awaken her each morning was not an option. Nor did she ever again want to hear him telling Robert he had trouble getting her up. Somehow, she would have to figure out a way to awaken without Jigger pounding on her door. There was a newfangled invention called an alarm clock that someone had patented—but she had never seen one. Now she wished she had paid closer attention.

Determined to get herself together before facing Robert and the men again, she decided to use this short reprieve to put away her clothes and have a quick wash. She was embarrassed by the way she must have looked this morning.

It wasn't that she was the least bit interested in impressing Robert as a man, but she did need to impress him as a boss. As soon as her feet were rested, she intended to dig clean clothes out of her trunk, take a sponge bath, and properly brush and plait her hair. It would be two hours before the bread would rise enough to bake. Lord willing, when Robert saw her again, she would be a different person.

She had barely caught her breath when she heard pounding coming from outside. She jumped up to take a quick look. There, behind the cabin, was the man she had heard the others calling "Tinker." He was building what looked to be a privy.

So, Robert was keeping his word in spite of his irritation with her this morning. Interesting.

Tinker had a young man's build and agility, but his hair was snow white. She had noticed this morning at breakfast that he hadn't eaten anything except flapjacks so saturated in sorghum that they were practically mush.

Tinker saw her and raised a hammer in a salute. Embarrassed to be caught watching, she nodded and then ducked away. A few moments later, there was a knock on the door and she opened it to find the man she had heard others referring to as "Blackie."

"Edward Blackburn at your service, ma'am." He bowed from the waist, a short mountain of a man with blue eyes that danced beneath brows so bushy they looked like giant black caterpillars. His teeth were a startling white against the swarthiness of his skin.

"How can I help you, Mr. Blackburn?"

The poor man had rivulets of sweat pouring down his face and neck. Unfortunately, he smelled as though he had been involved in something requiring great exertion for a very long time. It was all she could do not to cover her nose.

"Call me Blackie, ma'am." He held up a fancy piece of iron-work. "Got that lock made that Foster said you needed."

"Thank you, uh, Blackie."

"Hey, Tinker!" Blackie yelled. "Come here and help me install this bolt and lock for the lady!"

Tinker came scurrying around the corner of the cabin, a mile-wide grin on his face. Close up, she could see the reason he had eaten only softened flapjacks this morning. The poor man appeared to have no teeth except a couple in the front. With his thick shock of white hair, he had the look of a rabbit—except for his eyes. There was a look there—she couldn't put her finger on it—but she decided that this was not a man she would want to cross.

"Did you want me to hang this on the lady's door?" Tinker inspected the ornate lock Blackie had created. "Or display it in the town square?"

Blackie frowned. "Just put it on."

"You sure there's enough iron in this thing?" Tinker stuck his finger through one of the many curlicues. "I had no idea the lady was in danger of getting et up by a bear."

Blackie punched Tinker in the chest with a massive fist. Katie took a step backward and threw a hand over her mouth.

Tinker quickly recovered from the blow and rubbed his chest. "I deserved that," he said.

Blackie wore a mulish expression. "I can make more than just horseshoes."

"You are an artist, Blackie." Tinker pulled a fistful of nails from a pocket. "Now, tell me where to hang this thing."

Katie's dream of a couple hours of respite evaporated. Tinker stopped teasing Blackie, and she tried to stay out of their way while the two men cheerfully installed the lock. There was, she decided, going to be even less privacy here than she'd expected. And these shanty boys were . . . well, interesting.

But at least Robert had kept his word.

—೧ ೧—

The beans were steaming hot and seasoned with plenty of fatback, just like he liked it. Bowls of raw, chopped onions complemented the beans. Platters were piled high with wedges of crusty cornbread that had been baked in iron skillets coated with copious amounts of bacon grease. Baskets filled with spicy molasses cookies as big as dinner plates sat side-by-side with raisin pies—one of his all-time favorites.

He was beginning to suspect that everything Katie made was going to become his all-time favorite. After slathering a hot wedge of cornbread with brine-preserved butter, he sprinkled a spoonful of onion on top of the beans and dug in.

Robert was delighted both with the meal and with the woman who had prepared it. Unlike this morning, she was neat and tidy. Her dress was fresh, and she was as businesslike as any camp boss could hope for. He was proud of her and proud of hiring her.

In spite of the morning rain, things had cleared during the day, and the skeleton crew had gotten a lot accomplished. With Skypilot's help, Ernie and Cletus had managed to smooth some of the worst spots on the tote road while Sam went back into town for more supplies.

Tinker had finished Katie's outhouse and a sturdy new lock had been installed on the cabin door. Perhaps now she would relax and not be so skittish around him.

Horatio Barnes, a tall, thin man known to the camp as "Inkslinger," had arrived this afternoon to set up the office and camp store. Real names weren't important in a lumber camp. It was a rare man who didn't get some sort of nickname before the winter was over. Inkslinger was a Michigan dirt farmer with a gift for numbers. He left a family of six daughters and a wife behind to run his farm each winter while he ciphered lumber camp numbers and kept track of the board feet the loggers cut each day.

Inkslinger was the kind of person who tended to see the dark side of things. Robert had never seen the man smile. He couldn't help but wonder if the wife and daughters weren't a little relieved when Inkslinger tramped off to the camps each fall.

Two skilled axe men, one from Canada, the other from Maine, had hired on today. They were happily slurping bean soup at their assigned places at the table. They had heard about the new cook, they said, and had decided to check things out at the Foster camp. They didn't seem to be the least bit disappointed. He hoped Katie could continue to keep up when the rest of the crew arrived.

_⊱⊰_

Katie didn't know what she was going to do.

The kitchen was clean, the tin plates and cups washed and replaced, facedown on the table. The sourdough sponge Jigger had insisted she use for tomorrow's flapjacks was setting up. She'd sliced the bacon and readied a kettle of oil for doughnuts to add to the men's breakfast. She had swept out the entire cook shanty and rinsed out the dishcloths and hung them to dry. Ned was in bed, as were all the men. Everything was ready—except her.

She had no idea how she was going to go to sleep and wake up promptly at 2:00 a.m. On her father's farm and at Fallen Oaks, she could at least depend on a rooster crowing to awaken her before dawn. But there were no roosters here, and even if there were, they wouldn't be doing any crowing in the middle of the night.

After lighting a candle, she cupped her hand around it and made her way through the darkness to her cabin. It was a little eerie being alone in the dark in this wilderness. But it was a short walk to her cabin, and there was a light glowing in the window—the lamp she had lit when she had put Ned to bed.

When she stepped into the cabin, she entered a room filled with warmth and light. The lamp and her little brother's sweet, sleeping presence made the cabin feel like an oasis. She stuck the candle into an empty candleholder on the bureau and hung up her cape.

She had come up with a plan to make herself wake up in the middle of the night. Before leaving the kitchen, she had drunk two large glasses of water, and with any luck at all, that water would start nudging her awake in time to get an early start on breakfast!

9

We have fine girls, I own 'tis true.
But, alas, poor things, what can they do?
For if they want an honest man
he can't be found in Michigan.

> "Don't Come to Michigan"
> —1800s shanty song

October 9, 1867

Katie dreamed she was floating in a boat and fell into the water. As she thrashed around, she awoke and realized that she needed to go. Bad. Perhaps her plan to drink two glasses of water before bed was going to work after all!

She put on her shoes and checked the little pocket watch her father had given her a lifetime ago. Midnight. It was only midnight. Disappointed her plan hadn't worked, she used the chamber pot and got back into bed. How in the world was she going to make herself get up in two more hours?

At first, her sleep was fitful, with many glances at her watch by the light of the candle. Then she once again tumbled into a deep sleep.

Suddenly, there was a loud pounding on her door, and Jigger's voice broke through her consciousness.

"Hey! Yer sleepin' in again. Way past time to start breakfast!"

She sat bolt upright. "Coming!" she yelled. "I'll be right there." She checked her watch. Three o'clock. She should have been up an hour ago. But at least this morning she was already dressed. Fearful this sort of thing might happen again, she had slept on top of the covers, fully clothed.

She splashed water on her face from the basin she had filled the night before and smoothed her hair down with her damp hands. She had deliberately not taken it out of its bun before she lay down. She blew out the candle and bolted into the darkness.

Jigger had already started the fire in the stove. She set her largest pot on top and dumped half a bucket of lard in to melt for the doughnuts she had told him she was making this morning.

A half pound of bacon for each man, she figured, so the eight pounds of bacon she had thick-sliced the night before should be enough. She threw two huge cast-iron skillets on the range and began layering the bacon in the bottoms. While that began to sizzle, she mixed up the flapjack batter Jigger told her the men would expect every morning. She checked, and the lard was beginning to get warm, but it wasn't yet hot enough for doughnuts. There was time to get the flapjacks finished first. About six per man, from what she had seen yesterday morning.

"Is the sorghum and butter on the table?" she asked without turning around. It took all her concentration to keep the flapjacks from burning while frying the bacon.

"Already did it," Jigger said. "While you was still a-snoozin'."

"Take over the bacon, please." She ignored his comment. "I'll cut out the doughnuts."

Even with only one hand, Jigger was capable of frying bacon. It could be worse, she thought. She could be left alone with no help at all.

"Can I help?" Ned wandered in, rubbing his eyes. She had not wanted to awaken the little fellow so early, but now that he was up, at least Robert couldn't complain.

"Bring more firewood from outside," she said. "The stove needs to be extra hot for the doughnuts."

"Doughnuts?" Ned's eyes widened. "We're having dough-nuts?"

"Just as soon as I can make them."

Ned trotted happily off to do his chore.

"The men like 'em extra sweet," Jigger said. "And I like to put vaniller in mine."

"Me too." She reached for the sack of sugar and dumped in several cupfuls. She had often helped her mother make dough-nuts, and she automatically doubled the recipe.

"The vaniller's over yonder on the shelf."

"Thank you." As she reached for it, she congratulated herself on the fact that they seemed to be finally getting along. If only she could figure out a way to wake up without Jigger's help.

She dropped a smidgen of doughnut batter into the oil and watched it sizzle to a golden brown. One by one, she slipped raw doughnuts into the hot lard and watched them puff up. The men would enjoy these *so* much.

She felt good about today. She was getting the hang of things, learning her way around the supplies and tools of the kitchen. Even though she had gotten up later than she wanted, thanks to her preparations the night before, she wasn't nearly as frazzled. Jigger was acting decent to her, so she hoped his pique was over. The comfort and warmth of the early morning kitchen washed over her, and she experienced a feeling of deep contentment as she presided over the vat of doughnuts.

A half hour later, Jigger went to awaken the men. Soon, they came tramping through the door. By that time, she had placed stacks of flapjacks, heaps of bacon, and mounds of doughnuts onto the table. It was a pretty sight, and she knew the dining room was redolent with good smells. She had even heated the sorghum this morning.

"Looks good," Robert said as he and the other men took their seats.

Jigger stood near the head of the table, ready to chastise anyone who spoke while eating. He, too, seemed to be in a good mood. She had even caught him smiling a couple times this morning. Maybe he was beginning to thaw toward her after all.

The men dug into the food, and she waited, looking forward to seeing the enjoyment on their faces. She was especially proud of how well the doughnuts had turned out.

Ernie was the first to help himself to the pile in front of him. But instead of groaning with ecstasy, he grimaced at the first bite and swallowed hard. Then he stared at the doughnut as though he couldn't believe what he had just put in his mouth. To her horror, she saw the same action being repeated up and down the table. Robert was the last to bite into a doughnut, and he couldn't spit it out fast enough. His eyes sought hers.

"What did you *do*?" he asked.

Puzzled, she reached for a doughnut, took a nibble, and understood what had happened. She had put salt in the batter instead of sugar. Four cups of it!

Jigger didn't reach for a doughnut. Instead, he stood at the head of the table, grinning from ear to ear—as though he had been expecting this all along.

The old goat had sabotaged her cooking!

Without saying a word, she went over to the sack of "sugar" and tasted a few grains. It was salt. She pulled the box of salt off the shelf and tasted. It was filled with sugar.

"You switched them!" she accused.

"I don't know what yer talking about." Jigger acted as innocent as a newborn babe. "You must've gotten things mixed up, getting up so late and all. It's easy to make a mistake when you're only half awake."

Robert rose, took the tray of doughnuts over to the garbage pail, and dumped them in.

"Come here." He motioned Jigger and Katie to follow him to a far corner of the kitchen.

"She won't get up in time to do her work properly," Jigger complained. "Never saw such a lazy woman. Even got the salt and sugar mixed up."

Katie opened her mouth to defend herself, but Robert put up a hand to stop her. "I have a lumber camp to run, hungry men to feed, and limited supplies and resources to do it with. If the two of you can't figure a way to work things out, you're *both* fired."

He looked back and forth between them. "Do I make myself clear?"

Katie nodded, her face aflame.

"Do you understand?" he asked Jigger.

"Yeah." Jigger was the picture of penitence as he stared at the ground.

"Good."

Robert went back to his meal. Silence once again descended as the men finished filling their bellies with nothing more than bacon and flapjacks.

A lump grew in Katie's throat and tears threatened at the injustice of it all. She had done nothing wrong, and yet Robert had judged her anyway. Determined not to cry in front of the men, she fled out of the back door to her borrowed cabin.

The moment she entered, she slid the bolt shut on Blackie's fancy lock so no one could come in. Then she lay facedown on the bed and burst into tears.

It was a cry that was long, long overdue. She had not cried when Harlan had mistreated her. She had not cried the day Ned and she had made that terrifying flight into the unknown. She had not cried yesterday when her feet and back had ached so bad she could hardly stand up.

She had worked as hard as she knew how, and all she had gotten for it was being chastised by a man she had thought might actually become a friend.

Years of frustration and anger poured out into the straw-tick mattress. The privations of war. The burning of her home by Northern soldiers. She cried over having to sell the valiant Rebel's Pride. She even cried over how much she missed her two good cows.

Never in her life had she cried so much or so hard. Part of it was because of extreme fatigue. She had slept but a handful of hours in the past week. And part of it was because it was overdue. She had had enough. It was hard to cook for all those men, let alone with Jigger sabotaging her efforts and Robert standing ready to scold her just because of Jigger's meanness.

It felt as though everything had come crashing down on her at once, and she cried until she was sick.

Then, as her sobs slowed, she hiccupped a few times, wiped her tears away with the edge of a pillowcase, and forced herself to think about what to do next. One thing she knew—self-pity wasn't going to fix anything.

She went over to the basin of water and washed her face again. She lit the kerosene lamp and took a good, hard look in the mirror. What she saw was a woman with a red nose, blotchy face, and swollen eyes. She was a mess, and it was well past time to head back into the kitchen to clean up and prepare for lunch. It felt as though she had already put in a full day's work and it was only five o'clock in the morning.

She didn't relish facing Jigger after his prank, especially with the aftermath of her tears still written all over her face, but she had to do something that would stop this nonsense. If she didn't get the upper hand, and soon, she would lose her job. Robert hadn't been joking when he'd threatened to fire both of them. After this morning's fiasco, she didn't blame him.

As she stared at her mottled reflection in the mirror, she decided that she was tired of being the victim. Sick to death of being some man's punching bag. A raw fury stronger than anything she had ever felt before washed over her. She'd tried being nice. She'd tried being polite. She'd even made excuses to herself for Jigger's bad behavior. But no more. That old bully wasn't going to cause her to lose her job without a fight!

If there was one thing she knew she could do well—it was cook. Jigger wasn't going to take this well-paying job away from her. If it came down to a contest of wills between her and the old man, he was going to lose.

─ೲ─

Robert saw the look on Katie's face as he scolded her and Jigger. He saw the tears threatening to spill over from her big blue eyes, and he saw her leave the cook shanty the minute she could escape.

All of this pain, just because of a stupid prank Jigger had played and his own overreaction to it. He knew she had not made a mistake. Jigger had deliberately engineered it. Practical jokes were common in a lumber camp. Many of them were pretty rough. He had seen half-frozen raccoons put into bedrolls and tins of lice poured down the back of an unsuspecting greenhorn's shirt. He'd seen grown men, bored with camp, make a game out of whacking a blindfolded logger on the backside with a stick and then challenging him to guess who had hit him. In a lumber camp, exchanging salt for sugar was pretty mild stuff.

But the tension between his two cooks was getting on his nerves. He had meant what he said. Katie was going to have to find a way to deal with Jigger or both of them were going to be out on their ear. He'd figure out a way to cook himself before he'd put up with any more of this nonsense.

He really did mean it. At least he had meant it when he said it, with the sting of salty doughnuts still on his tongue. Now, well . . . Katie was crying.

From outside her cabin, he could hear her sobs. He was certain she thought everyone was still in the cook shanty, eating her feather-light flapjacks, but he was here, outside her door, and her sobs had taken his appetite away.

The girl had been so plucky, had tried so hard, had worked nonstop since they had arrived—without one complaint. She had even endured his lecture this morning without a whimper or word of defense. She had stood there, absorbing his words. He wondered now how hard Jigger had made things for the girl when his back was turned.

He also wondered what she had experienced before coming to the camp to make her so stoic, so accepting of hardship. He knew next to nothing about her except what he had seen with his own eyes—her love for her brother, her skill in the kitchen, that lift of her chin the first time she had told him she was a good cook. Being a good cook was obviously something she was proud of—maybe the only thing—and Jigger had ruined it for her.

Robert had seen her look of pleasure as she had surveyed the table right before the men had dug in. Her eyes had lingered a little longer on the carefully stacked pyramid of perfect, golden doughnuts. She was proud of them. Proud of having made them.

After getting up in the middle of the night to create a wonderful breakfast for the men, after having done her level best to make a work of art out of nothing more than breakfast in a rough lumber camp—thanks to him and Jigger, she had been humiliated and chastised.

Her sobs were breaking his heart.

He raised a fist to knock on the cabin door. Then he pulled his hand away and jammed it into his pocket. If she opened the door, with those big tear-stained blue eyes, he would melt.

Pure and simple. In fact, he had already begun to melt. Katie was starting to occupy too many of his thoughts, and he was only two days into logging. In fact, he hadn't even *begun* to log yet. His crew wasn't complete. Not one tree had been felled. And already things felt as though they were spinning out of control.

The problem was, he couldn't afford to let Katie's sobs affect him, or the wall he had erected between himself and the rest of the world would crumble. As it was, it was all he could do just to keep putting one foot in front of the other long enough to support his family. Had he not possessed the ability to harden his heart, he would have already lost his mind.

The nightmares alone would have driven him mad.

He had looked into the eyes of men who were dying and whom he had no way on earth of helping. He had seen the pleas in their faces—begging him to save them for their wives, their children, their aged mothers and fathers.

He had watched good, decent men falling, men whose families were depending on them to return to their small family farms. Needing their strength at home to keep the children fed, the families intact. There were too many men whose wives had ended up like Katie, alone in the world and trying to keep body and soul together by any means possible. He had seen some of those war widows, out of sheer desperation, working in the brothels of Bay City.

He couldn't save everyone. He could barely save himself.

He shoved away the memories of the bloodbaths he had endured. He took a deep breath of the clean air of the pine woods and stared at the treetops in the distance—the giant pines in whose presence he felt cleansed and renewed.

Cutting logs, ordering supplies, hiring men. Taking his turn with an axe or a crosscut saw or a peavey. This was what he did now. This was who he was. If he were to make a success of this camp, he would have to be tough. Logging companies weren't built by men who fell apart over the sound of a woman crying.

Resolutely, he walked back to the cook shanty and took his place at the table. Katie would have to learn how to deal with the realities of life in a lumber camp, or she would have to go. It was that simple. And Jigger would have to straighten up, or he would have to go. Robert couldn't waste another minute worrying about either of them. He had children depending on him for support, and the only way he knew to do that was to float at least three-hundred-thousand board feet of timber down the Saginaw River come spring.

~c○o~

Katie swept into the kitchen after she saw the men leave, with her jaw set and her head held high. She was done with tears and finished with cowering and placating. The only person left in the room when she entered was Jigger, who was wiping off the table with a rag and a bucket of water.

"Where's Ned?" she asked.

"The boy's watching Tinker fixin' the steps out front." Jigger rinsed the rag out with one hand.

"I'm glad he's not here. I want to talk to you. Alone." She picked up a butcher knife from the worktable and tested the blade. "That was a good one, Jigger—your practical joke."

He grinned, proud of himself.

"You don't know me very well." She picked up the whetting stone and hefted it in her hand. "Do you?"

"Don't need to," Jigger muttered, going back to his work. "Women are all about the same."

"Not really." She began to hone the butcher knife with the stone, taking slow, steady swipes. "Once you get to know them, women are very different, one from another. Take me, for example." She tested the knife by cutting a small shred off an old newspaper lying nearby. "I used to be an innocent, trusting girl. Very sensitive. I could weep just at the thought of something or someone being in pain."

Jigger sniffed, dismissing her statement.

"Then my husband went to war, and I had to fend for myself. I nearly starved until I learned how to trap rabbits and gut them. I learned how to fish and how to clean those too." She held the newspaper in front of her face and slowly sliced off another sliver with the razor-sharp knife. "In order to survive, I had to become so hard-hearted that I could chop off a chicken's head and watch it bleed out without so much as blinking—already planning the dumplings I would stew in its broth."

Jigger's hand that had been wiping off the table stilled—and she saw that she had his complete attention.

"What're you saying?" he said.

"What I'm saying is—and you need to listen carefully here—that sweet little boy out there is the only close relative I have left on this earth. If anyone is foolish enough to force me into a corner, I'll do whatever I have to do to take care of him." She brought her hand down suddenly, plunging the butcher knife into the work counter with so much force that it quivered. "If you ever try to sabotage my cooking again, by even so much as one teaspoonful of baking soda, you will regret it."

He tilted his head back, his eyes squinted. "What do you think yer gonna do?"

She stared him down while enunciating very slowly. "You don't want to find out, old man."

He turned away and continued to wipe the table.

And then she saw Robert standing stock still at the back of the room. Had he heard her threats? Did he believe them? Did it matter?

She straightened her shoulders, lifted her chin, and looked

him square in the eye. It might do *him* some good to be a little wary of her too.

Robert was wearing an old slouch hat. Without taking his eyes off of her, he lifted a hand and tipped his hat in a sign of deference and respect. Then he left, quietly closing the door behind him.

10

With patched-up clothes and rubber boots
and mud up to the knees
with lice as big as chili beans
fighting with the fleas.
　　　"The Jolly Shanty Boy Song"
　　　—1800s shanty song

Robert couldn't help but smile over the look of alarm he had seen on Jigger's face as Katie had subtly threatened him with a butcher knife. Anyone who had heard her sobbing in her bunk an hour ago wouldn't be worried. That sweet girl wasn't capable of hurting a fly. But if her threats kept Jigger in line, Robert would never tell.

He had gone to the cook shanty intending to let Katie and Jigger know that two teams of axe men, four men total, had arrived and would be needing dinner. But Katie seemed to have things well under control. His guess was that after this morning's disaster, she would outdo herself for dinner and supper. If Jigger's expression was any indication, he would be quite the helper too.

Hopefully, the tempest that had been brewing in the cook shanty was at an end and he could attend to more important things—like scrounging up a second teamster and praying that

102

more good men, some who had already promised to come, would materialize.

As he made his way through the camp, the sun broke out over the distant trees. In front of the sunrise, coming from the east, rode a man driving a team of horses. The sun blinded Robert, and he shaded his eyes to see who it was.

He was a little surprised when the man drew closer and he saw that he was black—not one of the various shades of brown worn by many freed men Robert had known but the inky blackness born of Africa. He was well-muscled and his team of horses shone with health. It was not unheard of for black men to work in the lumber camps, but it wasn't common.

"Nice-looking team you've got there," Robert called as the wagon drew near.

The man gave a low whistle, and the horses came to a complete stop. Robert was impressed. No harsh tugging on the reins, no customary string of curse words.

"I hear you's hiring."

"I am." Robert checked out the wagon, which was in excellent repair. "What's your name?"

"Mose." The teamster's face was expressionless, but his muscles were taut as though steeled for rejection.

"Where are you from, Mose?"

"Josiah Henson's." He jerked his head toward the north. "Up in Canada. We lumbered a deal of black walnut 'round his place. I'm a right good hand with an axe, as well as a team."

Robert had heard of Josiah Henson, who had escaped North before the war. Henson had managed to buy land upon which he had founded a cooperative colony of former slaves. The quality of work done there was legendary. From what Robert had heard, if Mose had been trained by Josiah Henson, he would be worth hiring indeed.

"There's no more work at Henson's?" Robert asked.

"Gettin' a little crowded. 'Bout five hundred of us there now. 'Sides, I's figuring on travelin' south come spring."

"I am in need of another teamster," Robert said. "And I can always use a man who's good with an axe. Take your horses on over to the barn and give them a good feed." He paused for a split second. "You can put your bedroll in the bunkhouse."

This last statement hung in the air between them. They both knew that there might be men in that bunkhouse who would object to Mose sleeping beneath the same roof.

If anyone did mind, Robert decided that he would no longer need their services.

"Thank you kindly," Mose said, "but I'd rather stay with my horses."

Mose wouldn't be the first teamster to prefer the fresh hay of the barn and the wholesome smell of the animals to the smoky, noxious bunkhouse—but Robert needed to make sure that was what Mose wanted.

"You're welcome to bunk with us."

"I 'preciate that, but my horses get nervous if I'm not around. They like me being with 'em. Keeps 'em calm." He gave Robert a shadow of a smile. "Keeps everybody calm."

"The pay is a dollar a day and all the food you can eat."

"I'm obliged." Mose gave another low whistle, and the animals responded immediately.

Mose's style of driving horses was different than what Robert had ever seen before. He liked it.

His camp was turning into an interesting place—but then lumber camps always drew a variety of men, all with their own personal reasons for seeking out work in the tall timber.

A few were hiding from the law. Some might be avoiding a shotgun wedding. Many were war veterans, like him, trying to get back on their feet. Others were farmers trying to piece together a stake to help them make it on the land another year.

He didn't know what Mose's story was, but he probably would before the winter was out. Everyone would know more than they ever wanted to know about one another—after working together for seven long months.

─୦·୦─

Every time Katie glanced out of the cook shanty, she saw more men arriving. They were rough-looking men, carrying sacks over their shoulders and axes in their hands. There would be a full table tonight. The work was beginning in earnest now, and it was going to take everything she and Jigger could do to get enough food together. There was no time to quarrel, and they both knew it.

She absolutely could no longer afford to sleep past two o'clock, and she had a plan she thought might work. When Jigger wasn't looking, she had taken a washtub and an old teakettle out to her cabin, along with some thick string she had found in a drawer.

The rich aroma of slow-cooked roasts, carved from a side of beef Sam had hung in the storage shed, drifted from the Dutch ovens she had just pulled from the stove. Three giant wooden bowls piled high with baked potatoes sat steaming nearby. Dried-apple pies cooled on the table where she had placed them at intervals. She had cooked, pared, mixed, and baked all afternoon.

"We're ready," she told Jigger.

He pulled the Gabriel horn off the wall and headed out the door. A few loud blasts later, and nearly thirty hungry men crowded in. Jigger took over the task of assigning each new man his permanent place at the table.

She was so busy carrying platters of biscuits to the table that she barely took notice of all the new loggers. The places were filling up fast, and she was preoccupied with wondering whether or not she had prepared enough.

As she brought the trays of potatoes to the table, she scanned the crowd, seeing many unfamiliar faces. At the end of the table, sitting beside Robert, she was surprised to see a large black man. At that very moment, the man glanced up, their eyes met, and she put out a hand to steady herself.

She knew him.

Not only did she know him, she could have recited the exact number of whip marks on his back. There were thirty. Her husband had put them there. She had counted them one dreadful evening, when the sound of each slash echoed against her own soul as her maid, Violet, sobbed in her arms.

She had listened to those thirty lashes, wincing with each one, wishing she could block out the sound. Her temples pounded with the worst headache of her life, and she had vomited afterward.

But her husband had been in high good humor when he came to her bedroom that night, and she had hated him for it.

She and Mose stared at each other, bitter, mind-scorching memories hanging in the air between them.

"Mrs. Smith," Robert said, bringing her out of her trance. "Could we have some of those biscuits down here, please?"

Mrs. Smith? Robert seldom called her that. She supposed he did so now because he was trying to establish a line of respect for her with all the new men. She saw a look of puzzlement pass over Mose's face. No doubt, he was wondering why she was calling herself "Smith."

This man knew who she was and where she had come from. He had ample reason to despise her. Would he inform Robert that she had been the mistress of a plantation where he had been brutalized?

She hurried to the end of the table and set the platter of biscuits down in front of Mose and Robert.

"We could use some more butter too," Robert said.

"I'll be right back." She saw Mose reach for a biscuit as she scuttled toward the kitchen. She would butter that biscuit for him herself, if only he wouldn't tell Robert who she was. She ran back and placed the butter at Robert's elbow while shaking her head slightly at her former field hand's silent, questioning gaze.

The last time she had seen Mose, it had been a summer evening, near twilight. Harlan had forced him to go back into the fields the very next day after the whipping. That evening, her husband had gone into town. Unable to abide sitting alone at their formal dining table, she had taken a container of lemonade and a packet of food down to the river, planning to have a solitary picnic where it was a few degrees cooler.

It was a lovely spot with willows overhanging the shallow water. The ripples made a sort of music that always calmed her. There was a small bench beside the river, where she sat and prepared to eat her cold supper.

As she gazed into the brush on the other side of the stream, she realized that a man was crouching very still. He reminded her of a deer, pausing motionless, hoping to be invisible, waiting for a threat to pass.

The wounded Mose had almost—but not quite—succeeded in blending into the shadows.

She had known instantly that she had caught him in the act of running away.

For as long as she lived, she would remember the look in his eyes when he realized that she had spotted him. Those eyes had pled with her to keep silent, to let him go. It was as though he had shouted at her—so strongly did he beg her with his eyes to ignore his presence.

And she, the young bride of the largest plantation owner in the county, had held the man's life in the balance. God forgive her, she had actually debated what to do. She had heard all the pro-slavery arguments from Harlan and the other plantation owners while desperately trying to fit into the incomprehensible social circle into which marriage had thrust her. She had tried hard to believe in those arguments.

But to her credit, she said nothing when she saw Mose frozen on the other side of the creek with terror written on his face. With the sound of the whip still ringing in her ears, she had gotten up from her seat, deliberately leaving her food and drink untouched upon the stone seat.

She had walked toward the big house without turning around, and as she walked, she had sung a hymn she had learned at her father's knee, "Savior, Like a Shepherd Lead Us," until she heard a slight splashing in the river and knew Mose was gone.

She did not turn around until reaching the big house. Then she allowed herself a glance over her shoulder. Although she was far away by then, she could see that the picnic she had prepared for herself had disappeared, and so—she hoped—had Mose.

That night, Harlan had returned very late. As she lay beside him, she prayed for Mose's safe escape and for his deliverance to a kinder place than the plantation in which she lived.

She never said a word about what had happened. Not to her angry husband the next morning, nor to the house slaves when she heard them chattering amongst themselves about the field hand's disappearance. Her own maid, Violet, whom she suspected of being in love with Mose, went into a quiet mourning, and Katie could not risk assuaging even her grief.

Looking back, she believed that the moment when she had left her picnic behind and turned her back so Mose could run was one of the few truly fine things she had ever done in her life. With all her heart, she wished she had been strong and brave and smart enough to have done more.

Now, it was *her* eyes that pled for silence. And it was Mose, after his initial surprise, who silently turned away.

Like most camp owners, Robert had built the bunkhouse without windows. There was no need to go to the expense and bother of transporting and installing panes of glass for the long building. Winter days in Michigan were short. The men living in this shanty would be awake and at work long before daylight. They wouldn't come back to the bunkhouse until after dark.

A long seat called a "deacon's bench" made of split logs ran around the inside of the room, flush against the bunks. In the middle, a barrel stove squatted in a box of sand with its stovepipe shooting straight up through an open hole in the roof. The stovepipe funneled some of the smoke out, and the hole let fresh air in. After men's intestines had absorbed the full effect of eating meals consisting of beans and bacon, the bunkhouse was always in need of a little fresh air.

There were twenty double bunks made of rough-sawn pine lining the walls. Each was built to hold two men. It was common for strangers who might not even speak the same language to sleep two to a bunk. They slept fully clothed, cushioned by sawdust or straw, doubling up their blankets, and kept from freezing by sharing body warmth. He would have a crew of thirty, so he had room to keep a bunk to himself. His personal supply of wool blankets was thick enough that he thought he could survive the winter without a bunk partner.

Several of the men lined the deacon's bench. Some lay in bunks. The logger from Maine was sharpening his axe on the grindstone that sat in the middle of the floor. Ernie, one of the few men who favored a mustache instead of a beard, scraped at his jaw with his own newly sharpened axe blade. Cletus was carving something that looked like a miniature horse. A Dutchman named Klaas was hanging his wet socks with all the others over the stove on a wire that stretched the length of the bunkhouse. Soon, the socks would begin to steam and add their own ripe aroma to the smoke and sweat.

Henri, one of the new men, was sitting cross-legged on a top bunk, his back against the wall, his eyes closed, playing a soft tune on his fiddle. Come Saturday night, the tune would become more raucous, but this was a work night and there would be no dancing and singing.

Skypilot was lying in his top bunk, reading a ragged Bible by the light of a kerosene lamp hanging from the ceiling. This behavior was out of the norm. Few shanty boys owned a Bible, let alone read one.

"So—you think you're a preacher." Sam sat on the deacon's bench, picking his teeth and watching Skypilot with mild curiosity.

Skypilot licked his finger and turned a page. "Nope."

"That's what Ernie and Cletus said."

"Ernie and Cletus were wrong."

"If you ain't a preacher," Sam said suspiciously, "then how come they call you Skypilot?"

Skypilot kept his eyes on the page. "Because I used to be a preacher."

"How can anyone used to be a preacher?" Sam probed. "Either you are or you ain't."

"Not if you get fired, you're not."

"You got fired? From a *church*?"

Skypilot sighed and put his finger in the Bible to mark his place. "Yes."

"What in thunder did you do, man?"

"I was not happy about the institution of slavery."

"A lot of us up here in the North weren't," Sam scoffed.

"I wasn't in the North." Skypilot laid his Bible on his chest, folded his arms behind his head, and stared at the ceiling. "I was living in Richmond."

"Wait a minute. You mean you were trying to be an abolitionist right smack dab in the capital of the Confederacy?" Sam's jaw hung open. Henri's fiddle playing stopped. All paused to stare at Skypilot.

"I preached some sermons against it, yes. I thought there were things that reasonable Christian people ought to think about before they started shooting at each other. But according to my father-in-law-to-be, I was a 'fire-breathing, dyed-in-the-wool, wild-eyed, raving lunatic' who was trying to destroy him and everything he held dear."

"Then what happened?" Sam asked.

"It got my dander up. Within twenty-four hours of a sermon in which I compared my father-in-law and others like him to the Pharaoh who tried to keep Moses and the Hebrew children in slavery, my engagement to his daughter was cut off and the leaders of the church gave me the boot."

"What did you do then?" Cletus's eyes were huge.

"I lived up to my former fiancée's father's low opinion of me by escorting over fifty slaves across the Ohio River and I made certain that several were his."

"How come you're an axe man now?"

"I put myself through Bible college on one season of timber-cutting at a time. I'd work a year and go to school a year. Took me a while."

"We ran two preachers out of my camp last year." Sam spat a stream of tobacco juice into the sand beneath the stove. "You planning on tryin' any of that convertin' stuff on us?"

"Nope."

Sam leaned back against the deacon's bench. "How come?"

"Here." Skypilot tossed his Bible at Sam. "Read it for yourself. Make your own decision. I'm done with preaching." Skypilot turned his back on Sam and faced the wall.

Sam gingerly laid the Bible on the deacon's bench as though it might bite. "Think I'll get some shut-eye." He pulled off his shoes and crawled into his bunk.

"That woman cook." The big logger from Maine spread his blanket on the bunk he had chosen. "She's a widow?"

"Yes," Robert answered.

"Pretty little thing."

Sounds of affirmation came from around the bunkhouse. Robert kept quiet. So far, no one had said anything out of place. Katie *was* a pretty little thing, and she *was* a cook.

"A man could get used to having a woman like that around," Mainer said.

More sounds of affirmation. Robert was glad now that he was sharing the bunkhouse with his men. He could keep the talk about Katie from spiraling downward.

Henri hung his fiddle on a peg on the wall. "Where is the girl from?"

"Ohio," Robert said.

"That's odd," Tinker said. "There seems to be some Southern in her talk."

"Ohio's south of us."

"Not that far south."

"Do you think she'll make flapjacks again for breakfast tomorrow?" Ernie asked.

"Or more of 'em fried potatoes," Cletus said. "I love 'em fried potatoes."

Robert relaxed. Their questions and comments were normal for a group of men whose interests lay, to a large extent, in what they put into their stomachs. He allowed himself to settle down in his bunk. Tomorrow morning would come soon enough. He hoped to start felling trees tomorrow.

As the men settled down for the night, Skypilot quietly climbed down out of his bunk, knelt beside the deacon's bench, bowed his head, and began to pray. It wasn't loud, and Robert couldn't make out the words, but he could hear Skypilot's voice softly conversing with God.

Out of the darkness, someone threw a shoe at the kneeling logger. It hit him square in the back. Skypilot stopped praying, picked up the shoe, looked at it, set it down, and resumed his prayer. A few moments later, another shoe came sailing out of the same bunk. Robert knew it was Sam doing it. This time, the shoe hit Skypilot in the back of the head. Again Skypilot picked up the shoe, looked at it, rubbed the back of his head, and slowly got to his feet.

"Now, Sam, why'd you have to go and do that for?" Skypilot said.

This time it was Sam's wet, dirty sock that was flung, hitting Skypilot square in the face.

There was an intake of breath all around the bunkhouse as they waited to see what Skypilot would do. Almost reluctantly, Skypilot walked over, grabbed a fistful of Sam's shirt, punched him twice in the face, then calmly went back to the deacon's bench and resumed his prayer. This time, the bunkhouse remained silent. Nothing else was thrown, and Skypilot was allowed to finish in peace.

Robert went to sleep with a smile on his face. This camp was going to be a very interesting place this winter.

11

About four o'clock our noisy little cook
cries, "Boys, it is the break of day."
With heavy sighs from slumber we rise
to go with the bright morning star.

> "A Shantyman's Life"
> —1800s shanty song

October 10, 1867

A loud clatter awoke Katie from a sound sleep. It sounded as though the roof had fallen in. She lit the lamp beside her bed and checked her watch. It was a few minutes past two o'clock in the morning.

Finally! After several experiments, her makeshift alarm had worked. Never again would she be late for preparing breakfast. Never again would she have to rely on Jigger to awaken her.

She was smiling as she went to investigate the contraption she had rigged. The candle had burned to within an inch of the base, to where she had imbedded the string in the candle wax. The string, which had been tied to her bedpost and strung up over the rafter, had caught fire when the candle had burned down to the point she had marked after letting a similar candle burn through the previous night. This had released the old teakettle to plunge against the washtub she had turned upside down beneath it.

It had made a quite satisfying clatter. She was delighted with her own ingenuity.

"Is it time to get up?" Ned's sleepy head emerged from beneath the covers.

"Go back to sleep, little brother," she said. "I'm getting such an early start I won't be needing your help this morning."

Without argument, he snuggled back down beneath the covers.

Once again she had slept in her clothes, but that would stop after today. Now that she knew she wouldn't have to rush around in the morning, she would take the time to put on a proper nightgown at night and brush and braid her hair instead of keeping it in a tight bun.

After putting a couple more logs into the stove, she splashed some water on her face, grabbed a shawl, and stepped out into the starry night. There was a sharper nip in the air than what had been there yesterday morning. If she wasn't mistaken, there was even a scent of snow in the air.

She let herself into the cook shanty and began lighting the lamps that would illuminate the work area. Then she lit the tinder in the wood box and set the teakettle on to heat. The potatoes she had boiled last night after supper had cooled to the point that she could peel them to fry. The ham she had sliced yesterday, she layered into a large, covered pan and slid into the oven to heat.

Last of all, she set a vat of lard on the stove. This morning she would make doughnuts. *This* time she would taste the contents of the sugar jar to make certain it was sweet before dumping it into the batter.

There was something peaceful about working alone in the silence of this rough kitchen. There was something strengthening in knowing she was capable of making her own living. Something about the familiarity of the preparations for the men's breakfast that made her feel strong and capable.

Deep in the recesses of her heart, she realized that she had made an important decision during that wild crying session in the cabin yesterday. She would never allow herself to be bullied again. From this moment forward, with the help of God, she would take control of her own life.

With the butcher knife held loosely in her hand, she walked over to Jigger's room. She quietly turned the knob, then she kicked the door so hard it banged against the wall.

The light from the kitchen spilled into the room over her shoulder, illuminating the wild-eyed expression on Jigger's face as he took in the fact that she was standing in his doorway with a sharp butcher knife in her hand. It took everything she had not to laugh when she saw the startled and fearful expression on his face.

"Time to get up, old man," she said with satisfaction. "We have work to do."

⎯ ⌒⌒ ⎯

The doughnuts were perfect and plentiful. The fried potatoes crisp and golden. The ham was tender. The biscuits fluffy. The tea was strong and scalding hot. Katie surveyed her table with pride as the men shuffled through the door.

Then she spotted Mose again.

He seated himself next to Robert in the same place Jigger had assigned him. Ernie was sitting next to him. He wasn't acting perturbed about being seated next to a black man—and she was grateful. Mose deserved the respect of the other men. More than any of them realized.

Once again, she studied Robert's face for some sign that Mose had told him about her, but all she got was a morning nod.

"Pass the 'taters."

"More sorghum."

"Butter—down here."

116

"Gimme more of 'em doughnuts."

The sound of forks scraping plates, the occasional burp, and requests for food was all the noise allowed.

Still, the enthusiasm with which the men ate was really something.

The logger from Maine startled Katie when he broke the silence. "Best doughnuts I ever et in my life, ma'am."

"No talking!" Jigger smacked the man on the back of the head. The logger gave Katie a wink before grabbing another fistful of doughnuts.

After the men had finished, she and Ned washed and dried the dishes and reset the table. When she went outside to dump the pan of dirty dishwater, it was still dark. Starlight and the dim glow of lantern light slanting out of the cook shanty windows illuminated her way to the edge of the camp.

She threw the dishwater into the brush that surrounded the camp and heard a disturbing, rustling sound, as though someone or something was walking through the brush.

"Who's there?" she asked.

It seemed unlikely that a shanty boy would be skulking about in the morning darkness, but it didn't sound like the footsteps of an animal. The hair of her neck stood up, and she backed away, holding the dishpan like a shield in front of her.

She had almost decided to turn tail and run into the kitchen when she caught a glimpse of a person emerging from the brush. She couldn't tell if it was a man or woman, but whoever it was walked hunched over and had a pronounced limp. The only people she had ever seen move like that were old and feeble.

What would an elderly person be doing walking through these woods in the dark?

As the figure emerged from the shadows, she saw what appeared to be a woman dressed in rags. Her long hair hung in tangles, and her face—what Katie could see of it in the dim light—was so dirty she couldn't begin to guess the woman's age.

As the woman held out her hand, cupped, in a gesture of supplication, her sleeve fell away, and Katie saw that her arm was as thin as a stick of kindling.

"Who—who are you?" Katie backed away.

The woman looked like she might be an Indian.

It was cold outside. Katie didn't know what else to do except open the door and allow her to enter. Maybe Jigger would know what to do with her.

The woman, Katie saw as they came into the lamplight of the cook shanty, was slight of build and much younger than Katie had first thought. Her limp seemed to come from an injured foot, and she was hunched over a bundle of clothing.

Ned's eyes were as large as saucers as Katie seated the woman at the worktable, where the leftovers from the men's breakfast lay. She pulled off the dishcloths with which she had covered the piles of food. The woman gasped, but she didn't reach for the food. Instead, she first looked at Katie for permission.

Katie grabbed a tin plate and filled it. Ned rushed to pour a cup of lukewarm tea.

"Here," Katie said. "Eat."

The woman hesitated, still clinging to her bundle of rags. Katie reached to take it from her, but the woman resisted. Then, with the saddest eyes Katie had ever seen, she relinquished it to her. She immediately snatched a piece of ham from her plate and began to eat—chewing and swallowing but never taking her eyes off the bundle Katie had lifted from her arms.

Katie, unwilling to have the filthy rags in her clean kitchen, started to set the bundle in a far corner of the room but was startled by a weak mewling sound from within. She pulled a ragged corner away and saw the wizened face of a starving baby.

"Dear God," she breathed. "Tell me what to do."

With the mother watching every movement, she unwrapped the rags from the tiny, yellow infant—a little boy. What on earth was she going to feed him?

Jigger appeared in the doorway of his room. "What in tarnation?"

"They're starving," Katie said.

"They?" Jigger stalked toward her and the baby. The mother jumped up from the table and threw her body between Katie and Jigger.

"I ain't gonna hurt your baby, woman." He turned his palms up. "I just want to see it."

Reluctantly, the woman moved away. She stood, wary and nervous, while he peered at the infant Katie held in her arms.

"Scrawny little thing, ain't it?"

"What can we feed him?" Katie asked. "We don't have a cow."

"Don't need a cow," Jigger said. "Go get me a clean washrag, boy."

Ned ran to get one of the cotton squares with which they washed dishes.

"Dip it in that pot of tea and wring it out good."

Katie watched as her brother did as instructed. The mother, in the meantime, was eating fried potatoes by the handful, standing, never taking her eyes off her baby.

Ned brought the moistened cloth to Jigger, who scooped a small pile of sugar into the middle of it, and twisted it into a cone shape. Drops of sugary liquid appeared on the outside of the cloth.

"Here," he said, sticking the pointed end of it into the baby's mouth.

The infant began to suck, weakly. A tiny, birdlike claw of a hand closed around Jigger's finger.

"He can't live on sugar water," Katie said.

"No, but it'll buy him some time." Jigger touched the tiny

scrap of black hair on top of the baby's head. "The mother might have some milk for him once she gets some food into her own gullet."

The mother, now wolfing down biscuits, seemed to relax a little about the fact that two strange adults were hovering over her child.

A door slammed and Robert entered. "Katie," he said. "I'm taking the men into the woods today. We'll be cutting too far out to waste time coming back here for dinner. You'll need to bring it out to . . ."

He stopped in his tracks as he saw the tableau before him. The woman cowered against a wall, watching him wild-eyed. Katie saw that she was grasping a butter knife.

"Looks like we got us a stray squaw and a starving baby," Jigger explained. "Got any good milk cows handy?"

Robert came closer. The mother tensed even more as he approached the infant. Katie could tell that if he made one wrong move, the mother would spring at him—butter knife and all.

"May I look at your baby?" he asked in a soft voice. "I promise I won't hurt it." She stared at him a long moment, then she laid down the butter knife and returned to filling her stomach.

Robert reached for the ragged bundle.

Katie handed it over. "I—I don't have much experience with babies."

The makeshift sugar teat dislodged from the baby's lips, and he began his pitiful mewling again.

"I do," Robert said. "Where is the evaporated milk?"

"I put it in a cupboard," Jigger said. "Your fancy cook here hasn't seen fit to use it."

"Evaporated milk?" Katie asked. "I've never heard of such a thing."

"Some guy named Borden invented it before the war," Robert

explained. "The Union soldiers had it. The Southern soldiers didn't."

"Oh." She hoped he didn't realize what he had just said. Presumably, if she were from Ohio and the widow of a soldier, she should have known about this new thing.

Jigger returned with a squat tin can in his hand.

"Dilute it with water that's been boiled," Robert told him. "It needs to be thinned down so it won't give the baby belly cramps."

"All we got is this tea water," Jigger said.

"That'll do."

Robert took a spoonful of the diluted liquid Jigger brought and dribbled it into the corner of the baby's mouth then he gave him the small sack of sugar to suck until the milk disappeared. He alternated the sugar and milk until the baby fell asleep.

Katie realized she had been holding her breath and let it go in a long sigh. "Will he live?"

"That depends." He glanced at the mother. "I hope so."

His finger, feather light, grazed the baby's cheek as he handed the bundle back to Katie. "I have a new crew heading out, I have to go."

"What will I do while you're gone?" She glanced down at the baby, then back at him. "I don't know how to do this."

"If the baby tolerates the milk and sugar, give him a little more every two hours. Let the mother eat whatever she wants." He headed toward the door. Just before he got there, he stopped and turned around to face her. "As far as whether or not the baby survives—it might be a good idea to pray."

The door closed behind him.

Katie and Jigger's eyes met. She knew that hers were pleading.

"Don't look at me." Jigger shrugged. "You're the one that found 'em."

Robert went into the woods long enough to get four teams of men felling timber. Two axe men on either side of a giant pine tree would notch it in the direction they wanted it to fall, and then begin to swing their axes, first one, then the other in a syncopated rhythm. The steel blades cut into the trunk, spitting out white pine chips. Another two-man crew stood ready to chop off the limbs after the giant fell. Once they had the tree cleared of limbs, they would use a crosscut saw to cut it into sixteen-foot lengths. Little by little, they would chew their way through the forest.

After getting the work started, he built a campfire and set up an iron tripod from which he hung a bucket of tea. The work the men were doing was hard and sweaty. It was customary for loggers to break when they needed to for a short rest and a cup of tea. Many used the break to refresh themselves with a new plug of tobacco as well. Tobacco was one of the few comforts and luxuries the men had out here. He had made certain there was a good supply in the camp store.

Word had spread that he was hiring, and a few more men arrived. He had to make on-the-spot decisions about who to hire and who to turn away. The man's nationality or background meant nothing to him, or any other camp boss. The only thing that mattered was if a man was skilled and dependable. A lazy shanty boy would get others killed.

As the crew swung into full production, he headed back to make certain the noon meal would be arriving. He was worried that Katie might have become too involved with the Indian woman and that pitiful baby to fix dinner. If nothing else, he could feed the child again while Katie threw the meal together.

Halfway there, he was surprised to come upon her pulling the camp's dinner cart. Ned was pushing from behind. She stopped for a moment when she saw him, then took a tighter grip and continued on.

"It won't be time for the men to eat for another hour or so," he said.

"I wasn't sure how long it would take me to get there," she said, panting from the effort of pulling the wagon.

"Let me help," he said.

"I won't say no to that." She allowed him to grasp the handle. He was amazed that she had been able to get it so far. He hadn't thought, when he'd asked her to bring lunch to the men, how hard it would be for her. And all this time she had been dealing with that Indian woman and sick baby.

Things were never uncomplicated—even in the woods.

"How is the woman and her child?"

"Moon Song and her baby were both sleeping when I left—on a pallet I made on the floor of the cabin."

"Moon Song?"

"Henri found out. He's that French Canadian you hired yesterday—the one who always wears that red sash and carries a fiddle around?"

"I know Henri. He was late getting out to the woods this morning."

"That's because he talked to her for a few minutes after breakfast. Moon Song is married to a French Canadian trapper, so she speaks a little French. They had a camp a few miles from here. He left and never came back. She was pretty far along in her pregnancy when that happened and ended up having that baby all by herself. When the food ran out, she started walking. When she saw the smoke from our stove, she came here."

"Does the baby have a name?"

"Henri asked her that," Katie said. "Moon Song said that the Menominee don't name their babies until a counsel of elders choose a name for them."

"Wonder if her trapper husband left her on purpose."

"Who knows *what* a man might take it into his head to do!"

To Robert's ears, Katie sounded more bitter than the question or the situation warranted.

"Moon Song looks like she might have vermin."

"Hopefully not any longer. I helped her take a bath and wash her hair while the bread was baking. The cut on her foot wasn't as bad as I expected once I got the rags off. I think it'll heal. She's wearing one of the flannel nightgowns I bought in town. She seems to think it's a dress."

"Do you know where she came from?"

"Way up northeast. Probably over into Wisconsin. Henri says she's from something she calls the Crane clan."

"The baby is tolerating the food?"

"Pretty well." Katie sounded worried. "Moon Song is very weak."

"There isn't a lot to eat in the woods in October."

"You won't throw her out?" Her voice rose with concern.

"Why would I do that?"

"Some men would. She's another mouth to feed."

"My lumber camp isn't so destitute that I can't feed a starving woman, Katie. Of course Moon Song can stay—at least until she can get on her feet and we can figure out how to get her to where she belongs."

Katie heaved a sigh of relief. "You are a good man, Robert Foster."

⸺◌◌⸺

The camp was growing. And now she had inherited the care of the Indian woman and child.

She knew had her father been alive, he would have advised her to pray. The idea of prayer was an attractive one—except that she seemed too exhausted to compose a coherent sentence right now. All she could do was send a silent, heartfelt plea for help to an invisible God.

The dishes were done. The sourdough sponge set for more flapjacks in the morning, for which the men seemed to have insatiable appetites. Variety didn't seem to be big in their priorities.

She went out to the new privy and sat there in the dark, in quiet privacy, for a few blessed moments. Soon enough, she would have to face her cabin and the fact that an Indian girl with whom she couldn't communicate and a sick baby were also taking up residence there.

Still, it was a homey scene when she went inside. Ned sound asleep. Moon Song in the rocking chair before the fire—in Katie's blue flannel nightgown—trying to nurse the baby. Katie could hear the suckling sounds. She peered over Moon Song's shoulder, and unless she was mistaken, the baby's cheeks were taking on a faintly pinkish hue.

Moon Song glanced up at Katie. With Moon Song's freshly washed black hair pulled back into a braid, the grime washed off of her body, and her body clothed in something besides tattered buckskin rags—Katie realized that the girl was a beauty.

As Katie got undressed and pulled the covers up to her chin, the girl snuggled down into the pallet Katie had made for her. Having the presence of another woman in the cabin was comforting. Even if they couldn't communicate with words.

As she drifted off to sleep, it occurred to her that she hadn't remembered to set up her candle and teakettle alarm system. She sighed, started to get out of bed, then thought better of it. She did not want to frighten the baby or Moon Song in the middle of the night with such a racket. She would have to rely on Jigger once again. Tonight she was too tired to care.

—⟲⟳—

The cries went on and on. Katie tossed and turned in her bed, wondering if the crying would ever stop. Wondering, through

the fog of her sleep-deprived brain, where the crying was coming from.

Restless from the noise, Ned kicked out in his sleep. A heel
caught her in the side, causing such pain that she sat up gasping.

Her eyes caught the sight of Moon Song sitting in the rocking
chair, trying to nurse the baby.

"Is he hungry?" Katie asked.

Moon Song turned desperate eyes toward her.

Katie wearily climbed out of bed and checked her watch. It
was midnight.

Only two hours before she needed to get up. She'd had, at
most, two hours of sleep.

"Let's go see what we can find." She opened the door and
Moon Song followed close behind her, through the darkness
to the cook shanty. The only good thing Katie could see about
this whole situation was that the baby's cries were stronger than
earlier in the day.

She opened the door and lit the lamp. There was lukewarm
tea in the kettle. It took her no time at all to dilute some canned
milk and dribble it into the baby's mouth. The little thing spluttered and spit and cried. She made another little moist sack of
sugar for it to suck on.

It soon appeared that hunger wasn't the only thing making
the baby cry. It kept arching its back as though in pain. Katie
had no idea what to do, and the young mother seemed equally
mystified. Jigger peeked out of his room once, then retreated,
slamming the door behind him.

"I can help, missus," a deep voice said.

Mose was standing at the back of the kitchen. She had avoided
him, having no idea what to say to the man. Now here he was.

"I could hear the babe way out in the barn." He reached his
big hands out.

Moon Song looked at Katie with alarm.

126

"It's all right," Katie soothed. "This man won't hurt him."

Mose put the tiny infant over his shoulder and began to pace the floor, patting its back and crooning to him. In a few minutes, the baby gave a loud burp and snuggled into Mose's shoulder. In seconds, he was asleep.

"You're as good with babies as you are with animals," Katie said.

"I was always able to comfort a crying child. Don't know why."

Moon Song was getting restless. She shifted her weight, nervously wanting her infant back. Mose handed the sleeping child to her.

Moon Song melted into the dark, leaving Katie and Mose alone for the first time since he had arrived in camp yesterday morning.

"I helped my mama raise my little brothers and sisters till . . ." He stopped and looked uncomfortable.

"Until?"

"They went away."

"You mean until they were sold," she said.

"Yes, missus."

She looked into the man's eyes. Even with all she had endured at the hands of Harlan, he had endured more. As painful as the memories were for both of them, now was the time for words. She decided to face it head-on.

"I never agreed with what Harlan did."

"It were his daddy, missus, who done that to my family."

"I hated what I saw at Fallen Oaks, Mose."

"We knowed. You were only a girl child yourself. You did what you could."

"I did nothing."

"That's true. You did nothing when you seen me ready to run. You didn't call the foreman. You didn't tell your husband.

And that lemonade and food tasted mighty good. Took me a long way. I was up in South Carolina before I got a chance to eat again."

Tears came to her eyes. At least she had done one thing right in her life. "I'm so sorry for everything, Mose."

"Wasn't none of your doing. We knowed that. We was scared when we heard the master was bringing home some uppity Northern woman—didn't know what you would be—but we felt sorry for you when we saw you. Little scrap of a thing. We could tell you didn't know what you had gotten into."

"Harlan was a smooth talker."

"He never smooth-talked me. Saved his smooth talk for white folk."

"I ran away too, Mose. No one here knows where I came from." Katie glanced at Jigger's door, making certain the old man wasn't listening. "I lied to the boss about being a widow."

"I figured so." Mose's voice was soft with concern. "Mister Calloway hurt you too?"

"Yes."

"I sorry for you, missus."

She thought of the stripes on the man's back, ones that her husband had put there while she did nothing to stop it except cry. Dear Lord, she didn't deserve Mose's sympathy.

"Please don't tell Mr. Foster. I'm afraid he'll fire me—or contact Harlan and tell him where I am."

"I still scared of that husband of yours." Mose smiled. "Don't worry. I never laid eyes on you before, missus." Kindness fairly emanated from him—it always had. Katie marveled that he had even a drop of it in him after all he'd endured. "I best be getting on back to my team. You be all right now?"

"Yes, Mose. Thank you."

She watched him go, comforted by his promise. Mose knew how to keep a secret. All of Harlan's servants had.

"You ever hear where that Violet got to, missus?" He stopped right before he reached the door. "I'd surely like to find her."

Katie froze. He wanted to find Violet? That was far too risky—for both of them. As of a month ago, Violet was caring for an elderly woman a few miles from Fallen Oaks. If Mose went looking for her—if word got out that he had found out her whereabouts from Katie—Harlan wouldn't rest until he had beat the information out of Mose, and no one in the county would help.

"No. I don't know where Violet is." She hated herself for the lie. But she had to protect herself and Ned—and Mose. "I'm sorry."

There must have been something in her voice. Mose gave her a long look before he turned and went out the door.

Well—she was wide awake now, and afraid that once she did manage to get back to sleep, nothing would ever awaken her again. She might as well get a head start on tomorrow morning's preparations. There was enough dry bread left over from yesterday to make into a nice bread pudding and she had plenty of raisins. She could make a thick glaze for the bread pudding.

With all her heart, she wished she had a cow and chickens and hogs so that she could *really* show the men what she could do. Fresh eggs would be wonderful, and with a good cow, she could make fresh butter instead of that nasty stuff the men ate.

As she began her preparations, Katie felt a slight dizziness. She grabbed hold of the worktable and waited for the feeling to pass. Then she sat down and began peeling potatoes. There was far too much work to accomplish before four-thirty for her to coddle herself.

12

A beetle-browed bully he war 'n mean,
an' as dirty a fighter as ever war seen.
"Camp Thirteen on the Manistee"—
1800s shanty song

October 11, 1867

There was heavy frost on the ground when Robert stepped out of the bunkhouse. It was apparently going to be an early winter. Soon, if this weather held, it would be possible to coat the tote roads with ice and begin sliding the logs out of the woods.

The thing a lumberman dreamed of was a long, cold winter. Sometimes they had to leave tree stumps behind as high as a man's head when the snow piled up and axe men worked while standing on top of three or more feet of snow.

The thing a lumberman most dreaded, next to wildfire, was a mild winter with mushy roads and Michigan swamps swallowing up the logs they were trying to drag to the river. Give him twenty-degrees-below-zero temperatures instead of warm winter weather any day.

He was in high good spirits as he entered the cookhouse. The first thing that struck him was the interesting smells wafting from the kitchen. Katie had evidently made something new.

130

The table was covered with heaping bowls and platters. Katie and Jigger had outdone themselves and he was grateful. This morning, with a full crew, the camp would roar into production. It was fitting that the table be groaning with food.

At the far end, Skypilot was buttering a biscuit. He glanced up at him and grinned, then went back to the serious business of getting enough fuel in his stomach to get through the next few hours.

Katie, neatly dressed, flitted around filling cups, dishing up more fried potatoes from the stove top, checking on something she seemed to be concerned about in the oven. She was a pretty thing, with her flushed cheeks and her red hair curling around her face from so many hours standing over the stove.

He saw a lot of admiring masculine eyes turned toward her as she conscientiously went about her work. A woman as pretty as Katie would turn heads in the middle of a crowd in Bay City, but out here in the wilderness she was quite a jewel. Strangely enough, she seemed to be oblivious of her beauty.

She could probably collect at least a dozen serious marriage proposals on the strength of her cooking alone.

It was an unhappy thought. And a surprising one. What could it possibly matter to him, aside from how it might impact the camp, what romantic interests the woman might develop? He had only known her the biggest part of five days.

Moon Song appeared. She was still emaciated, but she was a different person from the ragged woman he had seen yesterday. Her face was clean, her hair neatly braided. She was wearing a long-sleeved, high-necked blue flannel nightgown, but she wore it proudly. Some red flannel material had been wound into a sort of papoose carrier, and when she turned, he saw a tiny face framed by the red material, gazing out at the room with bright, curious eyes.

At that moment, Katie came toward the table bearing a giant pan of something that smelled heavenly.

"Bread pudding," she announced.

She set it down in the middle of the table with a flourish, and the ones nearest it began to spoon the delicious-smelling mixture onto their plates. It had been years since he had tasted bread pudding. He was hoping there would still be some left for him—when he noticed Katie sway. She was deathly pale. As she started to slump toward the floor, he jumped up and caught her.

"When was the last time you ate? Katie!" She felt rough hands shaking her. "Talk to me!"

The insistent voice annoyed her. Someone was expecting her to answer questions, but she didn't want to. She wanted to sleep. She was shaken again, and she realized that she was lying on something very hard.

Somehow she had ended up on her own worktable, and approximately thirty pairs of concerned eyes were staring down at her. The most worried were those of her boss, Robert Foster.

The last thing she remembered was serving breakfast.

"When did you last eat?" Robert again asked. Then he uttered something so improper she could have died from embarrassment. "Are you pregnant, Katie?"

The curiosity in the sea of eyes surrounding her intensified. Pregnant? Obviously, her boss didn't know with whom he was dealing. Not that it was any of his, or anyone else's, business.

She struggled to sit up. "I'm not . . . with child."

"Did you sleep at all last night?" Robert helped her to a sitting position. "Jigger said you were in here banging around from midnight on."

"I was worried about getting breakfast for so many and I couldn't sleep, so I cooked," she said. "I—I think I might have eaten something yesterday morning. Sometimes when I get too busy, I forget."

"You always did, missus," Mose mumbled, to her horror.

"Here." Robert didn't notice Mose's comment. He had dished up a bowl of bread pudding and was poking a spoonful of it at her mouth. "Eat."

Hoping to pull Robert's attention away from Mose's remark, she obediently opened her mouth. It was humiliating having so many men watching, but she was afraid Robert wouldn't stop insisting until the bowl was empty.

She desperately wanted to escape into the privacy of her cabin. Robert should never have asked her if she was pregnant in front of all these men. Decent women didn't talk about such things!

"Are you feeling better?" Robert asked.

She swallowed another mouthful and nodded.

"Good. We need to get to work. Jigger, keep an eye on her. I've got to go."

"I only got one good arm, boss," Jigger whined. "And I didn't get a lick of sleep with her making noise in here all night."

Robert blew out a breath of frustration. "Ned?"

"Yes, sir." The boy said. "I'll watch her."

"I'm fine," Katie insisted. "I've eaten now and I'm fine."

"I hope that's true." Robert's voice was harsh. "I need a cook, not an invalid."

Katie bristled. She had thrown everything she had into this—and he seemed angry at her for fainting. It wasn't as though she had meant to.

"Go on back to the bunkhouse, boys, and get your tools. I'll be outside in a minute."

The men reluctantly tromped out, obviously hating to miss a good show.

"You have to feed yourself, woman," Robert said. "Will you try to remember that?"

"Yes."

"And one more thing. Evidently Jigger hasn't bothered to tell you this yet"—he cast an irritated glance at the old cook—"but camp cooks take a nap in the afternoon to make up for getting up in the middle of the night. You'll do that too from now on."

"A nap?" She hadn't napped since infancy.

"Doctor's orders." He closed his eyes and grimaced. "I mean—boss's orders."

She watched as he walked out the door. What an odd combination he was. One moment angry and gruff, the next minute filled with compassion. She hadn't figured him out yet—but she would. If she was to keep her job, she would have to.

⸻

"Timberrrr!"

The call went out as the behemoth hovered for a few moments, quivering, and then lost the battle against gravity and went crashing down into the clearing. Unlike the other types of forests, there was no underbrush in these ancient woods. The giant pines had blocked the sun from the earth and left such a thick carpet of pine needles that few things sprouted beneath them.

Once the trees were cut and sunlight was allowed to saturate the ground, all sorts of seeds, long dormant, would stir into life. It was a sight that never failed to interest him—the variety of plant life that waited beneath the centuries of old pine needles, ready to spring up, gasping for air.

After he finished here, he would sell the land to some farmer who would clear stumps and plant crops. The population of Michigan was growing and the people would need all the crops they could get.

Thinking about this made him a little less uneasy about the fact that he and his men were cutting down trees that had taken centuries to grow. Timber like this was irreplaceable in even their great-grandchildren's lifetimes. But the giant trees seemed to be everywhere. *Inexhaustible* was the word bandied about when lumbermen spoke about the millions of standing pine in the Saginaw Valley. More sawmills went into production every year as more lumber camps set up. He doubted the forests of Michigan were inexhaustible, but he hoped they would at least last his lifetime.

Of course there were those who complained that the Michigan soil was too thin for farming. There were a few who even believed that the lumbering should cease—but that was not his concern. His job was to get the trees out.

Ernie and Cletus set to work chopping off the limbs of the fallen tree, while the axe team started notching the next one. He inspected the tree that was on the ground. It was at least 5 feet in diameter, 150 feet tall, and as straight as an arrow.

"Timberrrr!"

Another tree came crashing down on the south side of the clearing. The work was progressing well.

The discarded pine limbs would be left where they lay and become as dry as tinder. There was always the danger that lightning might strike amidst a tangle of discarded boughs and start a forest fire. He worried that if something like that happened, the fire wouldn't stop until it reached one of the great lakes that bordered the state.

But there was nothing he could do about it except hope it didn't happen. Lightning and fire were things he had to leave in the hands of the Almighty. It was all he could do to keep the camp running. Lord willing, there would be no fires this season.

Today was the culmination of months of preparation. Everywhere he looked there were skilled men busy with their assigned tasks—a small battalion of woodsmen. It was like being in the army again, with all of the camaraderie but none of the bloodshed.

He breathed deeply of the autumn air as multiple axes rang out and men's voices shouted out to one another.

"Timberrrr!"

Another giant crashed to the forest floor. Its massive weight bounced against the solid ground, causing the very earth beneath his feet to tremble.

This army of loggers working beneath his command was steadily advancing upon an unresisting enemy of standing timber. He was proud of what they were accomplishing.

If he could just keep himself from dwelling on the past, he might have a future.

Henri sat cross-legged on his bunk once again, playing a happy tune. Tinker sat next to him, wailing away on a cheap harmonica. The notes were discordant and the musicians not particularly skilled, but it added a festive note to a Saturday night. The men were relaxed and happy because Sunday would be their day off.

"Best food I ever et in my life," Ernie said wistfully. "A girl who can cook like that sure would make a man a fine wife."

"Purty too," Cletus added, blowing the wood shavings away from a tiny carving he held in his hand.

Robert saw that Cletus had just finished carving a little bird. He set it proudly on the narrow shelf above his bunk. In the past few days, a small menagerie had formed on that shelf. All had names. Sometimes Cletus talked to them before he went to sleep. Robert had come to realize that Cletus was slower than his twin brother. It hadn't been noticeable at first because Ernie was quick to intervene whenever anyone tried to talk with Cletus.

"Whatcha got there," Mainer asked.

"This here is Whistlepete." Cletus picked up the bird and held it out for Mainer to admire. "He's a little sparrow."

"Looks like a play-pretty to me," Mainer said. "Never saw a logger talk to a bunch of toys before."

Cletus looked ashamed and hid the little bird behind his back. Ernie was leaning against the bunk. "Leave my brother be."

"I was just sayin' it's a mite odd." Mainer grabbed his double-bit axe and sat down for his turn at the grindstone. "Him being a logger and all."

"Henri fiddles," Robert said. "You sharpen your axe, Skypilot reads his Bible, Cletus carves. What a man does with his free time is his own business."

"I don't know about that," Mainer said. "His sitting here night after night talking to his little toy animals bothers me. A grown man shouldn't do that."

Cletus lay down in his bunk, clutching the little bird in both hands as though to protect it.

"Ain't none of your business," Sam told Mainer, "what that boy does."

Sounds of agreement came from around the shanty. Everyone knew Cletus wasn't the brightest man in the camp; none had been cruel enough yet to point it out.

"What do you think Katie'll fix for breakfast tomorrow?" Skypilot made an attempt to turn the subject back to their favorite subject—food. "I sure wouldn't mind more of that bread pudding."

"Who cares what she makes?" The big logger from Maine glanced up from the grindstone, where he was busy sharpening his double-bit axe. "What I'm wondering is if that little widow woman is lonely for a man yet."

One of the men in the back of the cave-like bunkhouse gave a long, low wolf whistle.

Robert had been expecting this moment. "Best leave Katie alone," he said. "She's a decent woman and she has enough on her hands without having to deal with the lot of you."

"You're blind, Foster, if you don't see she's planning on finding herself a man." Mainer ran his thumb along the edge of the

137

axe, testing for sharpness. "Why would a decent woman come all the way out here if she didn't have a whole lot more on her mind than cooking?" He glanced around at the other men for encouragement. "I seen women cooks at lumber camps before. All of 'em were married up to the foreman or boss." He polished his axe blade with his shirtsleeve. "Never saw a woman decide to live in a lumber camp all by her lonesome. I think our little cook ain't as sweet and innocent as she pretends. Or maybe"—he leered around at the other men—"Foster here already knows that and ain't willing to share."

Robert could feel the anger begin to boil in his veins, and he tried to shut it down. As much as he wanted to wipe the smirk off Mainer's face, he knew he needed to control himself.

"I promised Katie no one would lay a hand on her if she came to cook for us," he said. "I won't allow you or anyone else to talk about her like that or bother her in any way."

"Well, you're the boss—but that Indian girl ain't too bad," Mainer said. "She'll probably start looking better and better the longer we're out here."

"Leave the women alone." Robert stood up from his bunk and looked straight at Mainer. He hadn't appreciated the teasing of Cletus—but now with the insinuations about Katie and Moon Song, he was beginning to thoroughly dislike the man. "Both are under my protection. Cletus too."

"I thought you just said that what a man wanted to do with his free time is his own business." Mainer scowled. "You don't have no call to tell me what to do except when I'm cutting down trees."

"Either leave the three of them alone," Robert said, "or pick up your pay from Inkslinger and move on. That's an order."

"Don't think I'll take any more orders." Mainer stood up from his seat behind the grindstone. He was several inches taller than Robert and as strong as an ox. There was a dangerous glint in his eyes. "I already had me a bellyful of orders during the war."

Robert bristled at the man's vicious tone. Then he realized that Mainer was gripping the axe with both hands. One blow from it could hew a man in half, and both of them knew it.

It was not within Robert to back off, although he suddenly, deeply regretted hiring the man. "You need to find employment someplace else."

"I like it here just fine." Mainer had a self-satisfied look on his face. "I like having that pretty little widow woman a-waitin' on me hand and foot."

"It's my camp." Robert's patience was stretched to the limit. "And you're fired. Pack your turkey and get out."

Everyone grew still, waiting to see how Mainer would react. Robert wasn't sure he stood a chance against Mainer in a fair fight, but he knew if he backed down now, he would lose the men's respect for the rest of the winter. The work would slack and this would turn into a haywire camp overnight.

And then Mainer uttered something so vulgar about Katie that Robert's sense of danger evaporated. He had been born and bred in his father's lumber camps and he'd had his share of fights. Without stopping to count the cost, he lunged at Mainer in spite of the fact that the man was holding an axe.

Mainer was so sure of his superior size that he had evidently not expected the boss to charge him. That gave Robert an edge. He landed one good, hard punch to the man's stomach before Mainer swung his axe. Robert ducked and swerved just as the axe embedded itself two inches deep in the bunk above Robert's head.

"What the ding-dong?" Tinker leaped to the floor. "I was sitting there, man! Watch yourself!"

It was at that point that Robert knew he was fighting for his life. He lowered his head and ran at Mainer, butting him in the chest, a blow that wrenched the embedded axe out of the logger's grasp and made him stumble backward. Robert, quite literally, saw red as his eyes became suffused with a blood-thumping fury.

He'd watched his father take on loggers twice his size when they had questioned his authority. There was a bloodlust in the Foster family that caused them to lose all fear in a fight, as well as their common sense. Robert knew he couldn't win against an opponent so much larger, but he didn't care. That comment about Katie had been so dirty and vile—when she was so pure and fine—that it enraged him. His focus narrowed down to one objective—he was going to take that logger down, no matter how big the man was—if it was the last thing he ever did.

Mainer straightened up from the head butt and landed a blow so powerful against Robert's right eye that it sent him reeling backward against the deacon's bench. He sprang back from that hit, even angrier than before. He threw himself forward, grappling with Mainer as they fell to the floor, fists flailing.

Shanty boys loved a good fight so much that sometimes the fight would spread throughout the entire group for no particular reason. But the men stayed out of this one, except for shouting encouragement to Robert. It appeared that they all had been annoyed by Mainer's obscene comment about Katie and were united behind him.

Robert and Mainer fought up and down the center of the room, staggering into bunks, nearly overturning the stove. Mainer was bigger and stronger. Robert was faster and wilder, but his strength wasn't quite enough to overcome the big logger. Mainer knocked him down and stunned him just long enough for Mainer to wrench his axe out of the bunk. Robert, still lying on the floor, gathered himself to roll out of the way of that murderous axe when it descended—but it stopped in midswing, held in place by Skypilot, the only man in the bunkhouse bigger than Mainer.

"That will be enough, now, lad." Skypilot held Mainer's axe in an iron grip.

Mainer tried to wrest it out of his grasp, but Skypilot was

firm—a grown-up chastising a child. "I said—that will be enough!"

Robert collapsed against the floor, the fight draining out of him. He didn't feel any pain yet, but both eyes were beginning to swell shut. The last thing he saw was Skypilot and two others accompanying Mainer to his bunk to pack up his things.

"Katie . . ." he mumbled through a split and swollen lip. "And Moon Song. They're . . ."

"I'll keep watch," Skypilot said as he herded Mainer out the door. "I won't give this fellow a chance to touch them."

"Hope the wolves get him," Ernie said, and spat.

"Wolves don't like spoiled meat," Tinker said with disgust.

Robert wanted to laugh at that comment, but his ribs ached and it hurt too much.

Before his right eye swelled shut, he watched Cletus placing the little bird beside the other small carvings.

"Don't you never-mind, Whistlepete," Cletus said. "Mainer's gone. Just don't you never-mind."

13

There's the doctor, and he'll tell
great stories of his calomel,
of the great doses you must take;
'twill cure your fever there's no mistake.
                "Don't Come to Michigan"
                    —1800s shanty song

Moon Song's milk had come back. She was busy nursing her
baby, looking on with interest from where she sat on her pallet
as Katie rigged up her makeshift alarm system once again. Moon
Song seemed to be drinking in and processing this strange new
world of the lumber camp. Katie had tried many times to engage
her in conversation, to see if she understood any English at all,
but all she got was puzzled looks or shrugs.

"This," Katie said, "will keep me from oversleeping tomorrow
morning." She touched the unlit candle and the string she had
tied around it. "When this burns down to here"—she pointed
to the string embedded in the wax, then at the old teakettle
hanging above her head—"that will fall down, make a noise,
and wake me up."

Katie had no idea if Moon Song understood a word. She
had lost interest in what Katie was doing and gazed down at
her baby with adoration, caressing its downy head. The child

142

was swaddled in more of the red flannel from the bolt Delia had insisted she buy. Katie was grateful she had the soft cloth to use against the infant's tender skin, but she also wished she had purchased some white. It just didn't seem right, bundling the child into red diapers.

Ned lifted his eyes from a small, ragged magazine he was reading in bed. "Why do you talk to her so much if she don't even understand you?"

"Because it seems strange to be sharing a cabin with another woman and not talk to her—even if she doesn't understand a word I say."

"You never talked that much when we was living with Harlan."

"Saying the wrong thing always set him off so I said as little as possible."

"You never sang so much, either."

"I've been singing?"

"Sometimes. When you're rolling out piecrust or something."

"I didn't know." She must be enjoying her work even more than she realized. "I'm going to blow out the lamp now, so you'd better put whatever you're reading away, little brother." She realized that she had no idea what he'd been looking at with such intensity. "What is that, anyway?"

"I found it in the bunkhouse." Ned held up the tattered bundle of paper. "Laying on the floor."

"The *Police Gazette*?" She snatched it away from him. "Let me see that."

The date on it was from two years earlier. The front page was a lurid woodcut of a bedroom filled with people trying to protect the Secretary of State, William Seward, from assassination on the same night as Lincoln's murder. The picture was enough to give *her* nightmares, let alone a small boy. She flipped through the pages and was shocked at the pictures, many of which involved scantily clad women.

"This is *not* something you should have." She stuffed the offending sheaf of papers into the stove and was relieved when the shameful thing caught fire.

"But the shanty boys read 'em all the time," Ned protested.

"What the shanty boys choose to do, little brother, and what you are allowed to do are two different—"

Someone pounded on the door. It was very late for someone to be coming to the cabin. She heard a familiar voice. "It's Skypilot, ma'am."

Skypilot? At this hour? Something must be terribly wrong. Heart pounding, she opened the door. Skypilot stood outside, his axe in his hand.

"Has something happened?" She could feel Moon Song and Ned pressing in around her.

"There's been a bit of trouble over at the bunkhouse."

"Trouble?" It seemed only a few minutes ago that she had envied the sound of laughter and music coming from there.

"The logger from Maine said some things the boss didn't like. There was a fight and Foster threw him out of the camp. We think it's best I keep watch outside your cabin tonight. I didn't want to scare you if you looked outside."

"I don't understand," Katie said. "What does this have to do with me?"

He shifted his weight. "Mainer said some things about you." He stared hard at the wall, unable to look her in the eye.

She was still confused. "What did he say?"

"Some . . . off-color things." He held up a palm. "Don't worry, though. The boss took care of it."

"Took care of it?"

"The boss fought him."

"But Mainer is bigger than Robert."

"Yes, ma'am. By a long shot."

She couldn't wrap her mind around what Skypilot was telling

144

her. She repeated it to make sure she understood. "Robert fought a man much bigger and stronger than himself—just because the man said something about me?"

"That's about it."

"Is Robert all right?"

"He won't look real pretty tomorrow, but Mainer will look worse." Skypilot grinned. "The boss was so riled, he went after Mainer like a wolverine with rabies. We wanted to make sure Mainer didn't try to get back at the boss by hurting you or the Indian girl."

She couldn't believe it. Robert shouldn't be risking himself over a few off-color words. Not to mention, she had heard that Mainer was one of his most skilled axe men.

"The boss couldn't let it slide." Skypilot seemed to be reading her thoughts. "We shanty boys might look and act pretty rough, but we have a code, and that includes treating decent women with respect. There's not a man in the bunkhouse tonight who doubts that the fight was necessary. If Foster hadn't taken him on, one of us would have."

"But how did he beat him? That man must have a hundred pounds on Robert."

"It was kinda strange." Skypilot's eyes lit up at the memory. "None of us knew the boss had it in him. One minute Mainer was saying . . . what he said about you, and the next minute Foster was all over him."

She had no idea how to take in this information. The fact that Robert had fought for her was startling. Robert was even more a man of his word than she had thought. He had promised that the men would treat her with respect, and he had backed that promise with his fists against overwhelming odds. Mainer was a brute. It was a miracle Robert hadn't gotten himself killed.

"You'll catch cold." She rubbed her arms, chilled as much by the story as by the night air. "I have some extra wool blankets. Robert left several in a chest here in the cabin."

"I'd be obliged, ma'am."

Ned, listening in, had already lifted two blankets out of the chest. Katie pulled one of the chairs outside so Skypilot wouldn't have to stand or sit on the ground.

As Katie closed the door, Skypilot was leaning back against the cabin in the chair, with his axe across his lap and the gray blankets draped across his shoulders.

Moon Song stared at the door for a long time, a thoughtful expression on her face. Katie couldn't begin to fathom what the girl was thinking.

"I'm sorry about reading that *Police Gazette*," Ned said.

"That's all right." In her surprise over Robert fighting for her, Katie had forgotten all about it. "Just leave those things alone from now on. They aren't fit for a boy—or a man."

"Yes, ma'am."

As Ned and Moon Song settled into sleep, Katie nervously paced the bit of remaining space on the floor. The news Skypilot had given her was unsettling. Imagine. Robert fighting for her honor!

In the past, when Katie couldn't sleep, she would read—but there was nothing here to read. She almost, but not quite, regretted burning the *Police Gazette*.

As she paced, she caught a glimpse of something she had never noticed before. A corner of what appeared to be a book stuck out from beneath the eaves. The color of it blended into the wood, making it almost invisible. Climbing on a chair to investigate, she discovered a leather journal and a long wooden box shoved in beside it.

She placed both items on the table. The box was heavy, and something inside of it clinked softly. She hesitated over opening the book. It could be anything, she supposed. A personal diary, perhaps, but considering Robert's no-nonsense attitude, she thought it more likely that it was a ledger of some kind—perhaps of camp expenses. It certainly wasn't any of her business. Her hand hovered over the leather strap holding it together, but she didn't open it.

The box also piqued her curiosity. It was varnished and smooth around the edges but worn in the middle as though from much handling. There were nicks and scratches in the surface and it was unlocked. This mysterious wooden box drew her with an almost magnetic force. She had never seen anything like it before. The curious girl within her surfaced, and the box begged to be opened. It wouldn't hurt, she supposed, just to take a quick peek. It might even be something Robert needed and had forgotten where he had put it. Some sort of logging tool. Maybe something for measuring timber. He might have great need of it, she rationalized as she wrestled with the decision of whether or not to open it. He might even be pleased that she had found it. It must not be too personal if he hadn't taken it with him to the bunkhouse.

With one finger, she nudged the latch open and then lifted the lid. She gasped as the front of the box fell away, revealing a row of gleaming, wicked-looking metal instruments—all nestled in individual compartments. She had seen just such an array in a doctor's office many years ago.

It was a box filled with surgical tools, and for the life of her, she couldn't figure out why. Shuddering, she closed the box and shoved it back up among the rafters. Those saws were made for cutting through human bones. The probes and scalpels were for digging out bullets, but what were they doing here?

Her interest in the leather journal took on a deeper fascination. Hoping it would hold the answer to the presence of the box, she undid the leather strap and opened it to the first page. The writing was small and precise.

Claire has taken to her bed, upset over my eminent departure with the troops that will soon be leaving en masse from our town. She does not understand that I am these men's doctor and friend, and I cannot abandon them now. If they have ever needed me, they will need me more in the coming days on the battlefield. Perhaps I can save some of their lives. I would never forgive myself if I did not try. Claire's anger and hurt is made worse by the fact that she is heavy with our second child.

Katie knew she should not continue to read Robert's private journal, but she couldn't seem to make herself stop. She wanted to know who this man really was. She turned the page and devoured the second entry.

The men and I pulled out of the train station early this morning amid cheers and a crowd of well-wishers. The local brass band added more noise to the chaos. It was enough to make a man feel like a hero—without having yet done anything except sign papers and put together some sort of uniform.

I do not feel like a hero. I felt like the worst kind of traitor, abandoning my wife only a month before the baby is due. I never realized it would be this hard. She did manage to come to the station long enough to see me off, waving good-bye, swollen with our second baby, her eyes red from weeping.

I have made arrangements for my sister to stay with her until the child is born. It does little to ease my conscience. I know that Sarah and Claire do not get along, but Sarah will at least do her duty to her sister-in-law. I am grateful that our house is in town, near Dr. Herman Walker, a man I trust to bring her safely through childbirth without infection. I have told him about my previous professor, Dr. Oliver Wendell Holmes, and his belief that childbed fever is brought on by unsanitary conditions. Also, I have made certain he will have access to what he needs.

I fear that the amount of carbolic acid I am able to carry with me will not be enough if I have to sterilize my surgical instruments very many times. Still, hopes are high that it will not take long for the North to quench the fire for secession.

Although I am taking my surgical supplies, I am hoping the men will not see battle. If the carbolic acid I have packed is not enough, I don't know what I will use for sterilization. I fear that the government will not provide anything like it—too few doctors accept the theory that unwashed hands and unsterilized instruments cause the spread of infection. My friend Dr. Walker and I are the odd men out.

I have also packed a goodly supply of opium to use in the case of dysentery—which I have read is the scourge of men in battle.

By the grace of God, I will do what I can. By the grace of God, and Dr. Walker's care, Claire will survive her confinement and I will return, having fulfilled my duty to my country and my townsmen, to a healthy wife and two robust children. I will be praying, daily, to this end. It is the one thing I can do for my family, even though I am far away.

That was enough, Katie firmly told herself. The journal was none of her business. Robert's marriage was certainly none of her business. Of course, it did answer her question about whether or not he had children. Evidently there were at least two.

She closed the journal and placed it, reverently, where she had found it—beside the box of surgical instruments. With her mind whirling over her discovery about the personal life of her boss, she lay back down on the bed and closed her eyes. Robert had not misspoken when he had said the words "doctor's orders." That's what he had meant. But why hadn't he been open about that fact? Being a doctor wasn't something to be ashamed of.

It appeared that she was not the only one with secrets in this camp.

14

The boys were glad when Sunday came,
that they might have a rest;
some would go a-visiting
all dressed up in their best.

"Turner's Camp on the Chippewa"—
1800s shanty song

October 13, 1867

"Get up, you lazy shanty boys," Jigger yelled into the pitch darkness. "It's daylight in the swamp!"

A blast from the Gabriel horn awakened everyone in the bunkhouse and set up the rustling, throat clearing, and passing of wind from men awakening from a deep slumber. Robert heard feet hitting the floor as the men on the top bunks hopped down. He heard the pouring of water into the washbasins and the spluttering of men splashing cold water on their faces—the full extent of bathing most of them would indulge in until they reached Bay City in the spring.

Robert waited until the men had gone out the door before he sat up. He was grateful that they had left him alone—probably assuming he wanted to stay in bed after the beating he received last night. He had no intention of staying in bed all day, even if it was a Sunday, but he did want some privacy in which to inspect the damage.

As he arose from his bed, he discovered that he had been hurt worse than he had realized. He gritted his teeth against the damage. Every bone and muscle and tendon in his body cried out.

As his eyes adjusted to the dim light of the lantern, he realized that his eyelids were swollen so badly he was barely seeing out of slits. He gingerly ran his tongue over his lips and found that they were split and swollen.

He made his way to the sliver of mirror nailed over the washstands. The first glance made him start in surprise.

"The women are fine." Skypilot came through the door and peered over his shoulder. "Which is more than I can say for you."

Robert grimaced. "Been a while since I was in a fight."

"You held your own."

"Barely."

"Still," Skypilot said, "you won't have any trouble with the men from this time on. They respect a boss who's handy with his fists."

While Skypilot unlaced his boots, Robert dumped a basin of leftover soapy water out the door, unearthed a clean cloth, poured fresh water into the pan, and began to carefully dab at his face.

"Katie already fed me," Skypilot said. "I was hoping to catch a few more winks if you don't mind."

"It's Sunday, do whatever you want." Robert rinsed the washcloth out and watched the water turn rust red. He hated that color. There had been too many basins filled with bloody water in his life.

He applied the washcloth's wet coolness against his aching and swollen eyes. "Did Mainer come near Katie's cabin?"

"No. He started to, then he saw me waiting for him and had

second thoughts. He headed west. Probably thinking of going over to Buck Wallace's camp. He's worked there before."

"Buck is welcome to him."

"You lost a lot of skill when Mainer walked out of camp. I watched him split a lucifer stick with his axe yesterday. All the men were betting on whether or not he could do it. He halved it slick as butter."

"A good cook is worth more than that pig-eyed logger."

"True. I just hope you don't scare your cook to death when you walk into her shanty this morning."

"Are you planning on holding services of any kind today?"

"No." Skypilot shook out his blanket and crawled beneath it. "Why?"

Robert felt like the reason should be apparent. "Because it's Sunday."

"I'm not a preacher anymore."

"I know, but most of the men could use—"

His sentence was interrupted by Skypilot's snore.

—⟡⟡—

The shanty boys were filing out of the cookhouse about the time Robert went in to breakfast. All of them nodded with respect as they passed, except for Mose.

"You all right, boss?" He laid a hand on Robert's shoulder. "I got me some liniment out in the barn—it works real good on horses."

"It's that bad, huh?"

"Uh-huh." Mose peered at his face. "It's pretty bad."

"I'll be fine." Robert tried to smile to prove how well he was feeling, but the smile hurt.

Mose made a clucking sound with his tongue. "You tell me if you want some of that liniment."

"Thanks, Mose."

152

He went inside, hoping there would be leftovers. Come to think of it, he also hoped he could still chew.

Moon Song was clearing dishes, one-handed, while holding the baby in the crook of her arm. Jigger had already retired to his room. Katie glanced up as Robert came through the door. He saw her quick intake of breath when she saw him and realized that Skypilot's comment that he might scare her was a valid one.

So far, she had been slightly aloof with him—doing her job, an employer/employee relationship, which was as it should be—but this morning she came straight toward him, a look of concern on her face.

"I heard what happened." She wiped her hands off on her apron. "Are you all right?"

"I've been better."

"You didn't have to fight Mainer on my account."

"Yes, actually. I did."

"His words weren't going to hurt me—not like he hurt you."

"You deserve the men's respect, Katie."

Her eyes softened at that comment. "Ernie told me you got hit pretty hard in the mouth. I made something that will be easy for you to eat."

Robert eased himself down on the bench while Katie busied herself at the stove. Moon Song made another trip gathering up eating utensils from the table. He noticed she was still so weak that she could barely hold the baby and a handful of forks at the same time.

"Can I see?" Robert held out his hands.

Moon Song shyly offered the baby to him and he cradled it in his arms. Memories of holding his first child, little Thomas, flooded over him. He deeply regretted the fact that he had not laid eyes on his second child, a daughter, until she was walking. The war had stolen her babyhood from him.

He removed the red flannel wrapping and inspected the tiny infant. The baby's color was better now, although he still had that wizened look of babies who were malnourished.

"Do you have milk?" he asked.

Moon Song tilted her head, puzzled.

He cupped one hand over his own chest to help her understand. "Can you nurse your baby now?"

Light dawned and she nodded eagerly.

"Good." He stroked one little cheek. Like a baby bird, the infant blindly opened its mouth and turned toward the touch. The instinct, so strong in all baby mammals, never ceased to amaze him. It was one of the many things he had marveled at as he had studied medicine. One of the many things that had convinced him that there *was*, in truth, a God. Someone who had designed his creation with much love and care.

If only that God had cared as deeply when Robert had been trying to block out the screams of the soldiers upon whom he was operating.

It was the root of his greatest spiritual battle—trying to reconcile a loving God, the Creator of such an intricately crafted world—with all the suffering he had seen.

"Here." Katie set a bowl and spoon in front of him. "I made you peach dumplings. They'll be soft and easy to eat." Moon Song came and reclaimed her baby.

He took an experimental bite, and his cut lip cried out in protest. He discovered that two of his teeth were loose as well, but the feather-light dumplings with their sauce of stewed peaches were soothing and delicious.

"You didn't have to go to all this trouble for me," he said.

"I didn't. I made it for Tinker too. The poor man has hardly any teeth."

"You've begun making special meals for individual men?"

"Only Tinker. The others eat like billy goats. Tinker struggles to get enough food inside of himself to live—I'm hoping to fatten him up a little before winter's end."

While he dug in, Katie brought two mugs of tea and sat down across from him. He inhaled the delicate fragrance of the steaming cup and savored the experience of having a pretty girl sitting across from him instead of Sam and his tobacco-stained teeth.

As he took another bite of peach dumplings, he realized that she had flavored the dish with a spice he had not provided.

"Where did you get the nutmeg?" he asked. "I didn't order any."

"I bought some when I was getting my other supplies," she said. "I was afraid it wouldn't be on your list and it's a favorite of mine to cook with—when I can get it."

"My wife used to use nutmeg."

"Used to?" Katie's brow furrowed. "Doesn't she still?"

For the first time, Robert realized how little he and Katie knew about each other. "My wife passed away five years ago."

"I'm so sorry." Her eyes widened. "I didn't know."

At that moment, the door opened and a man strode in. He was wearing boots laced up to his knees, heavy pants, a beat-up coat, and he carried a tote bag that had been ripped, patched, and resewn many times. The bit of his face that wasn't covered with a heavy, brown beard was chapped and wind-burned. He had a cadaverous look.

"Charlie!" Robert called. "Where did you blow in from? Come have some breakfast."

The man stared at Katie, who stared back, as though she didn't know what to make of this apparition.

"This is Charlie Rhodes, Katie," Robert explained. "He's the best timber-looker in Michigan. And this is our new cook, Katie Smith," he said. "That's Moon Song over there. She and her baby are staying with us for a while."

"Pleased to meet you, ma'am." Charlie tipped a moth-eaten beaver hat. "I am powerful hungry and something in here smells awfully good."

"I'll just see what I can find," Katie said cheerfully. "I don't want anyone going away hungry from my table."

As Katie headed toward the stove, Charlie took a good look at Robert's face.

"What happened to you?"

"Some trouble in the bunkhouse." Robert shrugged. "It's over."

"Did the other fellow look as bad?"

"The other fellow is gone."

Charlie dropped his pack on the seat beside him and sat down. "That's the reason I scout the woods alone."

"You are a wise man." Robert spooned up another mouthful of peach dumplings. He was feeling better by the minute. "What brings you here?"

"I've been looking over some land west of here. Thought I'd stop by and get something to eat besides hardtack."

"You're down to nothing but hardtack? You must've been out there quite a while this time. Did you find anything good?"

Charlie smiled and remained silent.

"Ah," Robert said. "You found a good stand of pine, but you're not telling."

"I found an excellent stand, but I need to hurry and get to the land office to register it before someone else beats me to it."

"Anybody else in the competition?"

"If I thought so, I wouldn't be taking the time to eat breakfast."

"If I bring in a good tree harvest this spring, I might be interested."

"I'll do business with you."

Katie brought a plate of bacon, fried potatoes, and sliced

bread to the table along with a mug from which steam arose. "What's a timber-looker?"

Charlie, famished, dug into the heaping plate of food without answering.

Robert explained, "A timber-looker explores the woods looking for good stands of white pine."

Charlie nodded in agreement and kept wolfing down food.

Robert continued. "Men like Charlie here travel alone, sometimes for months. It's kind of like striking a vein of gold when they find one."

"How do you go about finding them?" Katie asked.

Charlie took a careful sip of the scalding tea and swallowed before he answered. "I listen."

"You listen?" Katie frowned.

Charlie saluted her with his cup. "That was an exceptional plate of food, ma'am."

"Thank you," Katie said. "What do you listen for? Trees don't talk."

"Haven't you taken her out to hear the trees yet, Foster?"

"There hasn't been time. We've been here less than a week."

Katie looked from one man to another. "I don't understand."

"And I can't explain it. Just go out to the deep pine woods someday and . . . listen."

She glanced at Robert to see if Charlie was joking.

"He's telling the truth. It's a sound you can't describe. I'll take you and Ned soon—before it snows."

Charlie held out his plate. "May I have seconds?"

"Of course." She rose from the table and busied herself in the kitchen.

"Is she married?" Charlie asked Robert in a low voice.

"She's a widow." Robert discovered that he wasn't thrilled with the question. "But you only come out of the woods a few weeks out of the year—you aren't looking to settle down, are you?"

Charlie laughed. "No, but a man can dream." His expression grew serious and his voice lowered again. "I found something while I was out there, a few miles from here. Not quite sure what to do about it."

"What was it?"

"A trapper." He drew his pack to him and extracted something. "Couldn't tell who he was. Looked like he had drowned while setting a beaver trap. I buried what was left of him. Have no idea who he was, but I brought this along. Thought someone might recognize it."

He held out a hunting knife encased in a homemade buckskin sheath decorated with intricate beadwork.

At that moment, Moon Song, who had been looking on during the conversation, became visibly agitated. She hurried over, snatched the knife from the table, looked closely at it, let out a wail, and then a river of unintelligible words came spilling out.

Katie heard Moon Song's cry and came running. The girl was so distraught, Katie pried the baby from her arms for fear she would drop him. Moon Song barely seemed to notice. She collapsed onto the bench and began to sob, holding the knife and its case in her hands and rocking back and forth. Katie patted her with one free hand, held the baby with the other, and made soothing noises.

"I guess her husband didn't deliberately abandon her after all," Robert said.

"What should we do?" Katie asked.

"It would take weeks to get her back to her tribe. As weak as she is, there's no way she could make it alone, and I don't have anyone to spare to take her. Do you mind keeping her with you awhile longer?"

"Not at all." Katie smoothed the girl's hair away from her tear-streaked face. "We'll do fine together."

Robert wondered how many women he had known who

would willingly take a stranger with whom they could not even communicate into their home—especially if that home had only one room. Katie was becoming one of the most intriguing women he had ever known.

───❦───

Katie draped a dish towel over the clothesline Tinker had strung for her between the cabin and the cook shanty. Several of the men had also hung their own dripping clothes around the camp. It felt good to be out in the morning sun.

There was a great deal of bright-colored clothes flapping in the wind today. The ever-present red flannel, of course, which fit right in with the logger's love of red. It seemed to be the color of choice for their heavy plaid shirts. Henri, the fiddler, and another French-Canadian wore red sashes around their waists for no apparent reason—a strange custom, but dashing. The blue nightgown that Moon Song favored hung alongside of Ned's two blue shirts. Of course, Katie had hung unmentionables discreetly inside of the cabin. She had no intention of treating the men to a show of her bloomers.

The colors were a treat for the eye against the mud-colored background of trampled earth and the weathered log buildings. It was her first Sunday in camp, and it gave both her and the men a chance to get caught up on camp chores. Many of the men sat around a large pot of boiling water into which had been shaved plenty of lye soap. A load of dirty socks and long underwear had gone into that pot. She couldn't help but notice they boiled the clothes all together, creating a sort of uniform gray color of anything that was dropped in—but killing at least some of the gray backs that almost always infested lumber camp shanties.

Lice weren't something she wanted to have, but she feared her close proximity to these men would make it hard to escape those annoying little creatures.

The men spent the morning telling yarns, drinking tea, spitting tobacco, or smoking "nose warmers," those short, stubby pipes shanty boys seemed to favor.

The small camp store Robert kept in the office, and which she had already inspected with interest, consisted primarily of an abundance of chew, pipes, and pipe tobacco. She had seen men spit the amber juice straight into small wounds in the belief that some imagined medical properties of the weed would make the cuts heal faster.

These men, although hard working, were—in her opinion—rather vile. They cursed, smoked, and—from what she had gathered—would drink anything that wasn't nailed down when they went to town. Evidently they also visited unsavory ladies when they were in town as well, or else places like the Catacombs wouldn't stay in business.

At least Jigger seemed to have unruffled his tail feathers enough to be of some help. Instead of watching her cook herself blind today, he'd informed her that he would prepare the noon meal—laying out leftovers and sandwich makings for the men's dinner. She intended to help with supper preparations tonight, but for now, she was enjoying her partial day off.

She laughed to herself about how most women wouldn't consider doing a week's worth of laundry on a day off, but after standing over a cookstove all week, the chore of plunging clothes into soapy water, scrubbing them on a tin washboard, and hanging them on the clothesline felt like play. She was also looking forward to heating and carrying enough water for a good bath this afternoon. Ned was going to take a bath too, whether he wanted to or not. Even if many of the shanty boys took pride in not bathing for the entire seven months, she had no intention of it becoming a habit for her little brother.

As she wrung out a pair of Ned's britches, she noticed that the muscles in her arms had become stronger and more defined.

Lifting the heavy cast-iron pots and kettles was getting easier each day. Standing there, admiring her clothesline filled with freshly washed clothes, she realized that she was feeling healthier than she had in years.

It was amazing what being able to support herself had done for her morale. The feeling of freedom in not having to fear Harlan's anger was downright intoxicating. Without realizing what she was doing, she straightened her spine and lifted her head higher.

Moon Song and the baby were napping in the cabin, still regaining their strength.

She breathed deep of the mid-October air. Even though it was a sunny day, there was a definite snap in the air. Robert had said only this morning that he was expecting snow soon.

Robert.

So far, she liked everything about the man, from the way he treated Mose and Moon Song, to the way he treated her—with respect and consideration. She liked the way he kept himself clean-shaven, when nearly every man wore a beard. She even liked the way his hair, already grown too long, curled against the collar of his shirt.

It would truly be something to be married to such a good man.

With sheer willpower, she shoved that daydream aside and stood up. She was not free, and that was that.

15

She was blessed with a bright little youngster
a pretty and sweet-natured lad,
whose voice was the joy of the pinery,
whose laughs made the wilderness glad.
        "Jim Brooks"—1800s shanty song

He was headed to the barn, intent on telling Mose that he needed to make a trip into town for supplies. He was hoping on getting a head start on the trip, maybe leaving right after their Sunday noon meal. As banged up and sore as the fight with Mainer had left him, he wasn't going to be much help in the woods tomorrow. Now that the camp was up and running, his plan was to leave Skypilot in charge and get some business finished in town.

At least that was his plan.

Then he saw Katie and stopped in his tracks. She was sitting on the top step of her cabin, her head thrown back, her eyes closed, drying her freshly washed hair in the sun. He had never seen her hair unbound, and his mouth went dry at the sight of the shiny, copper mass cascading down her back.

Even though she was fully dressed, this moment felt strangely intimate. He had rarely seen her outside of the cook shanty, where she was usually swathed in a giant white apron. He stood, drinking in the lovely, feminine sight of her.

"Enjoying yourself?" he asked.

She opened her eyes. "While I can." She reached up to twist her hair into a bun.

"Don't," he said.

Her hands paused. "Excuse me?"

"Go ahead and let it dry. I didn't mean to disturb you."

"If you say so." She dropped her hands.

With her glorious hair about her shoulders and her big blue eyes looking up at him with such trust, he could barely remember where he had been headed before he saw her. This was a different, softer woman than the one he watched wielding a rolling pin and meat cleaver in the cook shanty.

"Was there something you wanted?" she prompted.

He tried hard to remember what it was that he had come for.

"Yes." He cleared his throat. "I'm headed into town to finish getting in supplies before the weather gets bad. Is there anything you want?"

She pursed her lips in thought. "We're going to need a whole lot more potatoes and flour before the winter's over." She began to tick items off on her fingers. "Sorghum, of course—the men practically drink the stuff. At least two more tubs of lard. Maybe some cabbages and rutabagas and carrots—they would keep well in a cellar through the winter."

"Anything else?"

"Well . . ." Katie's voice took on a teasing tone. "I miss my cows. If you brought me one, we wouldn't have to rely on canned milk anymore, and I could make fresh butter. That stuff your men have to eat doesn't taste right. I think it's all the brine and saltpeter it comes packed in."

"No chance of getting a milk cow way out here. You might as well wish for chickens to lay fresh eggs."

Katie jumped into the game of make-believe. "And a couple of pigs to throw the leftovers to—not that the men leave much in the way of leftovers. Sometimes I worry I'm going to bankrupt you from cooking so much."

"You don't have to scrimp on food, Katie. I want the men to eat well."

"How soon are you leaving?" she asked. "I'd like to put together a menu and check it against the food we already have."

He had been in a hurry only moments ago. Then Katie ran a hand through those damp curls, and his rush evaporated. Now, the only thing on his mind was the fact that it was a lovely day, and he hadn't been for a stroll with a beautiful woman in years.

"I'll be leaving tomorrow morning." He glanced up at the sky. "We won't have many more days like this." He found himself fidgeting with his hat like an awkward boy. "If you'd like to take a walk, you could hear what Charlie was talking about. There's a nice place about a mile from here that we haven't lumbered yet." He cleared his throat. "We could discuss the things you'll need from town and it'll give you a chance to see a little more territory than just the camp."

"Oh, I'd like that." Her face lit up. "I'll go get Ned. He's been wanting to go exploring."

Robert felt a little deflated at the prospect of her little brother accompanying them. But he also saw the wisdom in taking the child along. It would discourage talk if any of the men saw them leaving together.

She got her brother, and the trio took off. Robert pulled out a small notebook and a stub of a pencil from his pocket so he could write down her list as they walked. She tied her still-damp hair back with a black ribbon. It made her look very young.

"Like I said, flour and potatoes. And I'm almost out of cinnamon."

"What about sugar?" Ned said. "I think we might need more sugar."

Katie laughed and ruffled Ned's hair. "My little brother has quite the sweet tooth."

"So do the men. We went through over a hundred pounds of sugar last year. I can't even remember how many barrels of sorghum."

"I can believe it."

The destination Robert sought was a particular stand of white pine—the finest he had ever seen. He would eventually have men working there, but for now, he wanted to share the beauty of it with Katie—and, of course, Ned.

Katie had a long stride and easily kept up with him as they made their way through the tree stumps that surrounded the camp. As they entered the shade of the hardwood forest, he realized that he was feeling very odd. He tried to figure out why and discovered, to his surprise, that the strange emotion he was feeling was . . . happiness.

It had been years.

He felt almost lighthearted for the first time since his daughter had been born . . . and his wife had died.

The technical name was puerperal fever, better known as childbed fever. Some doctors believed that it was caused by a woman's predisposition to the disease. Others believed it was a judgment from God. He, however, subscribed to Harvard dean Dr. Oliver Wendell Holmes's belief that puerperal fever was caused by the attending physician's unwashed hands.

His wife's life could have been spared by the simple, civilized ritual of soap and water.

Robert had observed, in his own practice, that simple cleanliness usually brought about greater health in a patient. He had shared this knowledge with Dr. Walker before he left, and cautioned him to wash his hands thoroughly before he delivered the baby. Dr. Walker had assured him that he had been especially careful during Claire's delivery. Unfortunately, his new assistant had not. Another medical emergency had drawn Dr. Walker away from Claire's bedside only moments after her delivery.

If the doctor hadn't been so overworked because of Robert's absence, he could have stayed and made certain Claire was well cared for.

If Robert had been there, where he belonged, he would have been at Claire's side, seeing to every detail, making certain that everything that touched her was clean.

But he had not been there.

While he struggled to save the lives of men on the battlefield, his own wife had died of something he knew how to prevent. The knowledge tore at his gut daily.

Therefore, this fleeting touch of happiness caught him by surprise. He started to feel guilty for allowing his burden of grief and regret to lift, even for a moment. But then the grace of this sunny Sabbath day once again washed over him and tore the darkness away—at least momentarily. It was impossible to walk through the bright colors of the autumn woods with the innocent companionship of this good woman and small boy without his spirits lifting.

Katie finished reciting her list of culinary needs, and he tucked his notebook away. He was looking forward to showing her the place he had been so struck by the first time he had explored this tract of timber. He had left it uncut as long as possible because it was a place he enjoyed coming to for solitude when the elbow-to-elbow existence with his men began to pall.

A flush of ruffled grouse flew up and then dove to deeper cover, startling Katie. She laughed at herself, which he found charming. Ned pointed out a soaring bald eagle, and they all marveled at its grace.

As they entered the pine forest, Katie stopped and stared.

"Oh, my goodness!" she exclaimed. "It's like a—a cathedral!"

"I've always thought so." He was pleased that she had reacted in the way she had. "Let's walk farther in so you can listen."

Katie was wide-eyed as they moved through the open, brushless forest. "I hear it!"

"Me too!" Ned exclaimed.

There was a breeze today, and the treetops shimmering so far above their heads created a strangely aquatic sound, like rushing water, almost like an ocean crashing against a seashore.

"This is what Charlie listens for?" she asked.

"People call it 'whispering pine,' but on days like today, when there's a little wind, the pines don't whisper, they roar. On days when there's wind, Charlie will climb to the top of a ridge and listen for the air to carry the sound to him."

"I think I might like to do Charlie's job," she said.

"It's a lonely existence."

"There are worse things than loneliness."

Robert wondered what Katie had experienced that was worse than loneliness, but there was something about her voice that cautioned him it would be best not to ask.

"There's more," he said. "I think I have a surprise both of you will like."

When they reached it, she gasped in awe.

"Oh, would you look at that!"

In front of them, surrounded by the soaring pines, was a pristine lake shimmering in the slice of sunlight that fell through the break in the forest. All around them was a carpet of thick pine needles.

The supply list was forgotten. Katie walked to the water's edge, stooped, and dabbled her fingers in the water. Then she sank to the ground and drew her knees up to her chin, gazing at the water, drinking in the sight.

"This place feels . . ." She searched for the right word. "Holy."

Holy. Robert turned the word over in his mind. Yes, that fit the place perfectly. It had always felt like sacred ground to him too. A place so ancient and primal that it was possible to imagine God walking through the trees as he had once walked with Adam and Eve in the Garden. That was the very reason why he had directed his men to cut on the other side of the section—to give him more time to come to this place before he was forced to destroy it.

Not the best attitude for a lumber camp owner. His father wouldn't have hesitated—this place with its valuable timber would have been the first to go.

"Can I go skip rocks?" Ned asked.

"Of course," Katie said. "Just don't fall in."

Ned ran off to the other side of the lake where there was a small, rocky beach. Robert sat down on the cushion of pine needles close to her.

"I needed this." She turned toward him. "But I didn't know."

"In a few weeks it will be covered in snow." He picked up a pine needle and shredded the end.

"This will be even more beautiful then." Katie turned her gaze back to the lake.

"Yes but colder than you can imagine."

"Oh, I can imagine it." She glanced over at him and laughed. "I was well warned. Wool was pretty noticeable on that list you gave me back in town."

Her smile was so enticing, her eyes so blue, the flush on her cheeks from their hike so attractive that he wished with all his heart that he had the right to kiss her. He had been imprisoned within a cell of loneliness for so long.

"Why do you do this?" The words burst out of her before she could stop them. "Why do you cut down trees when you could spend your life healing people?"

The moment the words were out, Katie wished she could snatch them back.

Robert looked at her with mild curiosity. "How do you know I'm a doctor, Katie?"

She felt herself blush scarlet. It was something she hated about having fair skin and red hair. It was hard to hide embarrassment. Her body betrayed her every time.

Robert waited for her answer.

She wished she had never opened his journal—a better woman wouldn't have opened his journal. And now he would know—because she couldn't lie about it. She would have to confess.

"I—I found your surgical kit and your war journal." She stumbled over the explanation. "I'm so sorry. I didn't read all of the journal, just the first two pages and . . ."

The kindness in his eyes made her stop. He wasn't angry. In fact, Robert was smiling at her—an understanding smile, as though he could see right through to her heart.

"It's hardly worth taking your time to read, Katie." His smile faded, and his expression grew grim. "You say you've only read the beginning?"

"Yes."

"I was quite full of myself during those first pages. It sickens me to read them now. In fact, I intended to burn the thing and just never got around to it. I look back and see myself leaving a pregnant wife and child when I didn't have to."

"You did what was necessary."

"No, I did what I wanted to do. The life of being a small town doctor wasn't enough. I thought I was cut out for bigger things. I actually felt like a hero, marching off to war to save my fellow man. By the end of the war, I felt like the worst kind of butcher, removing bullets, stitching together wounds with unsterilized catgut, and amputating men's limbs for hours at a time without proper sanitation or anesthesia. Another doctor and I operated in one private house near a battlefield until the floor was so saturated with blood that a river of it ran down the staircase and out the door. I knew how to save them—many of them—but I didn't have the tools, or the help, or the stamina to do all that I knew to do. I watched men die of gangrene for lack of the proper care. I watched other doctors moistening stitching thread with their own saliva and sharpening surgical knives on the soles of their boots—and there was nothing I could do. While I amputated limbs and handed out plugs of opium to keep the men from dying of dysentery, my wife died giving birth to my daughter—and I know that she never would have gotten ill had I been there. You have my permission to read the rest of it, but I promise you, my journal is not something you will enjoy."

"I'm so sorry you went through all that, Robert. But why cut timber?"

"Because it isn't medicine. Because I don't have to hold a scalpel in my hand. Because I have to make a living and the only other thing I know is timber. I grew up working in the camps with my father. Lumber put me through medical school."

"You still have your surgical kit, though."

"You *are* a curious little thing, aren't you?" He chuckled. "My father bought me that kit when I graduated from medical school. It's a good one. He had it shipped all the way from England. I guess I keep it because of that reason alone."

"Will you ever practice medicine again?"

He looked out at the lake and the trees and was silent for a very long time. "I wish I knew the answer to that, Katie. All I know now is that I am no longer capable of surgery." He held his hands out in front of him. They were strong and steady. "These hands can swing an axe or bridle a horse or do practically anything except hold a scalpel anymore. When I try, they shake as if I had palsy. I have no idea how to make it stop—but if I were to attempt to do surgery now, the patient would not live. Like most of the men out here, I'm just doing the best I can to survive."

⚬⚭⚬

With a few greenbacks borrowed from a cousin, Harlan de-cided to head north. It had occurred to him that Katherine, timid mouse that she was, would no doubt flee to what was left of her family still living up in Pennsylvania. He knew he would have no trouble ferreting her out. He chuckled as he headed north. It would be good to see Katherine again. He was already savoring the fear he knew he would see in her eyes when he found her.

16

For I don't care for rich or poor,
I'm not for strife and grief;
I'm ragged, fat, and lousy, and
as tough as Spanish beef.

> "The Jolly Shanty Boy"
> —1800s shanty song

October 18, 1867

It had been five days since Robert and the two teamsters had gone to town. With him in camp, she felt secure and safe. With him gone, she felt threatened and unsettled. There were too many men. Big men. Rough men. Loud men. It felt as though there were always hungry eyes staring at her while she went about her work. Without Robert there, she felt exposed and vulnerable.

She wondered what was taking him so long. Then there was a shout and the glorious sound of a wagon and horses drawing into camp. She ran to the door. Mose and Robert had returned, bringing with them—it couldn't be! Were her eyes deceiving her? No wonder it had taken them so long to come back!

Robert was tired and cranky and angry at himself for being such a dolt. He had been on the road two long days trying to get this blamed cow back to the camp. He couldn't make her go any faster than a slow amble for fear she would go dry. Add to that the milking twice a day and the time to graze whatever clump of grass they happened upon along the way, and he was fit to be tied.

And then there were the chickens. He had no idea if they would ever lay again after being carted around in those cages for so long. The constant squawking at each bump in the road had practically driven him to distraction. He was not cut out to be a farmer.

At least the two piglets hadn't been much trouble. They had happily slurped up all the cow's milk Robert had provided. He was hoping to fatten them up enough to butcher right before the spring drive when the men would need all the meat they could get.

He knew that it had only been wishful thinking on Katie's part when she mentioned him bringing back livestock, but the more he thought about it, the more sense it made. If the cow stayed fresh, the milk would be a welcome addition to the table, and fresh eggs had all sorts of possibilities.

He and Mose had gone to Saginaw where, in addition to picking up other supplies, he knew a farmer who might be willing to part with some of his animals. He'd sent Sam on in to Bay City to pick up some boxes of tobacco late in being delivered to his house, and more feed for the mules and horses. It had all seemed like a good, common-sense plan.

Now, however, he felt foolish coming into camp with a cow tied behind his wagon, her full udder swinging, the bell around her neck clanging, the chickens clucking, and the piglets grunting. Unfortunately, he'd managed to time his arrival just as the men were coming out of the woods for supper. They stood around, avidly watching, grinning with amusement. He knew that tonight, he would be hearing plenty of humorous comments about his arrival.

He had a Harvard education, was a skilled and experienced surgeon, and knew how to run a fairly successful lumber camp, but at the moment he felt as nervous as a green boy as he wondered how Katie would react to his gifts.

And then he saw her bolt out of the cookhouse, petticoats flying, running toward him with a look of ecstasy on her face. For a moment he thought she was simply happy to see him, until she passed him by without so much as a glance and threw her arms around the cow he had tied onto the back of his wagon.

"Hello, you beautiful thing!" She buried her face in the cow's neck. "What's her breed?"

"The farmer I bought her from called her a Milking Shorthorn."

"I'm going to take such good care of you, Miss Shorthorn!"

Then she rushed up to inspect the chickens. At her approach, they set up a flurry of protests and flapping of wings. Robert watched as she reached into a cage and drew out a hen, tucked the biddy beneath her arm, and began to stroke its head as she walked toward him.

"I can't believe you did this!" Her eyes were shining with happiness. "I've missed having animals to care for so much."

"That's not all." Robert was suddenly feeling much better about having dragged livestock all the way from Saginaw. He pulled one of the piglets out of the basket at his feet. "I brought you two of these."

"Oh!" Katie stuffed the squawking chicken back into the cage and reached out her arms for the piglet. "Let me have it!"

The piglet was still small enough to be cute, and she kissed it on the top of its head. "You say you brought me two of these?"

"I did." He grinned, savoring her happiness. He had seen Katie concentrating on her work, he had seen her awestruck by the beauty of the lake and pine, he had watched her compassionate and tender with Ned and Moon Song, and he had seen her, many times, annoyed with Jigger—but he had not yet seen her happy. And to think, all it had taken was a cow, a few chickens, and some pigs.

"What will I name them?" She cuddled the piglet like a baby as the men gathered around.

"How about Dinner and Supper?" Tinker suggested, winking at the other men.

Katie made a face. "Try again."

Tinker scratched his chin and pretended to think. "I know! Bacon and Sausage?"

"I'll come up with something, but not that. Which of you men are going to build me a pen to keep them in?"

All raised their hands.

"And I'll need a chicken coop. These biddies will need a good place to shelter before it gets any colder."

"That coop'll have to be strong," Blackie said. "Else panthers'll get 'em or bears."

"Tinker will see to it," Robert said. "Katie, I think these men would like to be fed and I know I would."

"Oh, my goodness. I forgot what I was doing." She handed the piglet back to him, standing on her tiptoes to reach up to the wagon seat. "Thank you," she whispered as the men wandered into the cook shanty. "This is the nicest thing anyone has ever done for me." Her eyes were shining but filled with yearning. An instant later she was gone—back to her work. Leaving him dumbfounded by what he had seen written on her face. That was the way a woman looked at a man she loved—not at a camp boss who had just brought her a few chickens.

⁓ↄ⌁

"You never brought me a cow," Jigger complained when Robert entered the dining room.

"You never asked for one."

"If I'd a' had a cow and some chickens, I coulda made some fancier stuff last winter."

"Your meals were fine." Robert sat down and reached for a bowl of fluffy mashed potatoes. "Let it go, man."

Jigger's jealousy over Katie's skill still appeared to be simmering, but unlike Mainer, Robert couldn't just send him away. There was a loyalty factor to be considered. Jigger had worked for his father thirty-odd years and sometimes dredged up old stories about him—stories Robert treasured.

Dealing with people was messy. Relationships in a lumber camp could be a headache. He hoped Jigger's latest snit would pass soon.

He had just taken a forkful of raisin pie when the door of the cook shanty flew open so hard it bounced against the wall. A woman stood there, framed against the setting sun, her fists firmly placed on her hips.

"Robert Rutherford Foster! I want to talk to you."

It was his sister.

The men all turned and inspected the tall, thin woman with great interest. He didn't blame them. His sister, Sarah, favored shiny black material for her clothing. Combined with her severely pulled-back black hair and her slightly beaked nose, she reminded him of a crow. Her voice even had a sort of caw to it when she was upset—and she was definitely upset.

Behind her stood Sam, looking a little wild-eyed. Evidently, she had decided to catch a ride to camp with the poor man. The big question was why on earth was she here? And who was caring for his children back in Bay City?

"Sam." He stood up from the table. "After you take care of the mules, come have some supper."

Before Sarah could say anything else, Robert took her elbow and firmly escorted his sister outside and pulled the door shut behind them.

"What in the world is the matter?" he asked. "Are the children all right?"

"The children are in the wagon," she answered. "Along with their possessions and their clothing. It is time they lived with their father."

He felt like she had hit him with a two-by-four. "They can't stay here," he said. "There's no school and no one to care for them while I work."

"That is no longer my concern." She sniffed. "I have other things to occupy my time now."

"What other things?"

"I have a beau," Sarah said with pride. "He has proposed marriage. But he thinks it best we start our life together without the children."

Robert was dumbfounded. His sister had been so humorless and unbending her entire life, he couldn't imagine anyone wanting to marry her.

"I was waiting," she said, "for you to come in for supplies—and then I planned to send the children back with you."

"I went to Saginaw with my other teamster."

"It would have saved me a very difficult trip." She sniffed, then looked at him closely for the first time. "What happened to your face?"

"You oughta see the other fellow," he joked.

As usual, Sarah saw nothing funny.

"Have you been brawling again, Robert?"

No matter how old he got or how successful he might become, his older sister had a way of making him feel like an unruly boy.

"I fired a logger, but he didn't want to go."

"Well, no matter." She waved a hand. "You can have your teamster take me back tomorrow morning, although I must say, he's certainly no conversationalist."

Robert wondered if Sarah's refined sensibilities could withstand

Sam's idea of conversation, and he gave the man credit for keeping his mouth closed.

"Have you thought this over?" Robert asked. "Are you sure you want to marry this man?"

Her face softened. "I'm forty-three years old, Robert. When am I going to get another offer?"

"Do you love him?"

"He's clean. He has a respectable job—as a butcher. We get along all right. That's enough for me."

"Papa!" Five-year-old Betsy, growing impatient, climbed out of the wagon and came running into his outstretched arms.

"Hello, sugar!" He swooped her up and nuzzled her neck. She smelled so good. His seven-year-old son came and stood near.

"Thomas." With Betsy on his arm, he ruffled his son's hair. In spite of the circumstances under which they had come, it was good to see his children again. He'd missed them, even more than he had realized.

"Father." Thomas stood ramrod straight before him, already a little man.

"I shall need overnight accommodations," Sarah pointed out.

"You can have my bed." Neither of them had seen Katie come outside. "Ned and Moon Song and I can sleep on the floor of the cook shanty."

"That's very accommodating, dear, but who in the world are *you*?" Sarah asked.

"I'm sorry to interrupt," Katie apologized. "I wasn't trying to eavesdrop, I just saw that another woman had come into camp and I wanted to welcome you."

"This is my sister, Miss Sarah Foster, and my children, Betsy and Thomas," Robert said. "Sarah, children—this is Katie Smith, our cook."

Sarah looked Katie over with interest. "I'll be grateful for the use of your bed for one night. I'll be leaving tomorrow morning." She glanced at Robert. "Without the children."

Robert wondered when he had lost control of his life. There was no way he could have his children here. The men were too rough, there was no school, and he had no time. He had no house. And all because the man Sarah was marrying didn't want the encumbrance of his children.

The thought made him furious. What kind of a man wouldn't want to be around these sweet children?

His daughter clung to his neck. His son stood taking everything in with solemn, dark eyes.

He wanted to curse but didn't, even though it wouldn't be the only curse word the children would hear if they stayed here in the camp. And of course, they were going to be staying in the camp. His children deserved a better life than living with some stranger who didn't want them.

"Your little girl could sleep with her aunt," Katie said. "And perhaps you can take your son to the bunkhouse just for tonight? But I don't know what to do about tomorrow and the day after. There isn't room in your cabin for all of us."

"Of course there isn't room," Robert said. "That cabin was never meant to house an entire family."

"Too bad!" His sister pierced him with a dark look.

He supposed he deserved it. He had asked too much of her—expecting her to take the place of Claire in his children's lives for so long. He also knew that when Sarah made up her mind, there was no arguing with her. It was one of the many things that had kept potential beaus away. He wished the butcher well.

"I'm hungry, Papa," Betsy said.

"Well, *that*"—Katie took Betsy into her arms—"is something I can fix." She reached out a hand to Thomas. "You can come with me too, if you want."

Robert watched Katie enter the cookhouse, his daughter on

her hip and his son in tow as she chatted easily with them about the cookies she had baked just that afternoon.

If only she were free to watch the children for him—but her duties were too heavy as it was. Somehow he would muddle through, he supposed. He just hoped his children wouldn't be too damaged by the experience.

—⟨⟩—

Robert saw the bunkhouse through different eyes tonight—his seven-year-old son's. The boy sat scrunched up against him on the deacon's bench in the dim light. Although Robert had been raised in lumber camps, he realized that this was the first time Thomas had even been in one. From the time he was three until today, Thomas had been raised almost entirely by women.

He noticed that his son was holding his finger pressed beneath his nose.

"Is something wrong?" he asked.

Thomas motioned for him to lean down so he could whisper, "It stinks in here."

"You get used to it after a while."

"I want to go home."

"I know."

It was not going to be easy having his children with him. He had known they would need tending to physically, but he hadn't realized he would have to deal with homesickness too.

At the men's request, Henri rosined up his bow and began to play a jaunty shanty boy song. The men joined in, more noise than melody. Ernie began playing a rhythm with a pair of spoons. It was a cheerful thing, but Thomas pressed even closer to his side.

Robert felt a flicker of irritation. It was just music, for crying out loud. Why was his son shrinking back? Then Inkslinger, sober-faced and lanky, began doing a jig in the middle of the floor. His body seemed to be made of two different parts—the legs, which were dancing like they had a life of their own, and the upper half, which Inkslinger held as rigid as his expression.

Thomas pointed. "What is that man doing?"

"It's called step dancing," Robert said. "It's something shanty boys like to do."

Robert went to put another log on the fire and noticed that Thomas watched him with worried eyes as though afraid his father would bolt out the door.

And suddenly, he knew that Sarah, regardless of her reasons, had done the right thing in bringing the children to him.

Back on the deacon's bench, with little Thomas tucked beneath his arm, he once again tried to see the scene through his son's eyes. Skypilot sat at the grindstone, sharpening his axe. Cletus was busy whittling out a tiny mouse, turning it this way and that as he carved. Henri was sitting at the end of the deacon's bench, sawing away on his fiddle. Ernie was playing the spoons. Inkslinger was making the floorboards groan beneath his heavy boots. Several men were lying in their beds, squinting in the dim light at orange-colored dime novels and dog-eared *Police Gazettes*. Blackie and Sam were across the room, sprawled easily on the deacon's bench, grinning at the carryings-on in the middle of the room.

Robert checked his watch. It was nine o'clock. "Time to hit the sack," he yelled over the sound of the fiddle.

The song ended. The fiddler hung his instrument on a peg in the wall. Skypilot blew on the freshly sharpened blade and polished it with a couple swipes on his sleeve.

"You got a story for us, Skypilot?" Blackie called after everyone had crawled into bed and the last lamp was extinguished. "You being a preacher and all. I betcha you got stories."

"Sure," Skypilot said. "What kind of story do you want?"

"Something to help us sleep good!" Sam growled. "None of that hellfire stuff you preachers like to scare people with."

"When have I ever said anything about hellfire?" Skypilot asked.

"You haven't," Sam admitted. "And you better not. Talkin' about hell gives me gas."

"Everything gives you gas," Ernie pointed out.

"I'm serious." Sam scowled. "I got a delicate stomach."

The men hooted at the idea of Sam's delicate stomach, which put the man in such a foul mood, he climbed into his lower bunk and hung an extra blanket from the top in such a way that it made a wall between himself and the rest of the men. It was obvious to Robert that the effort of toting Sarah all the way here in the wagon had frazzled Sam's nerves to the breaking point. He sympathized.

"You got any stories about men like us'n?" Cletus said. "'Bout men who cut down trees?"

"Maybe I could tell you about the Sidonians," Skypilot said.

"What about the Sid . . . Side—what was that word?" Ernie asked.

"The Sidonians. They were famous woodcutters."

Everyone got still. A good storyteller was a prize indeed, and they especially loved stories about men like themselves.

Skypilot sat up and draped his legs over his bunk. "The great Israelite king, David—"

"I heard o' him," Cletus said.

"Of course you have. Everyone's heard of David." Ernie smacked his brother on the back of the head. "Now shush."

"David wanted to build a temple for God, but God wouldn't let him because David was a man of war. God told him it would be his son, Solomon, who would get to build the temple."

"I been to war," a new man—an Irish immigrant named O'Neal—added.

"A lot of us have," Tinker pointed out. "You ain't nothin' special."

"Even though David wasn't allowed to build the temple," Skypilot continued, "he began to gather together all the building materials because he said that Solomon was too young and would need all the help he could get."

"That's a good father." Ernie nodded. "Helping out that way."

"That's true," Skypilot said. "Especially since David would never live to see the temple built, and he knew it."

"Kind of like me clearing a farm of tree stumps and planting an orchard," Inkslinger said. "I might not get to taste the fruit of it, but my six daughters will."

"You got six women in your house?" Tinker asked with wonder.

"Seven, counting my wife," Inkslinger corrected.

Tinker shook his head sorrowfully. "No wonder you head for the woods every chance you get!"

"Let the man get on with his story," Blackie said. "What about them Sid—Sido—"

"Sidonians," Skypilot continued. "They were the best tree cutters in the world. And they had giant cedars to cut—as big as our pine. Solomon paid Hiram, their king, to take the cedar logs down the river to the sea. They put the logs together in big rafts and then floated them where Solomon was building the temple."

"Even after Solomon's daddy had gotten all the stuff together?" Cletus said.

"I think Solomon had bigger ideas than his father."

"Like my oldest girl," Inkslinger said. "Can't keep her in the kitchen. Always working on something. She was putting together a small windmill right before I left. Said she'd seen it in a book about some Dutch people overseas."

"Windmill?" Klaas Jansen, another new man, spoke up. "We haff windmills back home. Dey work fine."

"Let the man get back to his story." Ernie was getting impatient. "So when did Solomon live?"

"About three thousand years ago."

There was silence in the bunkhouse as everyone digested this.

"There's been people cutting down trees that long?" Blackie asked.

"Pretty much the same way we do now," Skypilot said. "Things haven't changed all that much—even in three thousand years."

"How about that," Blackie said with wonder. "We even float logs to the mills in rafts just like they did."

"Four-thirty," Sam called out from behind his blanket, where he was still pouting. "It'll come soon enough. Quit your yappin'!"

"I wonder what kind of axes them men had," Cletus said. "I wonder if any of 'em had a Kelly Handmade. That's the best axe ever."

A murmur of agreement followed Cletus's statement.

"I don't think they had Kelly Handmades three thousand years ago, Cletus," Skypilot said. "But I'm sure those loggers would have appreciated one."

"Quit your yappin'!" Sam threatened. "Or I'll shut all of you up by myself."

As Robert pulled the covers around Thomas, his son turned and gave him a hug with his skinny little arms. "'Night, Papa."

"Good night, son."

Robert lay there, listening to his son's even breathing, thinking about the elderly king David trying to gather materials together for his son. Things hadn't changed all that much. In a way, that was what he was struggling to do. Thomas was at that age where he was all knobby knees and big eyes and he held his father's heart in his fist—just like his little sister. What kind of a legacy would he be leaving for Thomas and Betsy? The timber wouldn't last forever, and then what?

―⁂―

Moon Song was restless as they made their pallets on the wooden floor of the cookhouse. Her fidgeting upset the baby. As

Moon Song walked the floor with the fussy infant in her arms, Katie noticed that she kept pacing from window to window, looking out.

"What's wrong, Moon Song?" Katie asked. "What are you looking for?"

"*La fumée,*" Moon Song said. "*Je sens l'odeur de la fumée.*"

"I don't understand."

"*La fumée!*"

It was impossible. Moon Song knew no English, and Katie didn't know a word of French or Menominee. Katie had no intention of trotting over to the men's bunkhouse at this late hour just to roust Henri out of his bunk to translate for her.

But the girl's restlessness, combined with the hard floor cushioned only by blankets, made it difficult to sleep.

She remembered the layers of the soft, downy feather mattresses in her bedroom at Fallen Oaks before the war. The house slaves had fluffed and aired them periodically—as though she were some sort of European princess. Did she wish she could go back to the prewar days of being waited on hand and foot by people she owned? Frankly, she would rather sleep on a rock. She had hated it even back then.

"Is Mr. Foster's sister staying long?" Ned asked from his nest of blankets beside her.

"I hope not. This floor is miserable. I don't know how Moon Song stands it every night. I'm going to ask Tinker if he'll make her a little bed for the cabin."

Moon Song continued to pace the floor like a caged animal. It made Katie nervous. The girl had never done that before. Was there something, or someone, out there? Was there any chance that Harlan was waiting outside, and Moon Song, more attuned to danger than she, sensed it?

"What is it, Moon Song?" Fear laced Katie's voice. "What are you looking for?"

Moon Song stopped dead and pointed out a westward-facing window.

There was no moon and no stars out. No lanterns were lit anywhere in the camp. The night was so dark that Moon Song was barely a shadow standing at the window. It would be impossible to see anything moving around outside.

But Katie looked outside anyway—and saw the thing that was agitating Moon Song. It was a glowing reddish-orange line in the distance, a tiny, flickering light against the dark sky.

As she watched, the distant light grew a fraction larger.

Her breath stopped as it dawned on her what that light meant. She had seen it once before—as General Sherman had burned his way across Georgia. There was a forest fire, and unless she missed her guess, it was coming straight at them.

17

Where the flames in torrents flashing,
through the fields and forest 'round,
and the trees like thunder crashing
in great numbers on the ground.

> "The McDonald Family"
> —1800s shanty song

She ran straight for the Gabriel horn, flung open the door, and began to blow. The sound of that horn was loud enough to wake the dead—which was what all of them would be if she didn't sound the alarm. She kept blowing the horn over and over.

Where could they go? What should they do? How could they get away?

The horn frightened the baby, and it set up a howl. The men stumbled out of the bunkhouse in various stages of undress, some barefoot and carrying axes, some carrying their boots, hopping about on one foot then the other, putting them on.

"What's wrong?" Robert was the first to reach her. Thomas, big eyed, was at his father's side, clinging to his belt.

She pointed to the horizon.

When he saw the ominous glow in the distance, he groaned as though someone had thrust a knife through him. "Wildfire!" he shouted to the men.

There was a clamor as they all scanned the western sky.

"What's the plan, Foster?" Skypilot asked.

That's what Katie wanted to know too.

"I'm taking the children, and I'm getting out of here." Sarah's voice shook as she stood on the fringes of the group, clutching a shawl around her shoulders. "I'm going back to Bay City where it's safe. I can drive that wagon myself, if someone will help me get it hitched up."

"I can't let you do that," Robert said. "If the fire comes this way, you won't make it back."

"Yes, I will."

"A wildfire can travel faster than a horse can run, Sarah. Even if you made it to Saginaw or Bay City, they're both built of wood and sawdust. If the fire reaches them, they'll go up in flames."

"What will we do?" Sarah grabbed him and started shaking him, her eyes wide with fear. "What will we do?"

The glow was getting bigger, and the one safe place, the waters of Lake Huron, upon which Bay City lay, was two days away over a bad road. They didn't have two days.

"We could set a backfire," Tinker said. "Burn everything between here and the fire."

"We can't stop a fire that size, no matter what we do," Robert said. "Sam, Mose, let the horses and mules out of the barn to fend for themselves. We'll head to that inland lake in the uncut section east of here."

"That lake isn't big enough," Sam pointed out. "When those pines catch fire, they'll fall right in on top of us."

"Not if we're in the middle," Robert said.

"Do you happen to have a boat I don't know about?" Jigger said. "One that'll hold all of us? Tinker ain't even started building the wannigan for the spring drive yet."

"Bring your tools and head to the lake. If you have caulked boots, wear them."

As the men rushed to the bunkhouse to get their axes and saws, Robert grabbed Katie by both arms and stared intently into her face. "That lake we went to last Sunday—do you remember how to get there?"

"Yes!"

"Grab as many blankets as you can carry and head there as fast as you can. Don't change clothes. Don't stop for anything." He turned away from her. "Sarah!" he yelled. "Take Betsy and follow Katie!"

For the first time since she had seen the fire on the horizon, Katie realized that she was standing among the men, barefoot and wearing nothing but a nightgown.

"Go put your shoes on, woman!" Jigger shouted as he hurried past her. "And don't you dare take the time to get dressed and flounced up. If we don't get into that lake, and into it in a hurry, nothing else is gonna matter."

"What about my chickens and the piglets?" she asked.

"If the fire comes, they won't make it," Jigger said. "And neither will you if you try to drag them along with you. Hurry, woman!"

Moon Song stood staring at the glowing horizon, her baby secure in the back sling, her moccasins on her feet.

Katie grabbed Ned's hand, and together they ran into the cook shanty, where both donned their shoes and Katie grabbed an armload of blankets and stuffed them into an empty flour sack, wondering what Robert intended her to do with them. She also lit a lantern. They would need it to keep from stumbling over roots and rocks as they made their way to the lake.

"Do we have to leave our animals behind?" Ned asked.

"Yes, but we can open their cages and give them a chance. Come help me."

As Katie and Ned shooed the chickens out and let the piglets run free, she could hardly believe that she was, once again, letting her livestock loose to fend for themselves. Would she ever have any peace?

The camp descended into sheer chaos. Frightened mules and horses ran through the camp. Loggers loaded with peaveys, saws, and axes rushed toward the inland lake. Sarah, hair streaming, with Betsy hanging onto her, was running in the opposite direction.

Skypilot, axe in hand, pulled Betsy away from Robert's sister and hefted the child onto his broad shoulders. "Sarah," he said. "This way!"

"I'm going to Bay City!" she screamed. "Where it's safe!"

Skypilot calmly grabbed the woman and started leading her toward the woods. Katie saw Thomas still holding onto his father's belt, sticking to him like a burr, as Robert shouted orders.

Tethered in the back of the cook shanty was Katie's precious cow, and she could not make herself leave it behind. She jerked the stake out of the ground and with Ned close beside her began to hurry toward the lake as fast as the cow would go.

She had no idea what Robert's plan was once they got there, but she knew that getting to the water was their only chance. Both she and Ned were adequate swimmers. Cows could swim if they had to. The Shorthorn might have a chance if it would just . . . walk . . . faster!

She jerked on the rope, and the cow followed at a leisurely pace. The bell around its neck tinkled with every lumbering step—the cheerful, homely sound unreal against the backdrop of danger. She put the rope over her shoulder and leaned into it, straining against it, willing the complacent cow to hurry.

Cletus ran by. As he passed her, he smacked the Shorthorn on the haunches. "Git!" he yelled.

The cow, surprised, bellowed and bolted forward. Katie ran a few steps to keep up with it.

"You might have to leave her behind," Ernie said.

"I know," Katie said. "I will if I have to."

In his haste, Ned stumbled and fell directly in front of the upset cow. Ernie scooped him up and set him astride the Shorthorn, giving the cow a swat. "Sorry, old gal," Ernie said. "But the fire's gonna hurt a whole lot worse than a little spank if you don't get into the lake and fast."

The cow bawled and trotted faster, Ned clinging to her back.

"What do we do when we get there?" Katie asked. "Surely not everyone can swim." She looked around at the shadowy crowd hurrying through the trees, a bobbing lantern here and there. In the darkness, she realized that she had lost track of Moon Song. She could only trust that the Indian girl was following the rest of them.

Ernie looked at the brightening sky. "I hope the lake is big enough."

"It's a big lake," Katie said.

"So is the fire," Skypilot said as he passed. "Can I leave Betsy with you?"

"Of course."

"Time for a cow ride, little one." He set Betsy in front of Ned. "Hold on to her, son. Katie, don't stop for anything. If the cow can't keep up, grab the children and run."

It was a strange feeling to be striding through the hardwood forest in the middle of the night. She could just make out various woodsmen, all carrying their tools just like Robert had ordered. She couldn't imagine what they could accomplish with these implements. There was nothing at the lake with which to build a boat. Was Robert simply trying to preserve the axes and saws from the fire?

There was movement in the brush beside her. She raised her lantern higher to see what it was and realized that there was a tide of small animals heading away from the forest fire. They were single-minded in their purpose and appeared to be oblivious to the small army of humans striding across their path.

Foxes and rabbits, skunks, even two black bears lumbered past—completely unafraid of the humans. They seemed to realize that there was a much greater threat coming.

When she broke through to the lake, she saw a strange sight. Several axe teams were in the process of felling trees by lantern light. Robert, his sleeves rolled up, stood opposite Mose as both took turns with their axes in a quick staccato rhythm as they dug steel blades into the base of the tree.

This made no sense to her. Why would they be cutting down timber when a fire was on the way?

She had never seen Robert wield an axe before. Even though he was the camp owner, she had no idea he even knew how. But Robert, to her surprise, was every bit as adept as the others. His face was grim, his muscles taut, and sweat poured off his face even though the night was quite cool.

"Timberrrr!" someone shouted from beyond where Mose and Robert worked. She heard a loud splash, and then the sound of furious sawing whipping through the air. She could see the dim forms of two men thrusting a crosscut saw back and forth across the fallen trunk while other men swarmed over the tree, lopping off limbs.

"Got one!" she heard a man cry. In the dim light, she could see two other men using peaveys to roll the log into the water.

"Timberrrr!" she heard Robert cry out. Another tree. Another log.

This frightened her. The loggers might have the skill to balance upon and ride a log into the lake, but she and the children did not. Nor did Sarah. Even Moon Song would not be able to save herself while carrying a baby. Logs rolled when they were in the water. It took much skill to balance upon one.

Robert had to know that this was not going to work. There

was no way tiny Betsy could cling to one of those massive things. There was nothing to hold on to!

"Incendie!" Moon Song materialized beside her, jerking on her sleeve and pointing west. *"Incendie!"*

"She's saying 'fire.'" Henri hurried past with a crosscut saw bouncing upon his shoulder. "But you've probably figured that out by now."

The sky was growing more ominous by the minute. Even though it was the dead of night, it was now so light the lanterns were no longer needed to see. The men continued to frantically roll each freed log into the water. Some who were wearing caulked boots discarded their axes and saws, grabbed peaveys, and climbed upon the logs, doing a sort of desperate dance as the logs whirled in the dark water beneath their boots.

Now she saw Robert upon one. He wasn't as skilled as some of the others, but he could stay up. Thomas stood, abandoned, at the water's edge. She could tell the little boy was getting more and more agitated.

"Father!" the child screamed. "I can't swim!"

"Trust me," Robert shouted as he fought to keep his balance. "Wait on the bank."

Betsy, following her brother's example, stretched her arms out and also began to scream for her father.

Sarah seemed paralyzed by the scope of the danger. She stood, eyes glazed, staring out at the lake, rigid with fear.

Katie scanned the banks. When the fire came, it would burn right up to the edge of the water. The giant trees that ringed it would catch fire and topple in. The lake didn't look so large to her now. No place anywhere near the edge would be safe. The only hope was to get to the middle, away from where the flaming trees would plunge.

Even then, if the fire was hot enough—and Katie knew it would be unimaginably hot—they might not survive.

At least she and Ned knew how to swim well enough to stay afloat. They might stand a chance on their own, but she could never abandon the other children.

"Dear Father in heaven," she prayed aloud as she watched the encroaching fire. "I don't know what to do!"

"Papa!" Thomas ran back and forth along the bank. "Don't leave me, Papa!"

Thomas ran up to her, sobbing in fear, and she drew the child to her for whatever comfort she could give for the short time they had left. Ned faithfully held onto Betsy and the cow. Sarah stood beside them, a gaunt woman with her hands clasped in front of her chest.

"What did Robert shout to Thomas?" Sarah asked. "I couldn't hear."

"He said to trust him."

There was no light of hope in Sarah's eyes. "Then I guess that's all we can do."

Katie put her arms around all three of the children and drew them to her.

Trust me, Robert had said.

Trust him?

If she had ever met a man she thought she could trust, it would be Robert Foster. The problem was, the fire was flying toward them so fast it was hard to even think, let alone trust. As she held the children, she closed her eyes and prayed for deliverance. It was hard to pray, because the crackling of flames was now so distracting, she couldn't see any way, short of a miracle, that they could survive.

And then she opened her eyes and saw something so beautiful and brave, she could hardly believe what her eyes were telling her. Out in the lake the men who were most skilled at riding the logs were forcing them to come together, one by one.

Ernie rolled his log lengthwise flat against Cletus's. Then he used his hooked peavey to latch onto the log upon which his brother was standing. Cletus reciprocated by digging his into Ernie's. This made the two logs beneath them stabilize. Tinker rolled a third log over and secured it flat against Ernie's. Klaas thunked his against Cletus's and latched on. Then Henri brought his up against Klaas's, and O'Neal followed suit.

The moment any two logs came together, the man upon it secured it to the one next to him by digging the curved spike of his peavey into his neighbor's. Those woodsmen who were not as adept at riding the logs now climbed aboard and stitched the logs more firmly together by using only their sheer muscle and those amazing hooked tools.

A crude raft was materializing right before her eyes.

"An old trick." Jigger came up beside her. "When the river drivers are riding the river, a couple of 'em will latch onto one another's log when they get to a straight stretch and make a two-log raft to float down the river for a while. It gives 'em a rest from balancing so they can better handle the rough patches later."

"You knew this was what they were planning all along?"

"It's been done before." He spit, the ever-present wad of chaw tucked into his cheek, even in a crisis. "Forget the cow. She'll either swim or run. Better get those kids on the raft, and quick."

A gust of wind blew a leaf of ash against her face. "Come on." She grabbed Betsy and Thomas and ran toward the lake with Ned and Moon Song right behind her.

Skypilot and Robert were frantically weaving lengths of rope between the logs, stitching them together the best they could. It was hard to accomplish because the logs were so huge. It involved both of them spending much time fumbling around beneath the raft, completely submerged in water, blindly searching for openings. As they worked, other shanty boys started tossing their peaveys onto the logs and climbed on. With their added strength, the raft became more stable.

"We can hold it, boss," Sam said. "Leave the rope and let's get out of here."

"Let's hope it will hold." Robert tied a knot in the lengths of rope they had managed to secure. "Jigger—get the women and children down here."

The logs were wet and rough and nearly impossible to climb upon. The raft bobbed crazily with the shifting weight. Robert and Skypilot stood in waist-deep icy water, ready to help anyone who couldn't get on by themselves.

Betsy, terrified, clung to her father as he lifted her up.

"Not now, sweetheart." He forcibly pulled her away from him and shoved her into the arms of Blackie, who stood above to help lift the children to safety. "Come here, Thomas. I told you I was coming for you. Be a brave boy, now."

Ned and the sack of blankets were handed up next. Ned crouched, holding onto the bundle.

"I shall never forgive you for this, Robert," Sarah said as she struggled onto the raft with her brother's help.

"If we don't get out to the middle quick," he said, glancing up at the sky, which was now as bright as the sunniest day, "you might not need to."

Skypilot helped Moon Song up, the baby still securely tied to his mother's back.

Robert grabbed Katie around the waist and lifted her onto the bobbing raft without bothering to ask permission. She had not realized how strong he was until the moment she felt herself deposited upon a slippery log. Jigger complained that he could climb up on his own, but Skypilot lifted the old man in his arms like an infant and deposited him on the raft as well.

Then Robert leaped up, grabbed a peavey, and helped anchor a log that Sam was straining to control. As those loggers already on the raft helped hold it together, the rest of the men pushed it out into the water. When it became too deep, the powerful men began to thrash their legs, struggling mightily to shove the ungainly thing into the middle of the lake. Finally, they were able to climb on and add their strength to holding the logs together.

Katie hunkered down on a giant log, her knees drawn up beneath her soaked flannel nightgown, clutching Ned to her side. On the other side of her, Jigger was starting to shiver.

"Are you all right?" she asked him.

Jigger shook his head, his body trembling from the cold. She scooted closer to him and wrapped both arms around the sodden old man. She was shocked at how thin he felt in her arms. She realized that, in spite of his bluster and boasts, he was more frail than she had ever realized.

"Ned," she said, "give me a blanket."

The little boy pulled one out, and she wrapped it around the old man.

"Get on the other side of Jigger, Ned, and help me keep him warm."

Ned obediently wrapped his arms around Jigger, and together, the three of them held on to one another while the cold, wet logs moved and swayed.

As the fire roared toward them, she could hear trees crashing in the distance. Sarah clutched Thomas and Betsy, her eyes wide with fear. Moon Song sat nearby, her baby in her lap, ignoring its cries as she fashioned a sling she apparently planned to tie high on her back, preparing to attempt to try to swim without drowning the child.

Above Jigger and the women and children, the stalwart woodsmen stood like grim statues, peaveys crisscrossed, straining to keep the heavy logs from drifting apart. Robert's muscles were set like stone as he stood above Sarah and his children, forcing the logs to stay together.

"Take the other blankets and get them wet, Katie," he

demanded. "Then throw them over you and the others. This is going to be bad."

Jigger wasn't shivering quite as hard now. With much difficulty, Katie crawled over the rough logs, bruising and skinning her knees and legs along the way, until she could dip the rest of the blankets in the water. Gathering Moon Song, Sarah, and the children all together around Jigger, she covered everyone with the drenched blankets.

It was a desperate situation. No one said a word. It was as though everyone on the raft was holding their breath as they waited to see if they would live or die.

Katie marveled at the fact that the men were putting their own lives at stake in order to rescue her and the others. She knew that the loggers would be safer in the water, half-submerged, clinging to a log, their heads barely above the water. Instead, they held fast. She had never seen such courage.

There was Henri of the fiddle and merry spirit—now grim-faced and trying to hold on to his end of a log, even though the raft was constantly shifting beneath everyone's weight. Somehow, even in the midst of the chaos, he had managed to tie his red sash crookedly about his middle. Inkslinger held on to a peavey—his face as solemn as ever. Klaas, his blond hair glinting in the unnaturally bright light, his sturdy legs set far apart, reminded her of a picture of a Viking she had once seen.

Blackie seemed almost cheerful as he added the strength of a blacksmith to the human chain. "Come on, boys—this ain't nothing," he shouted, but he was not a young man, and Katie could see the cords of his muscles straining with the effort to hold the raft steady.

Cletus was grinning with childlike wonder at the glowing horizon. His brother Ernie was standing near, watching his brother with concern.

"That's pretty." Cletus pointed at the encroaching horizon. "Don't you think that's pretty, Ernie?"

"Yes, Cletus," Ernie said gently. "It's real pretty."

Katie saw that there were tears streaming down Ernie's face. And yet the man held firm.

These men, these rough, uncouth, tobacco-spitting, lip-smacking, cursing, stinking men—some of whom she had been half-afraid—grew to hero stature in her eyes as they stood their ground against the danger, holding the strange raft together. She wondered how long these men could endure. If they lost their grip, or their courage, she and the others would tumble into the lake with nothing to save themselves with except the spinning logs.

"Don't you worry none, missus." Mose was crouched nearby with the spike of a peavey dug into a log. "Anything goes wrong, you and the boy grab aholt of ol' Mose here. I can hang on to one of these big old logs for a long, long time."

A lump rose in her throat; she could barely speak. "Thank you, Mose," she choked out.

The fire sounded like a million howling wolves as it came toward them. Smoke swirled over the water while everyone watched for the fire to appear. Animals began to swim out into the lake. Fearful of being capsized, Skypilot had to shove away a wild-eyed, antlered deer that was trying to climb onto the raft. The deer gave up and swam to shore, where it disappeared into the woods opposite the fire.

And then flames burst out upon the shore. It was a terrifying sight—the giant trees suddenly engulfed in towering, swirling flames.

Katie had heard of forest fires so intense that houses spontaneously combusted from the sheer heat long before the actual flames reached them. She and the others were not safe here. Not by a long shot. Not even in the middle of the lake.

"Father, please," Katie whispered, gripping Jigger and Ned tighter.

"Sweet Jesus!" Skypilot faced the fire, raised his hand in the air, and shouted, "Have mercy upon these innocent children!"

"Lord of mercy!" Sarah cried. "Save us!"

Henri made the sign of the cross with one hand while gripping the peavey with the other. Hardened shanty boys, men whom Katie would have bet money had never seen the inside of a church, mumbled prayers. Surprisingly enough, so did Jigger.

She glanced at Robert. His eyes were closed, but his lips moved in silent supplication.

Her precious Shorthorn stood at the river's edge, bawling with fear, but she could do nothing for it. She doubted it would survive. She doubted that any of them would survive.

The heat was blistering against her face now. She could feel it drying out the sodden blanket she had draped around her. No one was cold now. It felt as though a giant, fire-breathing dragon crouched on the edge of the lake, blowing fire at them, licking their faces with its flames. Still the woodsmen stood firm, closing their eyes against the inevitable.

As the heat of the fire began to wash over them, she realized there was no hope unless they all went into the water. She also knew that the loggers would never jump in to save themselves as long as the women and children were still on the raft.

In her opinion, drowning was preferable to being burned alive. She began to crawl toward the edge of the raft, pulling Jigger and Ned with her, planning to plunge beneath the water before the fire could engulf them.

And then she felt the strangest thing.

A welcome coolness caressed her damp nightgown.

She opened her eyes and looked about her. There was a wind—a wind that held the hint of rain—blowing against the fire.

Could it be? The loggers were all staring at the sky, a glimmer of hope in their faces. A thunderclap ripped through the air and lightning shattered the darkness behind them.

Then she felt a drop of rain.

The heavens opened. A downpour drenched the raft. Never in her life had water felt so welcome. Katie could see a visible line of rain as it raced across the lake, blown by the wind, into the trees on the other side—the trees she had watched ignite. She lifted her face to the life-giving rain and drank it in.

The Lord of rain and sky and earth and fire had heard the prayers of the women and children and rough loggers and had chosen to save them.

It took a great deal of effort for the men to maneuver the raft back to shore in the rain, but soon, they were waist deep again. The loggers continued to hold tight while Robert jumped off and he and Skypilot helped lift everyone except the loggers off the raft. Katie was the last, and when Robert reached his arms up to her, she went into them gratefully.

"Are you all right?" Robert whispered into her ear as he lifted her down.

For just a moment, she allowed herself to cling to him, absorbing his strength and courage—and then she let go.

"Yes," she answered. "I'm fine now."

Even though it had lasted only an instant, Katie knew that she would hold dear the memory of Robert's arms around her for the rest of her life.

18

Our bodies are as hard as iron;
our hearts are cased with steel;
and hardships of one winter
can never make us yield.

"Michigan I.O."
—*1800s shanty song*

By the sheer grace of God, the camp was spared—but Robert knew no one would rest tonight. There was something about narrowly escaping death that kept the body and mind awake and vigilant for hours afterward. He had seen it play out over and over on the battlefield. No matter how exhausted the surviving men were after a battle, most had trouble sleeping.

And they had definitely fought a battle.

The rule about silence at the table was ignored, with Jigger's blessing, as the men talked about what they had done. The old cook had changed into dry clothes, but his teeth were still chattering. While Jigger huddled in a corner, wrapped in a blanket, trying to get warm, Robert took over the chore of boiling tea and keeping everyone's mugs filled. The men hunched over the steaming cups as though trying to absorb the warmth into their bodies.

Sarah had taken the children to the cabin to change. She was still madder than a wet setting hen.

Katie, realizing the deep need the men had to congregate

together in the cook shanty, tied an apron over her drenched nightgown and went to work—stoking up the fire and turning out one towering stack of flapjacks after another. She instinctively knew the need to fill the men's chilled stomachs with something sweet and hot. The unending flapjacks and deep puddles of warm sorghum nicely filled the bill.

As the men talked over the night's events, marveling over the miraculous appearance of the driving rain, Robert watched Katie concentrate on her work at the stove. Her hair hung down her back in one long, unkempt braid. Strands straggled around her face, and occasionally she would push them out of her eyes with the back of her hand. She was so slender that the large apron, made for a man, enveloped her. She had kicked off her sodden shoes and was working barefoot.

There was an angry-looking scrape on her right forearm from the rough bark of the logs upon which he had tossed her. She had been wet, cold, and terrified, but now her only thought was the care and feeding of the hungry men.

Moon Song helped by carrying platters back and forth. Skypilot held the baby, asleep and wrapped in dry swaddling, cradled in one arm while he talked with the men. Henri kindly translated some of the conversation into French so that Moon Song could understand and participate in the conversation.

While everyone was absorbed in the telling and retelling of what they had experienced, Robert refilled the teakettle and walked over to where Katie was working while he waited for it to come to a boil.

"Thank you for doing this," he said.

"You and the men put your lives at risk to save ours." Katie poured more batter onto the griddle. "Fixing an early breakfast is the least I can do."

"You didn't even take time to change," he said. "You must be miserable."

"It doesn't matter." Katie brushed another strand of hair out of her eyes. "What matters is that everyone is alive and unharmed."

"You'll catch pneumonia."

"You have obviously never stood close to this stove." She expertly flipped another flapjack. "I'm plenty warm. I'm surprised steam isn't rising off me."

Robert did feel the heat of the stove, but he felt another heat as well, brought on by standing so close to her and remembering the feel of her in his arms when he lifted her off of the raft.

Those life-changing minutes as he had struggled to hold the raft together, praying that they would survive the fire, had forced him to see with absolute clarity that each moment with his children was precious and holy. He had lost enough time with them. He had grieved their mother long enough. He had lived with regrets long enough. For all their sakes, it was time to re-enter the land of the living instead of spending his life reliving regrets from the past.

The God-given reprieve from death had also opened his eyes in other ways. As he had watched Katie holding Jigger, shielding the old man as much as possible from the cold, as he had watched her covering his children with the soaked blankets, taking no thought for herself as she made her way over the rough logs trying to care for everyone—he knew he wanted this valiant woman. The fire had burned away any doubts he had about the rightness of bringing Katie into his life.

The problem was convincing Katie of that fact. If he knew anything at all about women, it wouldn't be wise to announce his intentions to marry her, since, until a short time ago, they had been strangers. Fortunately, he had time on his side. Neither of them were going anywhere for quite a while.

"I hope what happened tonight didn't make you regret coming to work here," Robert said.

"I'm being paid a king's ransom to do a job I enjoy." Katie poured more batter that sizzled on the griddle. "I work for a man I trust and respect. I regret nothing."

He stood behind her and lifted his hand, longing to touch her hair, caress her face—but it was not the time or place. He let his hand drop.

"When daylight comes, I'll be able to see how much of my land has burned," he said. "If too many acres were destroyed, I won't be able to keep this camp going."

"Then you'll find more trees and build another camp." Katie grabbed a platter and flipped flapjacks onto it. "You have the tools, you have the knowledge, you have the crew, and"—she gave him a mischievous grin—"you have a great camp cook."

Robert felt his spirits rise. No matter what the morning brought to light, with enough hard work and this woman by his side, it would be all right.

_꒳_

The morning light was not kind. The fire had come so close to the camp that everything was covered in sodden ashes. The camp, never picturesque, was now an ugly, uniform gray.

Katie slogged out to milk her cow, the hem of her dress stained from the ashy mud. The cow, so frightened last night, amazingly still gave milk this morning. Tinker and Ned had gathered up all the chickens, most of which had roosted in the trees until morning light. One of the piglets had been found. The other one was still lost. Some of the horses and mules were missing. Some had wandered back. It would take a while to sort it all out.

The familiar routine of milking was comforting. As she squirted streams of foaming milk into the pail, she dreamed of all the things she would be able to make if the cow's milk held. Butter, of course, which she would keep chilled in the cold river out back, and buttermilk, which she knew the men would enjoy after a hard day's work.

She would also make cottage cheese and there would be fresh cream for their tea. A cow was a wonderful thing—a virtual grocery of culinary possibilities. And this Milking Shorthorn seemed to be giving well. Its placid nature, which had been such an irritation last night when she desperately wanted it to hurry, was now welcome. Unlike her two Jerseys, it hadn't even once tried to kick her.

She eyed the amount of milk in her bucket when she finished: two and a half gallons. This bode well for the future. A cow that gave five to six gallons of milk a day was a treasure.

Robert was out with the men, surveying the damage, deciding how much the fire had cost him. She prayed he would be able to keep this camp open—moving to another location would put him behind for the winter, and she had no idea if he had the resources to purchase another section of timber.

As she stripped out the final drops of milk, she heard the men returning to camp. There would be no timber cutting today, and it felt odd to have people coming and going all morning. As she started to carry the bucket of milk into the kitchen, she saw Sarah march out of the cabin with both children. The woman was dragging luggage with her, and both of the children were carrying smaller bags.

As Katie watched, Robert came out of the woods, begrimed and weary, and noticed that his sister was preparing to leave.

"What are you doing with my children?" he asked.

"I've changed my mind." Sarah hefted a leather satchel into the wagon with a grunt. "I'm taking them back home with me."

"No." He laid a hand on her arm. "You aren't. They're staying here. I don't want them to leave."

She dumped a valise into the wagon. "It's too dangerous."

"I want them with me."

"Since when?" Sarah stopped and stared at him.

"I've always wanted them here." Robert's voice was exasperated. "I thought I was giving them a better life by letting them live in town with you, but I don't believe that anymore. I know this is a rough place, but they need to be with me. And I—well, I need to be with them too."

From behind the cow, Katie saw the children watching, with wide eyes, this debate between their aunt and their father.

"Go marry your butcher and make a good life for yourself, Sarah. The children should be my responsibility, not yours. I'm sorry I didn't see that sooner."

Sarah's face softened. "Are you sure?"

He glanced down at Thomas and Betsy. "Do you want to stay with me or go back home with your Aunt Sarah?"

"I want to stay with you, Father," Thomas said solemnly.

"Me too!" Betsy said.

"Where will all of you stay?" Sarah asked. "Betsy can't sleep in the bunkhouse, and Katie already has a full cabin."

"I'll have Tinker build some bunks in the office. It'll be tight, but I think we can manage."

"Well," Sarah said. "I guess it's settled then."

Katie thought she heard some regret in Sarah's voice. Personally, she doubted the butcher was worth the forfeiture of the children, but that was Sarah's decision, not hers.

"How bad was it out there today, Robert?" Sarah asked. "Will you still have work?"

"Most of my land is to the east. I lost about eighty acres of pine. Maybe twenty acres of hardwood. There's still enough standing timber to give the men work over the winter and into the spring. I won't be a rich man when the spring drive is over, but if we have a good, cold winter, I'll get enough timber out to pay the bills and purchase another tract of pine." He closed his eyes in weariness.

"You need to rest, little brother," Sarah said.

"Thank you for everything you've done, Sarah." Robert put his arms around his sister and rested his forehead against hers. "I don't know what I would have done without you."

"It's all right, honey . . ." There were tears in Sarah's eyes and she patted her brother's back. "It's all right."

⸺ ○•○ ⸺

As Sarah rode away, Katie strained the milk and put it to chill in the river. Last night had made her want to know so much more about Robert—more than she was willing to ask. He had given her permission to read his journal, and so she returned to her cabin and pulled the journal from its place beneath the eaves. She began reading where the pages fell open, about halfway through. She wanted to get to the part where she could begin to understand why he had given up medicine.

There was a thumbprint of blood on the page. With a sinking heart, she began to read.

> *July 6, 1863*
>
> *I have been operating for days and have gotten most of the "butchering" done. I have been left here in charge of 500 wounded men, with few medical supplies and little help. I do not yet know the full extent of the carnage, I did not ask. I could not think beyond trying to repair the next ravaged body and the next and the next. I tried not to look into the pain-filled eyes or see the fear in the men's faces as I approached them with my cutting saw to remove yet another mangled limb. Had I allowed myself to see the men as individuals, with mothers and wives at home praying for their deliverance, I would have sunk into utter despair and been of no use to anyone.*
>
> *And still, no matter how hard I worked, the sound of the*

battle continued—the gunshots and shouts and screams
ringing in my ears—a vicious, evil machine churning out
body after body for me to try to piece together again. I
operated until the surgical instruments began to slip from
my grasp and my orderly forced me stop.

I am told that our division lost. A third were killed or
wounded. Many of these men were my friends.

God help us.

Katie closed her eyes, absorbing the pain from those words.
This is what Robert had endured. This was what so many had
endured.

Harlan had made it sound like a lark.

She wasn't sure Harlan was entirely human.

July 10, 1863

The orderly has just scrubbed all the blood out of my
hair with castile soap and bay rum and my scalp feels as
if a steam plow had been passed through it. When this
nightmare is finished, if it is ever finished, I will never
operate again. I have not the stomach for it. Not anymore.
I have seen more entrails in one battle than most surgeons
see in a lifetime. Lord willing, I will find another way to
support my family when I am relieved of this duty and
allowed to go home. At least I know that little Thomas
and the babe are safe in Sarah's care. May their blessed
mother rest in peace.

Katie gently closed the journal. She stuffed it back up under
the eaves alongside the box of surgeon's tools. Robert was
right—it was *not* easy reading. She had no desire to continue.
There was enough pain in those two entries alone to last her
a lifetime.

She had a few more minutes before she needed to start dinner.

There was one more thing she needed to do, a person she needed to see, a promise she had made to herself last night while crouching on the raft in the wet and the rain.

~ ∽ ~

Mose emerged from the woods, as weary as she had ever seen the man—but he had finally found his horses. She knew she had information that might take some of the weariness away.

"You found them," she said.

"They know ol' Mose's voice."

What she intended to tell this good man could get them both killed, but last night had taken away the option of keeping silent. She kept pace with him as he led the horses to the barn.

"Do you remember the time that Harlan sent you to old Mrs. Hammond's place to buy her husband's seed cotton after he passed?"

"It was a far piece," Mose said. "Mrs. Hammond's a good woman. The lady gave me a drink o' water from her well."

"Violet is with her."

He halted. Then he turned and looked at her as though he couldn't believe what he was hearing. "Violet, does she have a man?"

"Not the last I knew."

"I been savin' up," Mose said. "When I find her, I gonna buy us a piece of land somewhere nice. She can have herself a garden and I can plant crops and raise some animals. Maybe a family too."

It was a long way from Michigan to Georgia, but Katie had no doubt Mose would manage to get there.

"Violet will be a lucky woman to have you." Katie scratched behind the closest mare's ears. "You're a good man, Mose."

"I try."

"You always did. Even when it wasn't easy."

"Yes'm. So did you."

A silence weighted with memories filled the air. Katie felt the heaviness of those memories.

"I'm sorry I lied to you, Mose."

"Why'd you do that?" he asked.

"I'm afraid if you go to Georgia, Harlan will hear. I was afraid he'd find out where I am and come after me."

She saw a muscle in Mose's jaw twitch. "You don't have to worry 'bout that none."

"You aren't going to spend the winter here?"

"No'm."

"You know that if word gets back to Harlan . . ." Her voice trailed off.

"All I want is to find my woman."

"This is going to leave Robert shorthanded."

"There's plenty good teamsters—only one Violet."

"Be careful, Mose." She rubbed a palm over the mare's velvety nose. "The South is a dangerous place for a black man right now."

"It always was, missus," Mose said. "It always was."

─⟨∘⟩─

Harlan rode back to his overgrown plantation, hating the sight of what it had become.

The days he had spent trying to hunt down the elusive Katherine had been a waste.

He had gone to her people in Pennsylvania, certain she had run to them, but even though he used his most charming manner, those Yankee clods had stood looking at him with suspicious eyes, informing him that they had not seen nor heard from Katherine in months.

He started to take a swig from his flask, and thought better of it. He realized now that it would take all of his cunning to track her down—he could no longer indulge.

19

*We are lying in the shanty; it's bleak and it's cold,
while cold, wintry winds do blow.
The wolves and the owls with their terrible growls
disturb us from our midnight dreams.*

> "A Shantyman's Life"—
> 1800s shanty song

December 11, 1867

It snowed.

And it continued to snow. Although there had been smatterings earlier, this snowfall settled in, piling inch after inch against the log buildings. She had seen snow before, but she had never seen quite so *much* of it.

The snow was beautiful, smoothing over the pockmarks of stumps, brush, and trash piles, but the winter cold also seeped through every crack and cranny of the cook shanty and her cabin. Not for the first time, she gave thanks for the plentiful firewood and men who cut and split it.

The cold weather meant that the "road monkeys" who iced the road could now turn it into a glassy sheet so thick that one teamster with a giant sled could pull tons of logs at a time, the runners sliding within deep ruts deliberately cut into the solid sheet of ice.

These days, she usually found the road crew warming themselves and eating molasses cookies around the banked coals of her stove each morning when she entered the kitchen. They would have already helped themselves to so much of the hot tea that there would only be dregs left, and she would have to make more. After thawing inside and out, they would brave the cold once again, refilling the strange, box-like contraption out of which water drained from multiple holes as they rode upon the tote roads, icing them down with gallons upon gallons of river water every night while the other loggers slept.

She had to keep the cookies in a large tin container. Mice had become an issue as the rodents sought warmth and food. It was an ongoing battle.

With her in charge, Jigger had taken to snoozing a little longer in the mornings. Gone were the days when he tried to undermine her. His attitude had shifted the night she and Ned had kept him warm on the raft. She tried not to make too much noise in order not to awaken him. He had been more frail than ever since that night, and he needed his sleep.

Katie had begun to love these early hours when she had her kitchen all to herself. It gave her time to have a cup of wake-up tea, to jot down a few thoughts about the day's menu, and to ready the kitchen.

And she prayed.

Ever since the fire, her prayers had changed. Instead of nothing more than an almost constant plea for God to protect her from Harlan, she had begun to pray for the loggers. Sometimes when she had a few extra minutes, she would walk around the table, touching each downturned tin plate, breathing a quick prayer for the man who ate there. It was her quiet gift to them. Out in the barn, three of her hens were laying and she had been saving up the eggs. This morning she planned on making a special treat for breakfast, scrambled eggs and sausage. Bowls of canned tomatoes mixed with cubes of leftover bread sweetened with sugar would round out the breakfast quite nicely.

As she cubed the bread, she found herself humming a hymn from her childhood.

"Rock of ages, cleft for me." She sang softly so as not to awaken Jigger. "Let me hide myself in Thee."

She became so engrossed in her cooking and her song that she didn't realize that Robert had entered the cook shanty.

"You have a pretty voice, Katie."

She glanced up, and her heart skipped a beat. He looked so handsome and strong in his heavy coat, stamping the snow off his boots. A welcome sight in the early morning.

"Hello," she said. "You're up early."

"I couldn't sleep." He leaned against the corner of the worktable, watching her work. "I thought I'd check on the road monkeys."

Since her hands were occupied with her task, she nodded toward the pot on the stove. "Help yourself."

He poured himself a cup and pulled up a chair.

"How are the children?" she asked.

"Sleeping the sleep of the innocent. Funny thing—it seemed like they always had coughs and colds back in town, but they're healthy as horses here. Thomas is growing like a weed, and he's not as quiet and reserved as he was when he first came. He hardly seems like the same child."

"Boys love being around their father." She wiped her hands off on a towel. "I saw him walking behind you the other day, and he was taking great big steps. From what I can tell, he tries to imitate everything you do."

"Guess I'd better be careful, then."

"Yes, I wouldn't do anything you didn't want him to copy."

She greased two large iron skillets, set them on the stove, patted out sausage patties, and washed the grease off her hands. The smell of sizzling spicy meat soon filled the air.

"If it stops snowing, I'll be sending Sam back to Bay City again this week for more supplies," he said. "Is there anything you need?"

"I was hoping you'd ask." She reached into her apron pocket and handed him a list. "It's all written down." She was proud of herself for being ahead of him this time. She was getting more organized. She'd been adding things to a list for a while now, each time she thought of something the men would like.

He glanced at the list, then at her. "There's nothing on this except food. Isn't there anything else you want?"

"Like what?" She flipped the sausage over. "I already have my cow and chickens. The one piglet we found is fattening up nicely."

"I don't know." He looked abashed. "I was wondering if there was some woman thing you or Moon Song might like."

"Woman thing?"

"You know, something froufrou. Maybe a lady's magazine or something. Claire used to love getting her copy of *Godey's Lady's Book*."

"Moon Song doesn't read and I rarely have time."

"Well, what about a hair comb or a mirror or something."

Her hands flew to her head. "Is something wrong with my hair?"

"No!" He looked at her miserably. "I'm just trying to be nice here, Katie. You're living in a camp full of men. There must be something you miss—something you need—just for yourself."

Her heart melted. How thoughtful could one man be?

"You want to get me something nice?" She started flipping the other skillet of sausage. "Something I *really* want?"

"I do."

"I want a cat."

"A cat?"

She nodded emphatically. "A good mouser."

Understanding dawned. "Of course you need a cat."

"The mice are driving me crazy. I would absolutely love a nice, hungry cat."

"I'll put it on Sam's list."

The door to Jigger's room creaked open and the old man peered out at them, squinting at the light. His baby fine gray hair stood straight up. His baggy long johns hung off his bony body.

"If you two would quit flappin' your lips about a dad-blamed cat, maybe a feller could get some sleep around here!" He slammed the door.

The old fellow was so irate and yet had looked so silly that Katie threw her hand over her mouth to keep from laughing out loud. Robert was struggling too. He grabbed her hand and pulled her outside into the snow, shutting the door behind them.

He pulled his sock hat off his head, ran his hands through his hair until it stood straight up, and squinted at her, imitating Jigger. Katie was in such a good mood, she started giggling, and that set Robert off, and they laughed until they were leaning against each other and wiping tears from their eyes—even though it really wasn't all that funny.

And then the laughter stopped.

Both of them realized, at the same time, that they were standing alone, under a starry winter sky, with a virtual fairyland of snow falling around them. Katie had become so warm standing over the stove that the momentary cold felt refreshing to her. She watched, fascinated, as giant snowflakes fell on Robert's hair and lashes.

She saw his face grow sober, gazing at her in the starlight. He reached to brush a snowflake off her cheek and—just for an instant—she leaned her cheek against the warmth of his hand.

They stood there, stock-still, gazing with wonder into one another's eyes.

"Katie-girl." Robert's affection for her was in that word as he bent his head toward hers. She craved the kiss she knew was coming. With everything in her, she wanted to respond to this amazing man who had been so good to her.

Her mind whirled with rationalizations. Harlan was hundreds of miles away. He was a cruel and vicious man. Robert was loving, kind, and good. No one would know. Ever.

Except Ned.

And God.

And herself.

And yet—oh how she wrestled with herself! One kiss wouldn't hurt. Just one. One kiss to warm her memories in her old age.

At that moment, the smell of scorched sausage struck her nostrils.

"The meat!" She whirled, flung open the door, and ran to the stove. The way the men ate, she could not afford to burn even one piece.

She threw water into the skillet and watched it sizzle up around the sausage. Then she pulled both skillets onto the worktable and inspected the sausage patties. They were brown, but not ruined. It had been a very close call, indeed.

In more ways than one.

"I suppose I'd better get out of your way." Robert stood near the stove. He acted as though trying to decide if he should leave or attempt to take up where they left off. He waited for her to make the first move.

And she couldn't—not now, not ever. It had, indeed, been a very close call.

~ formula ~

Robert couldn't get the scene with Katie out of his mind. If only the sausage hadn't started to burn! It was very confusing. He saw the yearning in her eyes, but she always kept him at arm's length.

Maybe it would just take a little more time and patience.

He watched a load of logs slide away to be deposited at the roll way near the riverbank. The piles, carefully stacked to roll into the Saginaw tributary when the spring rains came, had grown. The weather had been perfect for timbering and the men had responded with enthusiasm. He was certain that a large part of their good cheer came from Katie's cooking.

Last night, her big surprise had been custard pies. It was rare to see custard pies in a lumber camp, and they had been hailed as a great delicacy. A fight had broken out over who would get the last piece. Jigger had stopped the near riot by taking the last piece for himself.

Katie had apologized for not having made more pies.

As though the girl had anything to apologize for. With her two hands, she had raised the morale of the camp to heights he had never seen before—not even in his own father's well-run camps. Well-fed, happy men worked well together. And they worked with enthusiasm. It was not unusual to hear a logger whistling as he sawed limbs off a fallen pine, nor was it unusual—even in this cold weather—to hear strains of "The Jolly Shanty Boy" being sung at the top of some axe man's lungs.

And Katie had done all this while also keeping an eye on his children while he was in the woods each day. Little Betsy was learning rudimentary cooking skills at Katie's side. Thomas had been put on the payroll along with Ned and was more confident now that he had chores to do.

Robert had taken on the responsibility of teaching his children what he could in the bit of time they had between the end of supper and bedtime. It wasn't as good as a formal schooling, but the children seemed to be enjoying his makeshift lessons well enough.

Today the men had found a curiosity—an ancient oak so large it must have been growing there for hundreds of years. It was hollow from rot, but the outer wood was still strong. When they found it, Cletus mentioned that it would make a good playhouse.

That comment stuck with him. During their noon meal, Robert took an axe and widened the rotted-out opening at the base of the tree. The inside of the tree was the size of a small room. Working with his hands, he cleared out the debris from the inside and created a clean, aromatic floor with fresh wood chips and sawdust.

The men watched what he was doing with interest.

"You planning on hibernating in that tree this winter, boss?" Tinker teased.

"No." Robert laughed. "It's for the children. I'm thinking it might be good to invite them all out for a winter picnic."

Skypilot rose from his seat. With a few well-placed swings of his axe, he turned the doorway into a giant heart.

"There," he said with satisfaction. "Christmas is coming up. Let's give them something to remember."

Today, Carrie Sherwood, the wealthy young widow he had been hoping to court, had announced her engagement to Harold Swank, a lowly private who worked as a handyman around her plantation.

If it weren't for Katherine, he would probably already be married to the woman and making plans for the use of her money.

On top of every other indignity he had endured, he had recently learned that Mose, a slave he had once owned, had returned and was living at old Mrs. Hammond's place. Mose had somehow managed to get himself a wagon and a team of fine horses. He was earning good wages hauling for various sharecroppers in the area while Harlan had nothing.

He wasn't stupid. He saw what was happening. He was turning into a laughingstock in his own hometown—and there was only one person to blame. Marrying that Yankee had been the biggest mistake of his life.

20

With axes on our shoulders
we'll make the woods resound,
and many a tall and stately tree
will come tumbling to the ground.
       "Once More A-Lumbering Go"
               —1800s shanty song

Over the next few days, many of the men, homesick for their families, had added their own touches to the hollow tree.

Tinker made a small table. From the store back at the camp, Inkslinger donated three wooden boxes that had once held chewing tobacco to be used as seats. The final day, the morning of Christmas Eve, Ernie nailed balsam branches in an arc over the doorway as a sort of rough decoration.

Far from their families, with only other lonely shanty boys for company, the Christmas season was always hard on the men, a time when frustration was close to the surface and fights could break out over nothing. Somehow, preparing this surprise tempered all of that.

Robert was surprised to discover, when he entered the ancient tree to deposit the presents he had purchased for the children, that some of the men had already added gifts of their own. Someone had whittled three small wooden plates and cups along with miniature forks and spoons. A new, red handkerchief was spread out as a miniature tablecloth. A tiny doll made of braided straw lay on one of the plates. A colt carved of hickory kicked up its heels on another. A tiny kitten sat beside the doll. A tiny wooden dog, curled up as though asleep, sat on the last.

The people in town saw the shanty boys at their worst, cut loose from the isolation of the pine, with money in their pockets and mayhem in their hearts. He got to see them at their best.

The top of the tree had broken off long ago, and as it neared noon and the sun rose overhead, light filtered down through the hole, illuminating the little table with a shaft of sunlight as though God himself was blessing this Christmas offering.

Robert added the small sacks of candy he had picked up during his last trip to town. Then he backed out of the tree and looked at it with satisfaction. This was the kind of thing he would have loved as a child. He hoped the children's enthusiasm would match the giving hearts of the shanty boys who had tried to create a Christmas for them out of the little they had.

"Hello the camp!" Katie called out merrily from beside the lunch sled. Moon Song was beaming inside the heavy, man's coat he had asked Sam to purchase for her at Katie's request. The girl also glanced down admiringly at her new thick boots that Sam had added. Jigger, to his surprise, had come along as well.

Robert had broken the news to Katie that he could not find a cat to buy anywhere. It was true. He had not been able to *purchase* a cat, but Sam had been offered one for *free*—a barn cat that the owner had insisted was an excellent mouser.

The cat was, at this moment, sitting in the bunkhouse rattling the cage Sam had gotten for it. The thing had quite a fighting spirit. Robert still had the scratches from trying to put it back inside the cage once he found out how wild it was. He hoped this meant it would be a good mouser. If not, his intended Christmas gift to Katie would be a dismal failure.

The children were rosy-cheeked and glowing from their walk. He glanced around and saw that two burly shanty boys were deliberately blocking the children's view of the playhouse.

Betsy ran toward him through the snow and threw herself into his arms. "Katie said you have a surprise for us!"

"Did she now?" Robert winked at Katie. "Did she tell you what it was?"

"No." Betsy pouted. "She said she didn't know."

Robert told all three children to cover their eyes, and then he placed them facing the entrance to the playhouse. They could hardly stand still as Robert motioned the two loggers to stand aside.

"You can look now."

"Oh!" The children's gasps of wonder were everything he and the other men had hoped for. They rushed toward the tree and clambered inside, exclaiming over each discovery.

Betsy came running back out with the little doll and headed straight for Katie. "Look!" she said.

"It's beautiful, sweetheart." Katie looked around at the ring of men. "Who made this?"

"My grandmere teached me," Henri said. "Long, long time ago in Quebec. I think maybe I forget how—but I remember!"

"I think you better go thank Henri, honey," she said.

Betsy ran to Henri, who stooped down low so she could hug his neck. He smiled happily. Then she ran back inside the tree to see what other wonders it held.

Ned came out reverently holding the exquisite little horse.

"I believe that's Cletus's work, son," Robert said.

"It's beautiful." Ned walked over to Cletus, the carving cradled in his hand. "How do you do this?"

"His name is Poppy." Cletus lovingly ran a finger over the tiny colt. "He likes to run."

Robert knew how hard it must have been for Cletus to give Poppy away, and a lump formed in his throat at the sacrifice.

"Could you teach me?" Ned asked. "I have a pocketknife."

"Sure!" Cletus's face lit up. "I can teach you real good."

Thomas, wearing a worried expression, walked over to his father. Robert got down on one knee so he could be face to face with his boy. "What's wrong, son?"

The little boy uncurled his hand. He was clutching the tiny dog. "Is this for me?" he said. "To keep?"

"Ask Cletus."

"His name is Hunter," Cletus said.

"Thank you." Thomas was enthralled with the little dog.

Cletus, happy with the boys' response, ducked his head into the opening of the playhouse and told Betsy, "There's a kitty in there. Her name is Buttons."

Robert smiled at the sound of Betsy's happy squeal.

"I brought somethin' too." Jigger produced a worn checker set from a sack he had carried along with him. "I'll teach you young'uns to play—that'll be my present."

Betsy came back out and motioned for her father to bend down. "There's candy too!" she whispered loudly enough for everyone to hear. "Can I have a piece?"

At that moment, Ernie's stomach growled. The men laughed as he looked startled and grabbed his offending middle.

"Why don't you wait until after we have dinner before you eat the candy, sweetie," Katie said. "I have baked beans, corn bread, and raisin-filled cookies."

She pulled out tin plates and opened the containers of food while the children ran back inside of their Christmas playhouse. After the men had all dished up lunch and were seated on various stumps and logs around the fire, she called to the children to come get theirs.

Robert loved it when he saw them coming with the little wooden plates and cups he knew Tinker had made.

"Tell Tinker thank you," he said. "He's the one who made those for you, and the table too."

Tinker had to balance his food in one hand while each of the children gave him a hug, but he didn't seem to mind.

"That's all right." He grinned and patted each child's back in turn. "That's all right."

The children's happy laughter and chatter coming from their playhouse was like music to Robert and the men. He noticed several with quiet smiles on their faces while they ate.

He allowed the dinner break to last a little longer than usual. It was cold today, but it was sunny and clear. The men lounged around, enjoying the hot tea from the kettle hung from the tripod while their food digested. Even Moon Song seemed to relish the camaraderie as she sat on the stump, rocking the baby to sleep and chatting with Henri in French.

Katie was cheerfully making the men guess what she would be serving for Christmas supper tomorrow—traditionally the best meal served all year. She seemed at home in this setting. In spite of the hard work and privations, she, like the children, seemed to be thriving in this rough atmosphere.

This struck him as slightly odd. He knew from observing his own mother and other women who had survived their husbands, that widowhood was not an easy thing. His mother had seemed determined to bring his deceased father into every conversation for years afterward, exalting him to a sainthood he had never enjoyed in life—not even by his wife.

Katie had never mentioned her husband. Not even once.

He had a feeling his lovely, talented cook was hiding something. He just hoped he discovered what it was before he allowed himself to fall any deeper in love with her.

Katie needed to get back to start supper, but the children begged to be allowed to stay longer.

"I'll keep an eye on 'em," Jigger promised. "It's been a long time since I was out in the woods with the men. I'll keep the fire going so's they can warm up if they need to."

"Robert?" she asked. "What do you think?"

"It's all right with me if they stay."

Somewhat relieved, Katie left for the camp. She had an enormous amount of work to do before tonight, and having the children gone *would* make things easier.

As she and Moon Song plodded through the snow, dragging the emptied dinner sled behind them, she planned her meal down to the last morsel for tonight. In anticipation of it being Christmas Eve, she had already baked several layers of a cake she planned to stack and decorate with vanilla icing. It would be quite an eye-catcher when she was finished with it—the fanciest thing she had yet attempted in camp. The children would love it.

And, of course, Robert would also be impressed. Which was the main reason she was attempting such a towering confection. His praise for her was becoming an obsession. She hungered for it as much as the shanty boys hungered for her flapjacks every morning. Every kind word Robert had ever uttered to her, every compliment, she turned over and over in her mind like jewels. She was ashamed to admit how starved for kind words she had been.

Yes, tonight, her cake would be a marvel of engineering and beauty, and Robert would be impressed by her expertise. She could hardly wait to get started.

⎯⎯◌◌⎯⎯

"Timberrrr!"

Robert jerked his axe away from the base of the tree and stepped back, listening to the satisfying cracking sound as the remaining fibers of the tree broke away and the giant pine hovered before it began its long, crashing descent through the surrounding tree limbs. He was the other half of a two-man axe team with Skypilot today.

He had just turned to make certain Ernie and Cletus were standing by to chop off the limbs when he heard a sound that sent a chill up his spine.

"Papa?" Betsy's voice called. "Where are you, Papa?"

He whirled, searching for his daughter. *Please, God, not in the path of the descending tree!*

And then he saw a sight that would haunt him for the rest of his life. Skypilot was running, faster than Robert had ever seen a man run, directly in line with the tree. The preacher who wasn't a preacher anymore must have spotted the child before she even called out.

Robert had never felt so helpless in his life. Even Gettysburg had not left him feeling as useless. His heart pounded as he watched Skypilot race to save Betsy's life.

Skypilot did not hesitate when he reached the little girl. He scooped her up without breaking stride while tons of pine plummeted toward earth.

And then it was over.

A tangle of limbs obscured Skypilot and Betsy. He didn't know if either of them were alive. He grabbed his axe and began to run.

Years ago, while still a child, he had seen a man crushed by a falling tree at his father's camp. It was, at that moment, deep in the Maine forests, far from any medical help, that he had decided to become a doctor.

He knew exactly the kind of damage a falling tree could do to the human body.

The other men were running too. Robert had prayed many times in his life but never as fervently or as desperately as he prayed now—that his daughter would be unharmed and alive and the man who had risked his life to save her would be spared.

Then he heard Betsy's screams. No words, just screams that went on and on echoing throughout the forest.

He had to crawl over the tree trunk to get to them. Skypilot was pinned to the earth, a broken limb across his chest, another limb across his legs. He couldn't see Betsy, but her screams were coming from beneath some pine boughs about ten feet from Skypilot. As Ernie and Cletus began to chop at the butt of the limb that was pinning Skypilot to the ground, Robert waded through the branches, oblivious to scratches and scrapes, frantically digging his way through the green boughs covering his daughter.

"Betsy! Lay still. I'm coming!"

Other hands parted limbs. When he saw his daughter, she was curled into a ball. At the sound of his voice, she stopped screaming and started sobbing so hard her body shook.

As he ran his hands over her tiny body, he found no broken bones, no puncture wounds. Only a multitude of scratches and one scraped knee.

"He threw me," Betsy sobbed. "Skypilot *threw* me!"

"He saved your life, honey." Robert gathered her up in his arms. "Skypilot threw you as far away from the tree as he could to save you."

"Boss!" Ernie shouted from behind him. "You'd better come here."

Betsy was clinging to him.

"Let go, sweetheart." He tried to pull her arms from around his neck. "I have to see to Skypilot now. I'll come back for you as fast as I can."

"No!" She fought and kicked at Klaas, who gently pulled her away from him. It broke Robert's heart to see her so upset, but he had to go to the injured man.

"Boss!"

"I'm coming."

227

Robert fought his way back through the limbs to where Skypilot lay. His time spent getting to Betsy had taken less than three minutes, but it was three minutes Skypilot couldn't spare.

Ernie had managed to saw through the two limbs that had crashed into Skypilot's body, and now Cletus and two others were gently lifting them off him.

It was bad.

Robert's heart sank as he took in the full extent of Skypilot's injuries. One leg was twisted at a horrible angle. More than a few ribs were broken. He'd sustained a head wound. But the worst thing of all—the thing that made Robert's gut twist in sympathy—was the large splinter of broken limb that had punctured Skypilot's stomach like a dull knife.

Abdominal wounds were notorious for becoming infected. During the worst battles, when the injured were too numerous to be removed quickly from the battlefield, those soldiers who had stomach wounds were frequently left behind to die—the chances of a doctor being able to save them was too remote to be a medical priority.

But he had to try.

"Let's get him back to camp," he instructed the men who were helplessly standing around.

"Is he gonna make it, boss?" Ernie asked.

"God only knows."

The men cut two straight poles from limbs and fashioned a makeshift stretcher out of their own coats. With a sober and frightened Betsy now quiet in Klaas's arms, Robert directed the lifting and carrying of the wounded man. The shanty boys were as tender and solicitous as women as they carried their fallen comrade away.

Robert walked by Skypilot's side, helping to keep the stretcher steady, as he tried to prepare himself, once again, to perform surgery under primitive conditions. He had sworn he would never touch those instruments again. He doubted he could do so now. The last time he had tried, his hands had trembled so badly he knew it was impossible.

There was a term coined, while he was a doctor in the Union army, for an emotional condition that made a soldier unfit for duty. Too many battles, too many fallen comrades, too many gunshots took a toll on a man. The government called it "soldier's heart," and some men never recovered from the tremors and nervous condition.

For him, it had been a different sort of hand-to-hand combat. He had been in charge of too many tents filled with dying and wounded. Too many men he couldn't save.

When he had dealt with patients who had this disorder, he, too, called it "soldier's heart." But when it came to himself, he called it cowardice. It was a sin to take his God-given talent and medical training and bury it because he wasn't man enough to deal with what he had experienced in the war. He knew this. He was ashamed of this. But he was incapable of ever operating again.

Except now—he had no choice.

The man who had saved his daughter's life was dying, and Robert knew that he was Skypilot's only hope.

21

We have sawmills all o'er the land;
they saw the lumber with a band;
they'll take your leg or take your hand
and leave you crippled in Michigan.

"Don't Come to Michigan"
—1800s shanty song

Katie had just finished a masterpiece. The cake had turned out even lovelier than she had hoped, and she was certain it was going to astonish Robert. It was worthy, in her estimation, of a fancy wedding.

It had been nice to have Jigger gone while she worked on it. No doubt he would have poked fun at her fancy white icing and the rosettes she had so painstakingly created. She had been forced to be extremely creative in finding the right-sized pans in which to bake the cake. A couple of skillets had been brought into play, and several cake edges trimmed to make the shape she wanted—but it had all been worth it.

What better than a beautiful birthday cake to remind them all of the traditional date for the celebration of the birth of Christ? There was little enough religion in this camp.

"What do you think?" she asked Moon Song, who was nursing her baby.

"Taste?" Moon Song asked. It was one of the words she had

learned recently and used often. Sometimes Katie wondered if Moon Song would ever get filled. In some ways, she was as bad as the men.

Katie gave her a spoon with leftover icing on it. Like Ned, Moon Song loved anything sweet. Then she proudly carried the cake to the table and set it smack dab in the middle where it would be the first thing the men and Robert would see when they came in this evening. She could already imagine the compliments she would get.

Humming, she went back to the kitchen area to finish supper preparations. She would make an oyster stew tonight, and would infuse it with plenty of good, fresh cream and sweet butter, thanks to her lovely cow.

She was so engrossed in her work that she didn't hear the shouts at first—not until Moon Song jumped up and ran to the window. When she did look out, what she saw made no sense.

The men were coming back in the early afternoon. The sun was still shining and several more hours of work could be accomplished. This had never happened before.

Klaas was in the forefront of the group, carrying Betsy, and the two boys and Jigger were trailing him. The others were all clustered around something they were carrying.

Her hand flew to her mouth as she realized what she was seeing. Someone had been hurt!

Frantically, she scanned the crowd and nearly wept with relief when she saw Robert walking beside the stretcher. She couldn't tell who the person was on the stretcher, but at least it wasn't Robert. They were heading straight toward the cook shanty.

Robert was the first through the door. "Clear this out of here!" He swept the carefully washed tin place settings off the table with his arm.

She leapt to grab the cake before he could send it crashing to the floor as well. Carefully, she moved it to the worktable.

Then she saw Skypilot—and the cake over which she had so lovingly labored lost all meaning.

She did not have to ask what had happened. This was a lumber camp. Men got hurt.

"Dad-blamed trees!" Jigger was practically in tears. "Ever last one of 'em is out to kill a fellow."

"Do you have any boiling water?" Robert asked. "Please say that you do."

By the grace of God, she did have water boiling. With the rare occurrence of all the men and children gone for the afternoon, she had finished her cake early, so that she and Moon Song could indulge in the luxury of a bath while they had the warm cook shanty all to themselves. It was such a bother carrying buckets of hot water from the kitchen to the cabin. She had already hung up a couple sheets for privacy just in case someone *did* wander in.

"Plenty," she said.

"Good." He yanked down one of the clean sheets she had just hung up. "Has this been slept on?"

"No." She was puzzled why that would be important. "I took it off the clothesline only yesterday."

"If it's been dried in the sun, it will do." He spread the sheet over the table and instructed the men to lay Skypilot upon it. The big logger was deathly pale and his clothes were saturated with blood. She could hardly believe the damage that had been done.

"Henri, there's a black medical bag beneath my bunk. Go get it," he said. "Katie, run and get my surgical tools from the cabin."

She hesitated, trying to process the fact that Robert was actually going to do surgery.

"Now!" he barked.

She bolted through the door and ran to the cabin. Scooting the chair over to the wall, she dug the surgeon's box out from beneath the eaves and hurried back. When she returned, Robert had cut off much of Skypilot's clothing. Jigger was holding the baby, and Moon Song was washing the blood off the injured man's face.

The three children were cowering in a corner. Thomas was wide-eyed, Ned looked pale, Betsy was sucking her thumb.

Robert seemed to notice their presence about the same time Katie did. "Somebody get these children out of here!"

Ernie quickly ushered them out of the cookhouse, glancing worriedly over his shoulder as he did so.

"Katie," Robert said, "put all those instruments in the water. Then build up the fire as hot as you can get it. They need to boil hard."

She had no idea why he wanted her to do this. The instruments looked just fine to her as she removed them from the case.

"Why am I doing this?"

"Just trust me, Katie!"

She did as he said. Trusting him was becoming a habit. "Is he conscious?"

"No, he passed out from pain on the trip here," Robert said. "Put a cup of your saleratus in as well."

Katie measured out a cup of the ingredient she used to make her biscuits rise and dumped it in the water. Like everyone there, she desperately wanted Skypilot to survive, but Robert's instructions were getting stranger and stranger.

"Found it!" Henri came running in with a black bag in his hand.

"Dip out a washbasin of boiled water," Robert commanded. "And bring it here."

Even with all the people crowding the room, there was little sound except for Skypilot's labored breathing and the sound of her dipping water into the pan.

As she placed the basin on the table, Robert pulled out a bottle of white powder and sprinkled it into the water.

233

"What's that?" she asked.

"Carbolic acid." Robert placed a bundle of silken-looking thread and a curved needle into the water.

And then he did the strangest thing of all. After being in such a hurry, he took the time to clean his nails with the point of a knife. While Moon Song washed as much blood as she could from Skypilot's broken body, Robert stood there meticulously paring his nails.

"What are you doing?" Blackie lunged forward to grasp the large splinter of wood from Skypilot's stomach. "At least take that pine stick out of him before you pretty up your nails. What's the matter with you, man?"

"Don't." Robert grabbed Blackie's dirt-encrusted hand before it could grab hold of the wicked-looking piece of wood. "If he gets gangrene, he doesn't stand a chance."

"What do you know? You ain't a doctor," Sam said. "You're not much more than a shanty boy like the rest of us. I'm gonna hitch up my mules right this minute and take him to Bay City to a *real* doctor."

The other men began to murmur about the length of time it was taking Robert to help Skypilot.

"He won't make it to Bay City." Robert clicked his pocketknife shut and slid it into his pocket.

"Well, he won't make it here neither. Not without a doctor. Bay City's the only chance he's got," Tinker said.

"Ah, shaddup!" Jigger cried. "Every one of you!"

The old cook handed the baby over to Cletus and forced his scrawny body between Robert and the mutinous men. His arm had healed, but Katie knew how fragile that bad arm was. The scrappy little man held up both fists and positioned himself in a fighting stance, ready to take on anyone who tried to interfere with Robert.

234

"You don't none of you know a blamed thing! This man here *is* a doctor, a Harvard ed-u-cated surgeon! Leave him alone."

Sam looked from Jigger, to Robert, and back to Jigger again. "Then what in tarnation is he doing running a lumber camp?"

"Givin' your sorry self a job, for one thing." Jigger jutted his chin toward the teamster, his fists in front of his face. "Leave him be!"

For the first time, Katie understood why Robert had put up with the old man for so long.

Ignoring the drama swirling around him, Robert laid a clean dish towel flat upon the top of the hot stove. Just before it scorched, he placed it across a metal tray and, using tongs, removed each surgical tool from the boiling water and placed it on the towel.

While Jigger backed the men away, Robert rolled up his sleeves and scrubbed his hands and forearms. Then, and only then, was he ready to operate.

Except to her horror, she saw that he was *not* ready.

He picked up a scalpel and his hand started trembling. He tried to steady the hand with his other, but the shaking wouldn't stop.

There was dead silence in the room as all who were watching realized that Robert—and Skypilot—were in deep trouble.

He laid the instrument down, closed his eyes, took a deep breath, and tried again. Katie's heart sank as she saw the trembling begin again.

Katie's father's church had been undemonstrative. The people had a deep faith, they lived righteous lives, but their prayers were private. Praying aloud was not something they did unless it was in a formal church setting. Before today, it would never have occurred to Katie to do what she was about to do.

Whether it was the Holy Spirit whispering to her, complete

235

desperation, or a woman's instinct, Katie put one arm around Robert's waist and grasped his arm with her right hand.

"You can do this, my friend," she said.

Their hands were so different. He had long, strong fingers, hers were short and stubby. His were tanned and brown. Hers were white, freckled, and still puckered from washing all her cake-making utensils. But her hand was the one that was steady and strong, and she willed that strength into him now.

"You can do this because I'm going to stand right here beside you and I'm going to pray for you as long and hard as it takes for you to get through this."

She put both of her palms flat against his broad back and began to pray aloud.

"Give him strength, Father. Give him heart. Give him confidence. Make his hands steady and sure. Help him save the life of this good man, your servant. Give us a miracle, Father. Please give us a miracle."

The trembling in Robert's hand ceased.

She continued praying aloud, her hands flat against his back, asking God to give power and strength to Robert as he began to fight for Skypilot's life.

"I'm fine now, Katie." Robert's voice was strong. She opened her eyes and saw that the hand holding the scalpel was as steady as a rock. "But I need more clean cloths and this basin of water needs to be thrown out and refilled."

With enormous gratitude, Katie fetched more boiled water, found more clean cloths, and helped Moon Song empty pan after pan of bloodied water. She watched as he removed the pieces of bark and wood. She cringed as he cleansed Skypilot's deepest wounds with the carbolic acid solution, and bit her lip as he began to stitch Skypilot back together.

One of the shanty boys fainted and was ignored until he came to on his own and wandered off. Two others left the cook shanty to throw up and never returned. By the grace of God, Skypilot remained unconscious.

At least he remained unconscious until Robert secured the last thread, bandaged his wound, and began to set the leg. And then Skypilot screamed.

The scream of a man, she thought, was so much more frightening than that of a woman. There was something primal and terrifying in Skypilot's soul-wrenching scream.

The blessed unconsciousness was gone, and the big man, disoriented and crazed with pain, tried to fight his way off the table.

"Grab him!" Robert struggled to hold him down. "Keep him still!"

Katie was grateful that so many of the men had stayed. The remaining loggers rushed to grab whatever part of Skypilot they could reach without injuring him, as the big man began to fight in earnest.

"He'll rip out his stitches if we can't hold him down," Robert shouted.

Even wounded, the former preacher, fueled by pain, was a match for all of them. It felt like trying to hold back a large, bucking horse. She clung to his undamaged foot, expecting to get kicked across the room at any minute, certain that Skypilot was going to scatter them all.

And then Moon Song intervened.

"No!" The Indian girl grabbed a handful of Skypilot's hair, jerked it down toward the table, and shoved her face directly in front of his. Digging into her small store of English, she said, "No! You hurt!"

Skypilot seemed startled to find this raven-haired beauty's face so close to his. He stopped struggling and stared at her.

"W-what?"

"You." Moon Song gave another tug on his hair for emphasis. "Hurt."

At that, Skypilot's eyes began to focus, and he took in the ring of people holding him down. His body relaxed against the table as, once again in his right mind, he assessed the situation.

"What happened?"

"You got in the way of a falling tree," Robert said.

Skypilot attempted a feeble joke. "Is the tree hurt?"

The men laughed a little too heartily. Once again, Skypilot scanned the circle of tense faces.

"How bad am I?"

"You might make it, with a lot of care," Robert said. "But I still have to set this broken leg."

"Feels like there's a fire in my gut."

"You have a stomach wound."

"Is it bad?"

Robert hesitated. "Not as bad as when we first brought you in here."

Skypilot lifted his head and looked down at the bandages covering his stomach. "Somebody operated?"

"I stitched you up," Robert said.

"You?"

"I used to be a doctor."

"Used to be? That isn't very encouraging." Skypilot grimaced from the pain. "Go ahead and set the leg, but give me something to bite on."

Cletus had a partially whittled woodchuck in his pocket. He drew it out, gave it a long look, and then lodged it between Skypilot's teeth.

"Too bad we don't have any whiskey in camp!" Jiggers said. "That would be real handy right now. Too bad our boss won't let us have any!"

"Ether would come in handier." Robert positioned two loggers to hold the top half of Skypilot's leg as he grasped the calf. "Are you ready, my friend?"

"Do it!" Skypilot spoke around the piece of wood clenched between his teeth.

Robert jerked Skypilot's leg and Katie heard the bone scrape as it slid into place. Skypilot turned white, his eyes rolled back in his head, and the woodchuck fell out of his mouth. Cletus picked it up and checked it for damage.

"We need to get this splinted," Robert said, "his head wound closed, and put him to bed before he regains consciousness."

He washed the cut on Skypilot's forehead, stitched it closed, and finally it was over.

"Thanks for the help, men." Robert looked exhausted after he set the last stitch. "I hope we've avoided infection. A suppurated stomach wound is a cruel way to die."

"It's all my fault." Jigger shook his head.

"That's true," Robert said. "If you had watched over the children like you promised, none of this would have happened."

"I deserve to be fired."

"You deserved to be fired a long time ago."

The old man looked so miserable, Katie pitied him.

"What can I do?" Jigger said. "I'll do anything."

"Then go pack your turkey."

Katie's heart lurched. As ornery as Jigger had been, she didn't want him to go.

"And move it over to the bunkhouse. Skypilot needs your room to recuperate in."

Jigger didn't argue about giving up his beloved room. If anything, he seemed relieved to stay on under any circumstances. She wondered if he had no place else to go.

"Anything you say, boss," Jigger said.

"We should get him moved before he wakes up," Robert told the remaining woodsmen. "Katie, go spread that other clean sheet over Jigger's bed."

Jigger's room, to her surprise, was remarkably tidy. She would never have expected it. She almost wondered if the old cook had been raised on a ship.

It was five o'clock by the time they got Skypilot settled and the table scrubbed and set to rights again. Moon Song was keeping watch over Skypilot.

"Do you have anything you can fix for supper, Katie?" Robert asked. "I know we interrupted you."

"I was making oyster soup before you came in. The oysters and onions are already fried up in butter. All that's left is to pour the cream and milk in and heat it. I have bread sliced."

"Let's get the men fed, then," Robert said.

Ernie came through the back door with a bucket of milk in his hand. "I figured you didn't have the time to do this and I wasn't doing anything."

"Thank you." Katie was astonished she had forgotten such an important chore. "Tell the men I'll have supper ready for them shortly."

"A little hot food would be real welcome right about now," Ernie said.

"What's the temperature?" She could feel the cold seeping through the cracks in the cookhouse. "Have you checked the thermometer?"

"Yes, ma'am." Ernie blew on his hands. "It's about two feet below zero."

"That cold, huh?"

Katie strained the fresh milk into the kettle of soup and banked the fire so the milk wouldn't separate. The entire time, she was intensely aware of Robert as he carefully dried each one of his surgical instruments and put them away.

She ran down to the cellar, brought up a wheel of cheese, and began to slice it into thick wedges. Soup, cheese, and bread should keep the men from getting too hungry until tomorrow morning.

And then there was her cake—her froth of a cake that she had been so proud of. Her vanity over it seemed so silly now. Life and death had a way of putting things into perspective. Still, it was the only thing she had for the men's dessert tonight, so she placed it back into the middle of the table.

Robert seemed to notice the cake for the first time. "Your dessert is beautiful, Katie. I'm sorry we ruined your surprise."

"A fancy cake is small potatoes compared to what Skypilot's just been through."

"I never should have allowed the children to come out to the lumbering grounds. It's no place for them."

"The children loved it. You couldn't have known Betsy would come looking for you . . . or that Jigger and the boys would get so involved in a game of checkers none of them would notice."

"She's my daughter." Robert ran his hand through his hair. "I should have looked after her."

"Regardless of what anyone should or shouldn't have done," she said, laying a hand on his shoulder, "thanks to your skill, Skypilot is still alive."

He grasped both of her hands, brought them to his lips, and kissed them. She caught her breath at the intimacy.

"If it weren't for the strength in these hands and your prayers, I could not have done this tonight."

She stared down at her feet, fearful that her eyes would betray the strong feelings she had for him. "You're an excellent surgeon, Robert."

"Thank you, Katie-girl. I'm glad you have such a high opinion of me." He kissed her forehead and stood back, a wry smile on his face. "Now, if only there was a way to carry you around in my pocket every time I performed surgery, I could start practicing medicine again."

22

They jump and sing and dance and shout,
to pass away the time,
to pass away the lonely hours
while working in the pine.

> *"Shanty Boys in the Pine"*
> *—1800s shanty song*

December 25, 1867

Christmas Day was always the saddest day of the year in a lumber camp. Robert had seen it time and again. No matter what pains the cook took to provide a special meal—and Katie and Jigger were apparently in the process of outdoing themselves—homesickness ran deep. Unable to go home, even the hardiest woodsman grew nostalgic and pined for loved ones—real or imagined.

The men never worked on Christmas Day. They spent it like they spent their Sundays—washing clothes, smoking pipes, telling tales, and reading the *Police Gazette* or various dog-eared dime paperbacks.

"Want to see a picture of my girl?" Ernie handed Robert a tintype of a narrow-faced woman with a stern expression. She did have a bow in her hair, which Robert hoped indicated a more fun-loving disposition than what he saw in her face.

"She's very pretty," Robert said politely.

"Naw, she's not pretty, but she is a hard worker," Ernie said. "And she's not against Cletus living with us when we get married. A man could do worse." He sighed and slipped the picture back into his pocket. "You suppose Skypilot is gonna pull through?"

"I hope so."

"That was something—what he did." Ernie pulled out his nose warmer and stuffed tobacco into the little pipe. "I never thought he'd make it to your little girl in time. I didn't know a man could run so fast."

"I didn't see her until it was too late," Robert said. "I wish it had been me who got hurt instead of him."

"But Skypilot couldn't have operated on *you*." Ernie lit his pipe with a coal from the bunkhouse stove. "How come you ain't a doctor no more?"

"I was a surgeon during the war. After about the thousandth amputated leg, I just couldn't make my hands operate anymore."

"Ain't none of us come out of that war the same as we went in." Ernie drew hard on his pipe. "Me and Cletus was at Antietam. He ain't been right ever since. Cletus was never all that bright, but it was after that battle he started talking to those little wood creatures he carved."

A long look of understanding passed between the two men. Antietam had been one of the bloodiest battles of the war. Nothing more needed to be said.

"Say." Ernie knocked the ashes out of his pipe and returned to everyone's favorite subject. "I wonder what Katie's cooking tonight?"

"Last time I checked on Skypilot, Katie told me to stay out and not let anyone else in."

"Well, that weren't very polite."

Robert laughed. "I think she and the children might be cooking up a surprise for us. Ned and Thomas looked like a couple of cats who'd swallowed a canary."

Ernie's face lit up. "Wonder what they're up to?"

"With Katie, who knows?"

"Speaking of cats." Ernie nodded toward the corner. "You certain that's what that animal in there is?"

The large orange cat glowered in its cage, mortally offended by the fact that it was incarcerated. Robert and the men had faithfully fed it scraps and tried to tame it—but it had razor-sharp claws and an ugly disposition. He was afraid that the surprise he had asked Sam to bring from Bay City for Katie's Christmas was *not* going to be a success.

—❧❧—

The amount of dishes on the dining table was staggering. It was everything she could think of to make and more. Jigger had surprisingly added the "more." He had worked beside her all day without complaint, and she had gotten to see firsthand that the man truly knew how to cook.

"Stew's done." He speared a small chunk of venison from the bubbling vat. Henri had killed, cleaned, and proudly brought in the fresh meat early that morning. "I'm makin' the dumplings now."

He whipped together the dumpling dough and began dropping spoonfuls into the aromatic brown liquid.

"If you'll move to the side, I'll take the turkeys out of the oven," she said. "They should be finished."

Jigger obediently stepped aside. All was harmony in the kitchen as the two cooks prepared a feast.

She lifted the turkeys, one at a time, from the oven. They were crisply browned and would add even more variety to the meal. They were a little skinny but were a special gift from Klaas, who had gone hunting yesterday when he could no longer abide watching Robert work on Skypilot. She made a mental note to talk to Robert about allowing a couple men a little time to hunt. Fresh game on the table was a welcome addition.

"I'll carve the turkeys when they cool," Jigger volunteered. "I got me a system."

"Carving meat has never been my strong point," Katie said.

"But you got them pastries and sweets down cold," Jigger said. "The best I ever et."

"Thank you." Katie couldn't help but smile at the compliment. If Jigger got any more penitent about what had happened yesterday, he'd be singing hymns.

"Can we put out the place cards now?" Thomas asked. He and Ned had been painstakingly writing each man's name on a piece of paper and Betsy had been decorating them with a scribbled drawing.

"Try to put them where everyone's assigned place is," she said.

"I'll help," Jigger offered, "if you young'uns can't remember who goes where."

Katie paused momentarily as she sliced pies. Who *was* this man and where had he been those first days in camp when she'd needed him? Oh well. Better late than never.

When the remaining items had been placed on the table, there was hardly enough space for the men's plates. They would be so pleased with the special Christmas supper. She had not attempted anything as fussy as another decorated layer cake. Instead, she had concentrated on variety, and plenty of it.

She and the children had gone to some trouble to decorate. They had little to work with, but with what scraps of paper they had, they made chains to loop over the windows, laid fresh balsam boughs on the window sills, and punched holes in empty tin cans and stuck candles in. These were placed on the window sills and every other surface that wasn't already covered with food. Ned had washed and shined the chimneys of all the lamps.

When everything was in place, she lit the candles, and the children's faces glowed.

"Ooh—this is pretty!" Betsy exclaimed.

Katie gave her a hug. "I think so too."

Very deliberately, she took the Gabriel horn off the wall and formally handed it to Jigger.

"Would you please call the men in to our Christmas supper?"

"Happy to do it." Jigger went outside to blow the horn he loved so much.

They all looked forward to seeing the surprise on the shanty boys' faces and were not disappointed. The men showed absolute delight with everything—from the boughs on the windowsills, to the candlelight, to Betsy's little drawings. Many put the little scraps of place cards in their pocket and told the children that they would keep them as keepsakes.

Robert stood at the head of the table after the men had settled themselves. "I know we don't usually do this—it's not traditional in most lumber camps—but I'd like to say a prayer before we eat."

The men nodded in agreement. No one objected. They had survived too much together. Several removed knit caps that rarely left their heads.

Robert bowed his head. "Father—for preserving my daughter's life, I give thanks."

Katie heard several soft amens.

"For keeping Skypilot alive, I give thanks and ask that you help him heal. For the great bounty of this meal, and the two cooks who prepared it, I give thanks."

Katie heard louder amens as though some of the men had just found their voice.

"Keep my crew and my children safe throughout the rest of the winter, and if it is your will—give us a good timber harvest. Amen."

She saw Henri make the sign of the cross right before reaching for the bowl closest to him.

There was something satisfying about watching people she cared about enjoy the work of her hands. And she did care about these men. Every last one of them.

The moment would have been perfect had it not been for the battered Skypilot lying in the room next to them. And yet, as she watched little Betsy spooning up mashed potatoes while cuddled close to her father, Katie knew that if the man had it to do over, he would put himself at risk for the child again.

As soon as he'd helped Betsy fill her plate, Robert went into the bedroom to check on Skypilot. Katie, with her supper successfully on the table, followed close behind.

Skypilot, although having dozed through most of the day, was now clear-eyed and awake.

"Was that a trumpet I heard?" He smiled weakly. "Am I in heaven?"

"Not yet," Robert said. "Although if any man deserved heaven, it would be you."

"The child. She's well?"

"With the exception of a few scratches, she's unharmed, my friend, thanks to you."

"Thank God."

"Indeed." Robert pulled the sheet down and inspected the bandages. "How are you feeling?"

"Thirsty. Sore."

"Will you get him some water?" Robert asked Moon Song, who was standing nearby. He made a drinking gesture with his hand.

The girl rushed back with a glass of water, which Skypilot gulped down. When he finished, he looked at Robert and said, "I don't remember much."

As Robert told Skypilot the story of how he had risked his

247

life for Betsy, Katie went back to the kitchen with a lightened heart. There was so much for which they had to be thankful.

───⋘⋙───

Inside that warm, candlelit room, filled with the camaraderie of the men and the presence of the precious children—all sated with the good food she had prepared—Katie felt such joy. How could life possibly get any better?

But it did. As soon as Robert bolted down his food, he rushed out the door and came back with a large cage hidden beneath a blanket. The men all grinned with anticipation as Robert approached her. She could not imagine what this bulky item could be.

"Merry Christmas, Katie!" With a flourish, he removed the blanket. Inside the cage was the most unhappy-looking feline Katie had ever seen. It was orange, with a spot of white on its nose. For Katie, it was love at first sight. The cat, however, seemed to have a very different opinion.

"Oh, my goodness!" Katie exclaimed, squatting down to examine it. "I thought you said Sam couldn't find a cat for sale."

"Technically, that was the truth. It was a gift from a farmer I know. Sam said the man said this one was an excellent mouser."

She reached for the latch, and the men scrambled to get back.

"You might want to be careful," Ernie said. "That thing's a mite wild. We tried to take it out of the cage, and things didn't turn out very well."

"Oh." Katie withdrew her hand.

"It must have lived in the barn most of its life," Robert said apologetically. "I don't think this is going to be a lap cat, Katie. At least nothing you can make a pet out of."

"I guess we'll see." Katie bravely opened the cage. "Maybe it will take to a woman."

There was a blur, a rattling of the cage, and an orange streak

248

flew across the floor and crouched in a far corner—hissing. Katie, taken by surprise, fell backward onto her bottom. "A mite wild? I'd say so!" She laughed.

"Something that fast has to be a good mouser!" Blackie reassured her.

"Hope it doesn't have any kittens in it," another said. "I'd hate to have a whole roomful of those things."

"Is it a girl?" Katie asked.

The men looked at each other. A couple of them shrugged. "None of us ever had the nerve to get close enough to check," Sam said.

"Thank you for the gift." She stood up and brushed off her skirt. "I do appreciate it. Maybe the cat will calm down after I give it a few good feeds of warm milk."

"I hope so," Robert said. "If it gets too bad, we'll catch it for you and get it out of here."

"Let's see what happens." Katie poured out a bowl of milk. With the men watching with rapt interest, she slowly approached the cat. It crouched in the corner, glaring at her, apparently deeply offended by her and everyone else in the room. The moment she stepped across some imaginary line, the thing was up the wall in two leaps. It hunkered on a rafter, looking down at them. It hissed again, just in case no one had gotten the message the first time.

"Well, I guess it will come down when it gets good and hungry," Katie said, leaving the bowl of milk in a corner. "I don't have to pet it. I just hope it'll hunt mice."

Dinner was finished, the show created by the presentation of the cat was over, but the men seemed reluctant to leave.

"Could I bring my fiddle over here—just for tonight, ma'am?" Henri said. "We could move the table up against the wall and have room for a stag dance—it being Christmas and all."

The other men nodded enthusiastically.

"A stag dance?" Katie asked.

"Stags are old boots we cut down to wear as slippers," Robert explained. "A stag dance is where half the shanty boys tie a handkerchief around their arm and dance the women's part. The other half dance the men's. Sometimes they'll switch around halfway through. It isn't pretty, and it isn't at all graceful, but the men have a good time and it gets rid of a lot of steam."

"Jigger?" she asked. "Do you have a problem with that?"

"It's Christmas." Jigger shrugged. "Let 'em do what they want."

The men helped Katie clear dishes, and then they moved the table and benches against the wall. Henri came back with his instrument and Tinker pulled a harmonica out of his pocket. Ernie brought out his spoons.

As the musicians swung into play, the men drew straws, and then some began tying red handkerchiefs around their arms while the children looked on with excitement.

"I think you're going to enjoy this." Robert led her to one of the benches along the wall.

"Aren't you going to participate?" Katie pulled Betsy onto her lap just for the sheer joy of cuddling her.

"No," Robert replied. "It's a lot more fun to watch."

The music began and Katie couldn't keep her foot from tapping. The music, which she had heard on other nights from a distance, was fast and furious, and as the woodsmen galloped around the room, she hugged Betsy tight and laughed aloud. These silly, wonderful shanty boys were outdoing themselves showing off for her and the children. It was all such fun!

Ernie put down his spoons, did a quick dance step over to them, bowed low, swooped Betsy up in his arms, and to her giggling delight, spun her around the room.

It was hard to sit on a bench with the music playing and all the feet stomping in rhythm on the wooden floor. She had never danced in her life, but her toe tapping escalated into foot stomping as she clapped her hands in time to the music.

"Can we dance too?" Ned asked.

"I don't see why not!" She jumped up, grabbed the two little boys' hands, and the three of them spun around in a circle. It was Christmas—a time to celebrate—even in the deep woods.

She glanced up, saw the orange cat glaring down from the rafters as she and the little boys danced, and she threw back her head and laughed, giddy from the sheer fun of it.

"You go ahead, Katie-girl," Robert shouted. "Enjoy yourself. You've earned it."

She did not hear the door open. It was only when she heard the music slowly die out that she turned to see what had made it stop.

A tall, blond-haired man, oddly arrayed in the dress uniform of a Confederate officer, stood in the open doorway while the winter wind whistled snow in around him. At first she couldn't grasp what she was seeing, and then her mind went numb with fear.

23

Now, all young men a warning take:
don't be in a hurry to wed,
for you'll think you're in clover till the honeymoon's over,
and then you'll wish you were dead.

"Boys Stay Away from the Girls"
—1800s shanty song

"Hello, Katherine." The man's voice was heavily accented with the drawl of the Deep South. He kicked the door shut. "I brought you a Christmas present. It's from your good friend Violet."

Robert heard the innocuous words the stranger spoke, and he saw Katie, whose cheeks had been flushed with the glow of happiness, turn as white as a sheet.

Whoever this man was, Katie was deathly afraid of him. Ned turned a ghastly gray as he stared at the man. With their eyes locked onto the stranger's, both Ned and Katie seemed to shrink back into their own skin.

The men, puzzled by Katie's reaction, shifted from one foot to the other. There had been plenty of strangers pass through the camp in the past three months. Katie had efficiently fed them all without missing a step.

"We've just finished our Christmas dinner." Robert rose from the bench. "There's plenty of good food left over. Would you care to share it with us?"

The man ignored him. His focus was on Katie. His left cheek twitched in a weird sort of dance of its own. "Don't you want it, Katherine?" His voice was almost a singsong. "Don't you want your Christmas present from Violet?"

He pulled an envelope from his pocket and extended it. She edged toward him and snatched it from his hand.

The man had a look of supreme satisfaction as she ripped open the letter with trembling fingers and scanned it. Robert saw her head droop, and the letter fell from her hand and drifted to the floor.

"Are you happy now?" The stranger's cheek was dancing even more uncontrollably. "Are you pleased that you went against my wishes and taught that girl how to read and write?"

"Where did you get it?" Katie's voice was low and choked.

"Don't you remember?" He sighed dramatically, his right hand resting on the hilt of his dress sword. "My second cousin is a postmaster now. He saw Violet come in with that letter in her hand. When he saw that the letter was addressed to Katie Smith, Foster Lumber Camp, Bay City, Michigan, he thought I might be interested—what with you and Violet being so close and all."

Robert had no idea what was going on, but he didn't like it. The Confederate uniform bothered him as much as Katie's terrified reaction. The man was either stupid or mad to come into a Michigan lumber camp in that getup. The twitch worried him too. There was something deeply wrong with this man.

"Do you have a name, sir?" he asked.

"Harlan Calloway at your service." The stranger seemed to have noticed him for the first time. "And that woman you are harboring, sir"—he clicked his heels together and gave a mocking salute—"is my wife."

Robert felt his stomach grow as heavy as a stone. "Is this true, Katie?"

She turned toward him, and he knew he would remember that haunted expression for the rest of his life. He had seen hunted animals with the same desperate, cornered expression in their eyes.

His heart ached as he saw the truth written there. This man with the out-of-place uniform was, indeed, her husband.

And she was terrified of him. No wonder she had never talked about him.

"I think you need to sit down, Mr. Calloway," Robert said. "We need to talk this out. You must be hungry after your long journey."

"I don't want food. I want my money and my wife, and I want them now."

Money?

Harlan jerked his head toward Katie. "She stole all my cash and my best horse."

"We're not going back with you!" Ned cried. "You can't make us go!"

"You can keep the boy." Harlan waved a dismissive hand. "I never wanted him in the first place."

Whatever Katie had done, or not done, Robert knew one thing. He would not allow this man to leave with her and Ned. From what he could tell, Harlan Calloway was more than a little deranged.

"I always knew you had something to do with Mose's escape, Katherine," Harlan said. "Now, thanks to Violet's stupidity, they've both paid you back richly. How many more of my slaves did you help run away before your Yankee government finished ruining me?" He turned the collar of his uniform up, preparing to go out in the cold weather. "Get your wrap. We're leaving."

"Not so fast." Robert held up a hand. "It doesn't appear that the lady wants to go."

"Since she's my legal wife, I don't think she has a choice, now, does she?" Harlan arched an eyebrow. "If she doesn't come, I'll have her arrested for theft."

"I still have your money." Katie moved toward the back door. "I'll go get it now." She fled out into the night.

A cold silence fell over the cookhouse. Ernie put a protective hand on Ned's shoulder. The men watched Harlan narrowly. Robert knew it would only take one spark, one ill-advised remark, to set off a powder keg. These men would willingly stomp Harlan into the dust for Katie—or just for the sheer enjoyment of it. A least six of them had served in the Union army, and that uniform Harlan was wearing was dredging up some bad memories.

Katie was back within seconds with a small sack of coins.

"Here." She tossed the sack toward her husband.

He caught it with one hand and spilled the coins out onto the table. "This isn't all of it."

"I needed some for the train."

Robert heard the disappointment in her voice and knew she had hoped Harlan wouldn't count it.

He could tell that the loggers were debating whether or not to intervene. Each was capable of picking Calloway up and throwing him out the door—but getting involved in a domestic quarrel was not part of their code. Still—Katie was the jewel of their camp, a woman a man with any sense would cherish for life. It was a conundrum.

"I'll give you the rest of the money," Robert said. "But Katie stays here."

"And who are you?" Harlan methodically dropped the coins back into the bag.

"I'm Robert Foster, owner of this camp."

Harlan turned a hard gaze upon him. "And how is *my* wife any of *your* business, Mr. Foster?"

Robert found himself looking into the coldest, most calculating eyes he had ever seen. He didn't really care. No matter what, this man was *not* leaving with Katie.

"She signed on for a full season as camp cook," Robert said. "I'm holding her to it. She can return to you after the spring river drive—if she so desires."

"And just what other jobs does she do for you, Mr. Foster?" Harlan's voice dripped with innuendo as he grabbed Katie by the wrist. "Besides cook?"

Robert's fists clenched. The utter arrogance of this man was astonishing.

He was ready to fight Calloway right then and there, but just at that moment, Ned threw himself in front of his sister, his little pocketknife open in his hand. It was only a boy's toy, but he slashed at Harlan's hand and drew blood.

Harlan dropped Katie's wrist and put the small wound to his mouth. "When I get you home, I'll—"

"You'll do nothing." Robert stepped forward. "You will leave my camp immediately. You will not take your wife or the boy."

"And who's going to stop me?"

"I am," Robert said.

Harlan looked him up and down. "Were you in the war, sir?"

"Yes."

"May I inquire as to your position?"

"I was a surgeon."

Harlan snorted with contempt. "I ate men like you for breakfast."

That was all it took. Robert rushed him, but Harlan had other plans. He threw open his coat, and as fast as lightning, drew out two Kerr's revolvers, aiming one at Robert's heart and the other at Katie's.

Serena Miller

Robert had seen those distinctive five-shot weapons before. They were a favorite among Southern cavalrymen, and he knew that at this close range they would be deadly.

"I wouldn't do that, if I were you," Harlan said. "Nothing would give me more pleasure than to put a bullet into you—and the woman." His voice was strangely disembodied. A voice that was not attached to any normal human emotion.

Klaas moved to intervene, and Harlan turned a gun on him.

"You all might want to reconsider," Harlan said. "I can take out ten of you before I have to reload. Katherine, if you want your friends to live, come with me. We're leaving."

Katie looked at the guns, and at Harlan, and then at the men. Her eyes sought Robert's, and there was defeat in them. "I'll go," she said. "Just let me get my cape. It's hanging on the wall." She sidled away. "Don't get trigger-happy, Harlan. I'll leave with you. Don't hurt anyone."

"Be quick about it," Harlan snarled.

She glanced at Robert and her eyes were pleading. "Will you take care of Ned?"

"Of course I will."

Harlan once again brought his hand up to his mouth and sucked on the small wound Ned had inflicted. "Hurry up, Katherine."

Katie pulled the wool cape down from the peg and wrapped herself in it. Harlan began to back slowly toward the door, still holding the revolvers trained on the men.

Out of the corner of his eye, Robert saw that Moon Song had managed to creep out of Skypilot's room without Harlan knowing. She now crawled along the floor, next to the wall, hidden by the men and the deep, flickering shadows cast by the lamps and candles. She was so small compared to the men, and Harlan was so preoccupied, he didn't see her.

Robert stared straight at Harlan so as to not give away her presence. Everyone else did the same.

"I'm sorry I ran away, Harlan." Katie walked slowly toward him, deliberately distracting him with her chatter. "I should never have done that. I'm so sorry about taking your horse too."

"I got Rebel back," Harlan said. "No thanks to you."

"Really? How?" Katie was taking her time tying a wool scarf over her head. She fussed with the knot.

Moon Song was crouched behind him now.

"People know Rebel, and word got back to me. Let's just say that the man who bought him saw the error of his ways."

"I miss Rebel's Pride." Katie pulled on a pair of woolen mittens. "Is he outside?"

"Of course not—Rebel's at Fallen Oaks where he belongs. I came by train and hired a hack from the stable in town."

At that moment, Moon Song turned into a blur. She leaped onto Harlan's back and went for his eyes. Two shots rang out as Harlan bent backwards. The bullets buried themselves in the ceiling before Harlan dropped the weapons on the floor and scrabbled to remove Moon Song's clawing hands from his eyes. From high above, the orange cat, startled by the shots, dropped from the rafters directly onto Harlan's chest with a yowl.

With Moon Song sticking like a burr to his back, Harlan flailed about, upsetting the cat even further. It clawed deep gashes into his face and neck. The men didn't intervene. All were thoroughly enjoying the spectacle of the battle between the cat, Harlan, and Moon Song. He was a big man, and Moon Song was not a large woman. It took only seconds for Harlan to fling the cat off, then grab Moon Song and drag her off of his back. But the damage had been done. His weapons were on the floor, and the men were no longer avoiding a domestic dispute—they had been threatened. And they were ready to kill.

Klaas lifted Moon Song up out of the fray and sat her to the side. Harlan was felled by one blow from Blackie's fist.

Then the stomping began.

Robert had seen this sort of scene more times than he could count. It was the way a logger fought. It always had been. It was called "putting the boots" to a man, and it involved jumping on an enemy with caulked boots—boots with spikes in them—the kind that loggers wore to ride the logs. Most shanty boys who liked to brawl had felt the sting of an opponent's caulked boots. The pockmarked scars they left behind were called "Logger's Small Pox." Jigger's back and chest were covered with them from all the brawls he had been in.

The men weren't wearing caulked boots tonight since no one was working on the river. But they stomped all the same. Harlan was curled in a ball, trying to cover his face.

Part of Robert wanted the man dead—the other part of him, the part that was the doctor who had sworn an oath to save lives, knew he needed to stop the carnage. He had just opened his mouth to call the men off when he heard Katie's voice.

"That's enough!" she said. "Stop it!"

He was surprised. She, of all people, must want this man permanently gone from her life.

The men stopped, surprised at the command in Katie's voice.

"The children." Katie nodded at a far corner.

Everyone looked at the three children huddled together. They had their arms around each other and were more frightened than Robert had ever seen them.

They were watching men they looked up to, men who had lovingly created a playhouse for them, men who had carried them on their shoulders—now single-mindedly beating a man to death.

The men backed away, leaving Harlan lying on the floor. He was bruised and battered but able to sit up.

"I'll come back," he growled between split and bleeding lips. "And I'll kill all of you."

Robert picked up the Kerr revolvers from where they were lying on the floor. "You've outstayed your welcome, Mr. Calloway."

Harlan started to reach for the bag of coins, still sitting on the table.

"Leave the money. I'm sure your wife earned it many times over."

As Harlan flung himself out the door and rode away, Tinker walked over to the window and watched the departing soldier.

"I seen that man before," Tinker told them. "Wished I hadn't, but I seen him, all right."

"Where?" Robert asked.

"At the battle of Spotsylvania. I fought under General right." Tinker sank down on the bench. "I'm sorry to say this, Miss Katie, but I watched that man walk through the battlefield after the Confederates beat us. He was finishing off Northern wounded like it was nothing. Never saw anything like it before or since. I managed to crawl behind a tree before he saw me."

"You got away?" Katie asked.

"No. Some other Johnny Reb found me and toted me on over to Camp Sumter."

"The POW camp at Andersonville?" Robert asked. "They let soldiers starve to death in there."

"Around thirteen thousand of them. I helped bury some of them."

"How in the world did you survive, man?"

Tinker's snow white hair crowning a young face was vivid in the lamplight. "Who says I did?"

"He'd better never show his face around here again," Blackie said. "We'll be ready for him if he comes again. Won't be no offer of food and drink, neither."

"Tryin' to take our Katie away from us," Jigger said indignantly. "Who's he think he is?"

"And talking about Ned thataway." Ernie said. "Any man with half a brain would want to call that boy his son!"

"And what Tinker saw him do." Sam stared out the window. "That's lower than a snake's belly."

Moon Song came out of Skypilot's room, cooing over the baby in her arms. It was hard for Katie to equate this loving young mother with the wild woman who had leaped onto Harlan's back.

She touched Moon Song's arm. "Thank you."

Moon Song shrugged as though it was of no importance. Or perhaps it was because she didn't understand the English words. Katie didn't know.

"Are you all right, Katie?" Robert rested the flat of his hand against her back as the other men's voices faded into the background.

"I never intended to lie to you." She turned around to face him. "But I had to get away from him. I thought this camp would be far enough away that he would never find me. I was wrong."

"I wish I had known."

"It wouldn't have made any difference."

"Oh, Katie-girl." Robert's voice was choked with emotion. "Couldn't you have just divorced him?"

"Harlan is a war hero and a Calloway. His relatives practically own his county. The local courts would never have listened to me."

Robert ran a hand through his hair in frustration. "I have no idea what to do except try to keep you safe. I'll post a guard tonight."

"No," Katie said. "Not this time."

"Why not?"

"This isn't your fight, and you need every man you've got to harvest the timber." She grabbed the two revolvers off the table where Robert had placed them. "These belong to my husband, and I'm claiming them. He'll never be able to force his way through that heavy lock Blackie made me, and if he tries to come through the window—I'll be ready for him."

"Are you sure about this?"

"I'm sick and tired of being afraid. I'm weary of carrying fear around in the pit of my stomach. It was hard seeing Harlan again. For a few moments I fell back into that old terror—but no more. Show me how to use one of these things, Robert, because I'm never, *ever* going to allow that man to lay a hand on me again."

24

He would not drink and he would not chew;
he would not even smoke.
But he swung his axe with the best of us,
with a firm and even stroke.

　　　"The Greenhorn"—1800s shanty song

December 26, 1867

Katie had decided to make cinnamon rolls this morning—great fluffy clouds of them drizzled with vanilla-flavored icing—as a special treat. It would take extra time for the dough to rise, so she needed to get to the kitchen even earlier than usual. She wanted to give everyone a special breakfast this morning. It was the only way she could think of to show how sorry she was for what Harlan had put them all through.

Regrettably, things would be awkward between her and Robert from this point on. There was simply no way to get around it. She had lied to him and been humiliated in front of him. She was also, unfortunately, in love with him. All she could do was finish out the year with as much dignity as possible.

She entered the darkened kitchen, lit a couple lamps, and began the ritual of stirring up the embers from last night into a blaze that would heat the oven.

And then she heard the whisper of a slow, steady crunching

coming from the darkened side of the cook shanty. It sounded like a man's footsteps breaking through the hard crust of snow. She crept to the window, but there was nothing there except unbroken snow stretching out into the forest.

She was puzzling about where the sound was coming from until she heard a loud hiss near her feet and saw that the crunching sound was the orange cat, consuming a mouse, bones and all.

Well, at least her Christmas present was, indeed, a mouser. No more chasing rodents around the kitchen with a broom!

Still, even though the crunching sound was only the cat having a snack, she was on edge. She did not believe for a minute that Harlan would meekly go back to Georgia. Her guess was that he was biding his time, waiting his chance to accost her when she wasn't surrounded by a battalion of loggers.

Because of that, she knew she couldn't let down her guard for an instant. She could not and would not expect any of Robert's men to stay behind to protect her—things were already too precarious for him financially because of the fire. Even Blackie and Tinker were doing double duty by going out in the woods when they weren't needed in camp.

If Harlan came while the men were out working, there would be only her, the children, Moon Song, the injured Skypilot, and Jigger. Two women, three children, an invalid, a baby, and an old man. Odds that Harlan would love.

She had lain awake thinking up ways to protect both herself and the vulnerable people who had fallen to her care. If Harlan came back, she was determined to fight.

After last night, she no longer saw the kitchen as only a place to fix food. This was where she spent most of her time, and it was filled with potential weapons. As she kneaded the dough, Katie took inventory. One meat cleaver. A heavy rolling pin. Several cast-iron skillets. Ten razor-sharp knives. A kettle of boiling water. In addition, she carried Harlan's loaded revolvers secreted within the pockets of her voluminous skirt.

Although she was not a large woman, she was determined to stand her ground. Orange cat wasn't very large, either, but loggers backed away every time it hissed and took swipes with its claws.

Like orange cat, she intended to scratch and claw and bite and let Harlan know that he was dealing with a different woman—a woman who would never again cower in fear from him.

She was bent over, placing another length of firewood in the stove's firebox, when she heard the door swing open. Every muscle in her body tensed.

"Hello, Katherine," a familiar voice drawled. "You're alone. What a pity."

Katie sighed in resignation. The confrontation had come even sooner than she had expected. Harlan must have been out in the woods for the past few hours, waiting for this moment. The man must be practically frozen.

"Aren't you going to call for help?" Harlan's voice dripped with sarcasm. "You seem to have collected so many men friends."

"No." She closed the firebox and stood to face him. "This is between you and me. I won't be calling for help."

Harlan looked bad. For the first time, she noticed that his uniform was frayed. The beating he had received from the loggers had taken quite a toll as well. But it was more than the bruises she saw on his face. He looked haggard and hollow-eyed, nearly unrecognizable from the glorious young man she had once followed into the Deep South.

"What about your Indian friend?" He glanced around as though half-afraid Moon Song would drop from the ceiling.

"She's sleeping."

Now that he was here, Harlan seemed unsure as to what to do next. Katie stood absolutely still.

The Scripture with which she had comforted Ned their first night in camp—about God not giving her the spirit of fear—rose to mind and gave her strength. She stiffened her resolve not to back down.

Harlan took a step toward her, and her hand closed around a meat cleaver.

"I don't want to hurt you, Harlan." Their eyes met and hers didn't blink. "There has been enough pain between us."

He laughed, but his laugh sounded hollow. "You think you can hurt me?"

"Yes, Harlan." Her voice was steady. "I know I can."

Once again, he seemed slightly unsure of himself. He was used to her cowering and pleading. The unwritten rules between them had shifted, and he wasn't ready for the change.

She decided to take advantage of his hesitation, to try to talk some sense into him. "I understand what you lost, Harlan. I was there. I suffered too. What Sherman did to the people in Georgia was unforgivable. I saw it. I watched the war strip you of everything you had—your wealth, your home, the only life you had ever known. But Harlan, other people have endured great losses and still found ways to live decent, good lives."

"You Yankees destroyed everything."

"I had no hand in it."

"You could have tried harder to save our home. My grandfather built that mansion."

"Your grandfather didn't build it, Harlan. His slaves built it while he sipped sweet tea and watched." She shook her head in disbelief at his attitude. "I stood no chance against that horde of Sherman's soldiers. All I did was survive the best I could. The slaves had all left. I was alone. I nearly starved after his troops went through. I hated Sherman every bit as much as you."

"You helped Mose escape." He dismissed her attempt to

reason with him and took another step forward as his cheek began to twitch. "Didn't you. Don't lie to me. I know you did."

So that was that. It was not possible to reason with Harlan. It never had been. She didn't know why she had even tried. His bitterness was too great.

"Yes," she said. "I helped Mose. My only regret is that I didn't help more of your slaves escape from you sooner."

His eyes blazed. They stared at each other, and she knew that the gulf between them was something she could never bridge.

Strangely enough, she felt no fear. She looked at the dark hollows beneath his eyes, saw the ragged hair and dirty fingernails, noticed the worn and scuffed boots, and felt nothing but sadness. This man was so broken compared to the dazzling young officer she had once known, that in that split second—regardless of all that Harlan had done—her heart broke for the man he could have been. Out of that sudden burst of compassion, she said the first thing that came to mind.

"You're hungry. Let me fix you something to eat."

"What?" He looked at her as though she had slapped him.

"The men won't be awake for another three hours," she said. "You're safe here until then. You're hurt and you're hungry. Let me get you something to eat."

He seemed bewildered by her words.

"Sit down, Harlan. Let me take care of you."

His anger seemed to evaporate. He sank down onto one of the benches.

The stove top was red hot, and it took only seconds to crack six eggs into a skillet of butter and scramble them. In the meantime she toasted two thick slices of bread, but not once did she turn her back on her husband.

She scooted the plate toward him and then stood back and watched him eat.

His good manners were gone. He reminded her of a starving

dog, a mean one, who had seen too many fights and bore the still-fresh wounds.

"Why did you try to kill me?" she asked. "I would have helped you rebuild."

"I needed money," he said simply. "Not you." He took a bite of bread, chewed, and then spoke with a nonchalance that was chilling. "With you dead, Carrie Sherwood would have married me and her resources would have come under my control. I could have rebuilt Fallen Oaks exactly as it was."

Katie was not shocked. She had suspected something along those lines.

"Did Carrie know what you were planning?"

"Of course not." He shoveled in another spoonful of eggs. "She's a respectable woman. I would have to be a widower in truth before she would even allow me to court her."

Everything made sense now.

The only thing that had ever been holy in Harlan's eyes was his beloved Fallen Oaks. The plantation was what he worshiped. It was his god and his sanctuary. In his twisted mind, it would make perfect sense to eliminate her in order to save it.

"Is Carrie still single?"

"Engaged to be married in four months." He wiped his mouth with the back of his hand. "Plenty of time to change her mind and get her to marry me. As you know, I can be quite charming."

Although she had been momentarily lulled by his beaten appearance into pitying him, she was aware that Harlan was still dangerous. She had tried to appeal to his better nature, but he was too far gone.

And yet, God was not only the God of power and a sound mind—he was also the God of love.

Still keeping an eye on Harlan, she went back to her kitchen. "Here's something I've packed for your journey." She laid a parcel of food on the dining table. "It's a long way back to Bay City." From her left pocket, she withdrew the pouch of silver coins she had carried with her just in case he came back. She dropped it onto the table. "This was from the sale of your land—it doesn't belong to me."

He hefted it in his hand.

"Forget about gaining control of Carrie's money. You could use this money to buy seed when you get home. You could hire some help and start over again. But you really need to quit feeling so sorry for yourself, Harlan."

His hand struck out before she could see it coming and curled itself around her left wrist. His grip was as strong as steel. "You're coming home with me, Katherine."

"No." Her right hand dove into a pocket. She withdrew the gun and pointed the muzzle straight at him. "I'm not going to do that."

Harlan's eyes were calculating as he stared down the barrel of his own gun. She knew he was weighing the chances of whether or not she had the nerve to pull the trigger.

"You'd better listen to her," Skypilot said. "I believe the lady's had enough."

Skypilot's splinted leg was hidden behind the doorjamb and his impressive bulk filled the doorway of Jigger's bedroom. In his hand was a steel-tipped jam-pike that Jigger had once used during his glory days when he had ridden the logs. In the right hands, it would be a formidable weapon.

Close beside Skypilot stood Moon Song, no doubt standing there to help keep Skypilot from falling down—but Harlan didn't know that.

Katie couldn't imagine what strength of will Skypilot had to draw on in order to pull himself out of bed and come to her aid.

"*Va t'en!*" Moon Song said.

Katie had no idea what the girl had said, but it sounded

ominous. Harlan slowly released his grip. She snatched her hand away from his grasp.

"You've outstayed your welcome, Harlan." She kept the gun trained on him. There was no way she was going to let him hurt Moon Song or Skypilot. She would shoot if she had to, and that determination was in her voice. "It's time for you to go home."

25

*Our lumber camps are all so nice;
they're filled, the bunks, with bugs and lice.
You'll scratch and dig them with your hands,
but you'll still have them in Michigan.*

"Don't Come to Michigan"
—1800s shanty song

February 10, 1868

Robert watched dark winter days dissolve into dark winter weeks, and yet Harlan did not come back. Logs, wet with snow, multiplied along the riverbank, piled into pyramids as high as a house, readied to be rolled into the water the moment the spring thaw came and the river rose.

Some days the temperatures were so low, the forest snapped and boomed as the sap froze within the huge pines in the savage cold.

Accidents had been held to a minimum. Some cuts and bruises. One case of frostbite in a young shanty boy too green to understand the need to stop often and warm himself at the campfire.

It was necessary to work in even the coldest temperatures. The snow was heavy this year. The men cut trees while wearing snowshoes on top of snow several feet deep. In the spring, the stumps left over would be as high as eight to ten feet tall—wood wasted from the men having to stand on top of deep snow.

There had been one very dangerous, but memorable, moment, when Cletus and Ernie fell through an embankment where the snow was especially high. They had fallen in on a black bear in its den, startling it out of its hibernation and scaring both men and bear out of their wits. He wasn't sure who had been the most shocked, the men or the bear, but there was a flurry of arms and legs and fur—until the bear and the men got themselves untangled and the bear ran into the woods.

He had no doubt that the bear was still wondering what in blazes had happened. The episode had provided conversation for the men for days. Cletus was now in the process of carving a small bear for his collection. Ernie said it calmed Cletus's nerves after his narrow escape.

The snow had long ago blocked the door of the children's hollow tree house. Perhaps, come spring, they could enjoy it for a few days until the entire camp made its way down the river.

As the weeks passed, Robert continued to worry about Harlan. He hoped that getting that money back from Katie would be enough to satisfy the man, but somehow he doubted it. It appeared that Harlan might have actually gone back to Georgia, but nothing about the man's demeanor had suggested to Robert that he would give up a fight so easily.

Skypilot, still on the mend and having nothing to occupy his time, had offered to teach the children. Skypilot was a gifted teacher, and he often wove in little Bible stories as a sort of treat. The children, with few chores and fewer toys, were entranced by their "school." During breaks from learning, they made a sport of trying to tame the orange cat. So far, the cat had spurned their advances, but it did take its job of mouse patrol very seriously.

Moon Song, bright as a button, sat in on the lessons, and her English was improving daily.

It was thrilling to Robert that Skypilot was healing with little sign of infection. There was definitely a new day dawning in medicine. He was convinced that this fledgling knowledge of sterilization that was slowly making its way into the medical establishment was going to save thousands of lives.

Yes, there was a new and exciting day dawning in the field of medicine. But he would not be part of it. His ability to operate on Skypilot had been a direct answer to prayer. He doubted that his struggle with his "soldier's heart" was over quite yet.

26

But when the winter days were past
then came the spring and thaw;
our drive was started for the mills
that lined the Saginaw.

"The Old Cass"
—1800s shanty song

April 2, 1868

It began with a change in the air. An almost imperceptible feeling that something deeply primal had shifted in its sleep and was beginning the slow process of awakening. It showed up on the thermometer attached to the cook shanty as the temperature slowly rose.

One morning, with the sun shining brightly, water began to run down the heavy icicles in rivulets—creating a constant drip, drip, drip—until they froze solid again during the night.

Then the snow turned to slush, and the faintest of green began to appear upon the bushes.

Katie could hear the rush of the river grow each day, as water melted from the thousands of acres of the Saginaw Valley and funneled down through waterways to feed the river.

According to Jigger, the men would spend a few more days getting out the last of this season's logs, and then each pyramid would have a key log knocked loose, and the logs would tumble into the river to be ridden and herded by river drivers, or "river hogs," until the bobbing logs flowed into the "booms" of Bay City—where they would be sorted and counted.

It would never have occurred to her to think to brand a log—but that was what she saw Blackie doing one day while she walked with Jigger to take the men their dinner. Blackie swung a heavy hammer into which was carved a sort of branding iron, gouging a design into the butt end of each log. Robert's brand was simple—RF surrounded by a circle.

This was done, according to Jigger, to keep river pirates from stealing the camp's logs. This seemed incredible to her that with so many trees still uncut anyone would feel the need to steal someone else's labor, but Jigger assured her it was true. He said they even went to the lengths of cutting the end of the trees off when they could get by with it, and then rebranding the fresh butt with a brand of their own. Jigger laughed when Katie said she thought that if the river pirates were going to go to all that trouble, they might as well go out and get honest work.

Tinker had been working for weeks on the wannigan, and it was ready. Soon, she would be living in and cooking and serving meals from the rough-looking flatboat.

It would not be an easy task. Jigger had told her that the men would be working so hard and spending so much time in ice-cold water that they would need four to five meals a day, instead of just three. She and Jigger would be cooking in nonstop shifts.

The moment she stepped foot on the wannigan would be the beginning of the end of her sojourn as Robert's cook. She and all the rest of his employees would be paid at the end with deductions for whatever they had purchased from the camp store. She had purchased nothing but a few bars of laundry soap, so her pay would be large. Three hundred and eighty dollars! Enough to keep her and Ned for quite a while.

She had hopes of cooking for another lumber camp in the fall—although not Robert's. It was too hard to be around someone you loved but could never have. She had heard that there were camps opening up in Wisconsin. Perhaps, if she went there, it would be too far away even for Harlan.

—❧❧—

"Timberrrr!"

Robert watched the giant pine crash to the ground. The crew swarmed over it, denuding it of its branches while the crosscut saw teams began their work of turning it into logs. Night was closing in. This would be the last tree his crew would cut this season. The extra river hogs had begun to arrive, men who were expert in the dangerous skill of herding the logs down the river. Some of his crew would stay on and ride the river as well; others, not comfortable with the job, would head to Bay City and await the river drivers' arrival, collecting their wages once he and Inkslinger had settled up with the milling company.

His men would then either turn the wages of the past winter into one glorious drunk lasting at most a couple of weeks, or they would tuck their pay away into their turkeys and strike out for the various small farms struggling to gain a foothold in the Michigan wilderness. He knew that there were families waiting, praying that Father would come home with his wages intact.

What the men did, or didn't do, with their wages was not something he could control. His biggest worry right now was getting the logs down the river without anyone drowning. Strangely enough, some of the best river drivers couldn't swim. They felt it was an unnecessary skill, since usually, when a river hog fell into the water, the crush of logs above their heads would make it impossible to surface.

He prayed his most fervent prayers at this time. He prayed that there would be no logjams—a lumberman's nightmare. If

276

even one log got hung up, the ones behind it could pile up for miles behind—the weight of them crushing the front logs into pulp, creating a nightmarish dam out of the splintered timbers, through which the river hogs would have to pick their way carefully, hunting for the key log holding the others back.

Unraveling a logjam was the most dangerous work of all. If the men were lucky or skilled enough to pry the key log out, they still had to have the reflexes of a cat to jump out of the way before the mountain of logs in the accidental dam poured down over them.

Few river drives took place without some deaths. He couldn't do anything about it except be as responsible as he knew how, keeping his men as well fed and cared for as possible. The drivers made three times the salaries of common shanty boys—and they earned every penny.

Tinker had made a good, solid wannigan. It would accommodate a kitchen large enough for Katie and Jigger to work. It had a deck big enough for Katie or Jigger to nap during their short breaks and to store supplies. The men would eat on shore and sleep in hastily erected tents.

The river hogs lived those few weeks in the spring constantly wet and chilled from the icy spray of the river. They never changed into dry clothes, believing that to do so would give them pneumonia. Instead, they chose to fall asleep sopping wet, awakening as miserable as when they had lain down. Rarely had he seen a river hog working past the age of forty.

He had already sent Skypilot and Moon Song ahead with Sam, along with the children. All would be cared for the next few days by his sister. She would not be pleased, but she would do her duty for a short time. She was, after all, living with her new husband in a house that Robert owned.

Most of Bay City and Saginaw would turn out to watch the river drive. Buggies and horses would line the rivers and creeks

277

waiting for the logs to roar down. Many of the townspeople would pack picnics. Sometimes they cheered a river hog from the banks for some especially heroic feat.

Yes, tomorrow would be a big day. They would break the logs loose from their frozen piles and watch their winter's harvest tumble into the water. He would set the wannigan and its occupants floating far behind the mass of logs, and he would ride his horse beside the riverbank, keeping an eye out for river pirates, helping shove logs away from getting hung up on the river's edge, and encouraging the men the best he could. Although he could hold his own with an axe or a saw, he had never mastered the art of balancing on the logs well enough to ride the rough waters of the river drive. He admired the brave men who did.

Soon, if everything went well, the season would be over. The logs would be delivered, and everyone would leave. It was a strange sort of life. Men lived and worked together, shared their stories and the details of their lives, learned the cadence of each other's snores, fought one another over the most trivial of things out of sheer boredom, and protected one another with their lives. They became a sort of supportive, brawling family—and then at winter's end, they parted ways, often never to see one another again.

He was used to it, but saying good-bye to Katie was another thing altogether. How could he leave her to just fend for herself? And yet he had no right to look out for her once they reached Bay City. She wasn't his sister, and she wasn't his wife. He didn't think she could initiate a divorce from Michigan since she didn't even have a permanent address in the state. And there was always the chance that doing such a thing might draw Harlan back—which could be dangerous. But it was her choice—not his. She had no ties to him at all. She had the right to disappear from his life completely. He had overheard her talking to Jigger about the new camps springing up in Wisconsin.

He couldn't ask any more of her. She had fulfilled her responsibility to him and the men. She was free to go where she wished.

And it would break his heart.

The thought of the vacuum her absence in his life would cause
was overwhelming. Not only for himself but for his children.
They, too, had grown to love her. How would they feel when
she walked away? And how would they get over the loss of Ned,
who had become as close as a brother?

He was good at solving problems. He could cipher out numbers better than most, and he had once been able to make split-
second life-or-death decisions during surgery. But this was one
problem for which he had no answer.

27

With tree-tops, logs, and ice piled high
while wild the waters roll,
every year the "old" Cass claimed
a driver for her toll.
   "The Old Cass"—1800s shanty song

April 6, 1868

As Katie feverishly prepared enough food for the ravenous appetites of the river drivers, she noticed Robert riding along the riverbank. It was a unique experience cooking on this crude flat boat. She was half afraid she would accidentally set the boat on fire and have to jump overboard, but all in all, cooking on a wannigan wasn't a bad experience. After being cooped up in the cook shanty for most of the past seven months, it was a feast for her eyes to watch the ever-changing scenery.

But the best part was getting to watch Robert as he worked. Sometimes he rode ahead to check on the men, sometimes he had to ride further inland to cross some small tributary or to avoid a steep embankment, sometimes he waded into the water to dislodge a log that had gotten hung up.

These few months of working with this good, fair man had been the pinnacle of her life. And so, as she kneaded bread, her fingers so familiar with the task that she barely had to think, she memorized every angle of his face, every line of his body, and allowed herself to grieve the life with him she could not have.

The river, for as far as the eye could see, looked as though it were made entirely out of wood. The thousands of logs sounded like pleasant thunder as they bumped against one another. Men in steel-caulked boots walked from one side of the river to the other across this tapestry of moving logs, almost as easily as she had once traversed the rough floorboards of the cookhouse. Other camps were driving their logs to market also.

The river was so full of pine logs that when she drew up water for cooking, it carried with it the scent and taste of pine.

A mosquito landed on her arm, and she smacked it before it could draw blood. Jigger said they were lucky this year to only be dealing with a few of the things buzzing around, instead of the clouds of them he had seen following river hogs during especially wet springs. Before they left, Jigger had prepared jars of yellow birch bark and sassafras root tea with which to dose anyone who might come down with the ague during the drive.

Some of the younger river drivers, with their cut-off "stagged" pants, would show off sometimes—birling the log beneath their feet until it was a blur every time they saw her looking at them. Jigger called the most skilled of the river hogs "catty men" because they were cat-like in their ability to leap around on the logs without falling in. He told her that good catty men boasted they could throw a bar of yellow soap into the river and ride the bubbles to shore.

She was thoroughly enjoying the show until at one bend in the river she noticed something odd as they passed close to the riverbank.

"There's a pair of boots tied up in the branches of that tree," she pointed out to Jigger, who was slicing potatoes. "Why in the world would someone go off and leave a perfectly good pair of caulked boots hanging up in a tree?"

281

He craned his neck as they floated past. "Guess the river got another one."

"Another what?"

He kept his eyes down as he finished the potatoes. "Another driver."

"What are you talking about?"

"I was hoping you wouldn't ask."

"Well, I'm asking now. Why are someone's boots hanging from that tree?"

"That's the only headstone most of these shanty boys will ever get."

"What!"

He sighed. "When a river driver falls in with all them logs grinding above him, he don't stand much of a chance of surviving. If his buddies find his body—and they don't always—they take his boots and hang 'em up so's others will know and pay their respects. If they got a few minutes, they'll carve his name in the tree after they bury him on the riverbank."

"Were those boots from any of our crew?"

"Nope. Not yet. At least not that I've heard."

"Does this happen often?"

He tossed a dollop of lard into the skillet. "Often enough."

An hour later, she saw another pair of caulked boots in a tree. From that moment on, she made it a point to never be caught watching any of the boys dancing about on the logs—their lives were dangerous enough without showing off for her.

———⟡———

The river was not as high and deep as Robert would have liked. The logs crowded together, bumping and complaining, at various narrow places. The only thing keeping the mass of timber from turning into a jam was the expertise and daring of the river hogs. As they worked atop of the floating logs with their long jam-pikes, or as they stood in icy water at the edge to help shove the pine along, the men were masters at keeping the river clear. So far, so good. Only a few more miles and they would reach the mouth of the bay.

And then he heard shouts up ahead and saw that the wooden river was slowing down. The few inches of water visible between the logs began to close up. Logs pushed against one another as though they were living things. Sick at heart, he urged his horse forward, toward what he knew was a logjam.

Half a mile later, he arrived at a place where river hogs were working frantically to free a jam. The logs had become intertwined as they made their way through a narrow place in the river.

"Someone put in a sinker," Ernie shouted over the sound of grinding timber. "I saw it, but I couldn't get to it in time."

"You'd think the other camps would know better than to put hardwood in with the pine."

"Some people are idiots."

More river drivers were arriving by the minute. A logjam was the most dangerous occurrence that could happen to a camp, next to wildfire. Several were working along the edges, trying to keep as much as possible from backing up. Ernie and one other river driver were directly in the center.

Robert knew the black-haired river driver working alongside Ernie. He had a red handkerchief knotted around his forehead and was as graceful as a deer. His name was Leaping Fox and he worked for another company. Robert was relieved to see him there. Indian drivers, in general, were reputed to be the most skilled and sure-footed of all. They liked to work a few weeks, make three times the money of a regular logger, and live on that income for the rest of the year. He'd watched Leaping Fox the year before, and the man was the best river driver he'd ever seen.

"Be careful, Ernie!" Cletus became more and more agitated

as he watched his brother. Although competent with an axe, Cletus was not a particularly good river hog, which was why Robert had him working only the edges of the river.

Of everything Robert had to do in regards to lumbering, this was the part he despised—watching good men risking their lives to break a dam. But there was no choice.

As Leaping Fox and Ernie probed the logs, trying to find the one that would unlock this mess, he prayed that they would not get crushed by a wall of dripping logs.

He glanced at Cletus, who was nervously rubbing a small wooden beaver against his cheek as he watched Ernie and Leaping Fox prying out a large log that had managed to get crosswise of the others.

And then the sinker that had started this mess was extricated, and Robert held his breath, knowing that the next few seconds could mean the difference between life and death, especially for Ernie and Leaping Fox, as the men ran for the bank on tipping, spinning logs.

Ernie almost lost his balance at one point, teetered for a heart-stopping second, regained it and began to run again, his caulked boots digging into the bark. Leaping Fox ran toward the shore too, leaping from log to log, as sure-footed as a cat, his legs as strong as steel springs. And yet, even the fastest, strongest river man was no match against the freak nature of a breaking logjam.

Slick, wet logs were their only bridge to safety as the two men and the others ran for the safety of shore.

They had almost made it when Ernie tripped. Robert watched, helpless, as Ernie lost his battle against gravity. As his head disappeared beneath the bobbing logs, Cletus began to jump up and down and cry.

Leaping Fox, safe, fell facedown onto the shore. Ernie had been close enough to shore that there was a chance he might survive if he could get out quickly enough. But as the almost solid mass of logs shoved their way down the river, directly above Ernie's submerged body, Robert knew the chance of him surviving was slim.

Then he saw a hand grasp a log, and Ernie's head reappeared, but the man was obviously in deep trouble. Blood streamed from a gash in his head, and he seemed too weak to do anything except hang on. The possibility of being crushed to death was great.

The force of water, once the dam had been broken, propelled the wooden river of logs forward at a breakneck speed. Robert ran alongside, watching that one lone hand clinging to the log, praying Ernie wouldn't disappear.

Even though he was not as skilled a river driver as others, Robert was preparing to leap out onto the logs to try to save Ernie's life when he saw Ernie manage to grab onto a sturdy, overhanging branch. He used it to pull himself back up onto the log to which he had been clinging. Half holding onto the branch with one hand, and half using the logs as a moving bridge, he unsteadily worked his way from log to log until he had reached shore. Robert saw that he was holding his other arm close to his body, as though something was wrong with it.

Together, Robert and Cletus helped Ernie climb up a slick embankment and collapse on level, dry ground. He was so limp by this time that he could not stand alone.

His head was bloodied, and the arm Robert had seen him favoring was broken in two places.

The other river drivers, including Leaping Fox, had disappeared, continuing to herd the timber that only minutes before had made up the logjam.

"You shouldn't a' done it." Cletus fell to his knees beside his brother. "You shouldn't a' gone out there in the middle."

"I'm fine, Cletus." Ernie, dripping wet, cold, and barely

conscious, reached out with his good hand and weakly patted his brother on the leg. "You can stop crying now."

Robert glanced up just in time to see the wannigan, far behind the bulk of the logs, float by. Katie rushed to the side of the boat.

"Is Ernie all right?" she shouted as the boat moved past.

Robert cupped his hands around his mouth and yelled back. "Yes!"

He looked down at the injured man. The arm could be set. Ernie would live. Cletus wouldn't have to face life without his brother.

Was cutting the timber worth it? Worth the danger and the sacrifice? Worth the deaths that everyone knew would take place during the river drive? Was it worth the accidents that happened out in the woods when the giant pines took their own revenge on the puny men trying to destroy them?

At this moment, he doubted it. And yet he knew that if he didn't take the timber out, someone else would, someone less careful of the men, someone less honest who would try to cheat them out of their wages. Regardless of whether he stayed in the logging business or not—the loggers and axe men and swampers and road monkeys and teamsters would continue to pour into the Saginaw Valley to mine the green gold that was putting Michigan on the map.

28

When navigation opens
and the waters run so free
we'll drive our logs to Saginaw
then haste our girls to see.

"Once More A-Lumbering
Go"—1800s shanty song

April 14, 1868

There had been no more logjams, thank the Lord, but Robert's men had found and apprehended two nests of river pirates. He had helped capture one of them.

None of the river drivers who had drowned were men he knew or for whom he was responsible. For that, he was grateful.

Jigger and Katie had successfully put enough meals together while floating down the river to keep his men healthy. The harvest he had brought to Bay City was some of the best timber he had ever seen.

All things considered, Robert felt good as he surveyed the islands of "booms" floating in the bay with the "sorters" separating the logs according to their branding marks. From a distance, it resembled a rough carpet made of logs woven together.

He could have had a better year—the fire had taken a toll, as had Skypilot's accident—but it could have been much worse. He had made it through another year and it had not been easy.

Soon, he would head home to his family. His crew and Katie had been paid and Moon Song was also given something. If nothing else, the girl deserved a salary for taking care of Skypilot so faithfully. He hoped she would stick with Katie. The two women would be safer together.

He intended to invite Skypilot to spend the rest of the summer in his house. The man was able to walk again, but he was still weak, and as far as Robert knew, had nowhere else to go. His house was large enough to accommodate one more, and if his sister's husband didn't like it—that would be his problem.

He didn't know what he was going to do with Jigger. There was a shanty song, called "The Boardman River," that had always haunted him. The words often ran through his mind when he thought about his old friend.

> Where is the money I have earned?
> Not a dollar can I show.
> It is scattered to the four winds
> while in my rags I go.
> If there's anyone I pity,
> it's the man that's old and gray,
> that must face the storms of winter
> to earn his bread each day.

Jigger was the only one Inkslinger had been instructed *not* to pay. Robert knew that with a wad of cash in his pocket, the old man would only end up in an alley behind some saloon, stone broke and, if he was lucky—still alive.

At the moment, Robert was avoiding Jigger's wrath over not being handed his pay until he could figure out what to do with him. Unfortunately, he hadn't hidden himself away soon enough.

"Hey," Jigger yelled. "How come Inkslinger won't give me my pay?"

Robert knew he would have to do battle with the old fellow, but the last thing he wanted was to spend yet another summer trying to keep him from destroying himself.

"About that . . ."

Jigger didn't seem to be all that interested in what he had to say—the old cook seemed more interested in a folded newspaper he had tucked beneath his arm. He shook it open and pointed to an advertisement.

"Katie showed me this. It's for a place called the Western Health Reform Institute. Just got started last year. Looks like some people way over in Battle Creek is making other people eat something called 'graham' crackers. I think I'm gonna head on out there and help them out. Imagine making people eat nothin' but a bunch of little bitty crackers and being charged big money for it. I bet if they were to have a *real* cook show up—someone what knows how to cook up plenty of beans and fatback—those people would think they was in heaven."

Robert wished he could be a fly on the wall when Jigger showed up at the health institute. "No doubt."

"Says here they're looking for someone they want to train to cook veg-e-tar-ian." He looked up at Robert. "I don't know what that is, but I bet I could figure it out. I learned a bunch from Katie and I'm a big enough man to admit it." He poked his chest with a thumb. "I learned *her* a few things too."

"So, you're wanting to go out to Battle Creek, then?"

"Yeah." Jigger lowered his voice. "But you'd better not give me no money yet. These saloon keepers will suck the blood right out of a man—and take his payroll while they're at it. What I want is some new clothes, a train ticket, and for you to send me my pay after I get myself out there."

"I'll be happy to, Jigger."

"You mean you don't mind?"

"Not at all."

"If they make me head cook, I might not be back this winter."

"We'll struggle along the best we can."

Jigger stared at the advertisement. "Wonder what veg-e-tar-ian is, anyway?"

Robert tried to keep the smile out of his voice. "Go get fitted for a new suit of clothes. I'll be along in a bit to pay for them. My treat."

"Thanks, boss."

Robert watched as his old friend walked jauntily down the street and into a store that stocked men's suits. He wondered if Jigger had missed the wording about the Institute being a temperance organization as well. If so—he wasn't going to be the one pointing it out to him.

Either this would be the salvation of Jigger, or Katie was getting a quiet revenge for everything Jigger had put her through at the beginning of the season. For now, he was just happy that Jigger had a destination in mind other than the saloons of Bay City.

Tinker had disappeared as soon as he had gotten paid, without a word to anyone. Sam would probably be broke within the month, but his mules were being cared for down at the livery, and when he sobered up, he would likely get some work hauling for the sawmills to tide him over until fall. Cletus and Ernie were headed back home to southern Michigan, their money safely stashed away, ready to hand it over to parents who were hoping to purchase more acreage for a family farm.

Inkslinger was taking Katie's cow back to his farm as a gift for his daughters and wife. The pig and chickens had been slaughtered right before the river drive to provide much-needed energy during the intense days.

Orange cat had bolted for the woods the minute Katie tried to coax it onto the wannigan. Robert could have told her there was no way that cat was going to tamely float down the river.

He was certain it was capable of taking care of itself in the woods, but still, he left the door ajar on the abandoned cook shanty before he left, in case it ever needed shelter.

They would not be coming back to that camp. He had logged all that he intended from that section of timber. The log buildings would eventually go back to the earth from which they had sprung.

Blackie, at his wife's prodding, had signed the temperance pledge right before coming out to the lumber camps. A man of his word, he had pocketed his money and caught a train home. Henri and two of his friends from Canada had already left for Ontario, their red sashes still jauntily wrapped around their middles—albeit, much worse for wear.

Bay City would enjoy several weeks of wild prosperity as hundreds of shanty boys from all over the Saginaw Valley descended on the various entertainments the town offered—throwing their payrolls around in one glorious, ill-conceived splurge. They were young men, most of them. If they survived a few seasons, they would get a little more sense when they came out of the woods.

It was Katie he was worried about. Where would she go? Would she stay in Bay City? Did he even *want* her in Bay City? Would he be able to stay away from her if she settled there?

He hated being in this no-man's-land of loving her and being unable to do anything about it. A lesser man and a lesser woman would throw morality to the wind—but neither of them was made like that. There were children involved, for one thing. It was either a legal marriage for them, or nothing. For now, it appeared that it would have to be nothing.

Robert decided it was time to go look up Charlie. He wanted to see the timber-looker's big discovery. Perhaps it would help take his mind off Katie.

29

But now the winter's ended,
and homeward we are bound;
and in this cursed country
no longer we'll be found.

"Michigan I.O."
—1800s shanty song

April 16, 1868

There was a stir down at the bay that drew Katie's attention. It appeared that something was being dragged from the water. A knot of people had formed. One man walked away and vomited in the bushes.

Was it the body of one of the river drivers? She hoped not, even though that seemed to be part of the expected price of bringing the logs to market. She didn't want to know what the people had found in the water. Shopping to replace Ned's outgrown clothing was her objective right now.

She was admiring a pair of shoes in a display window when someone touched her on the shoulder. It was Jigger, but she hardly recognized him. He was all dressed up in a new suit with a high, starched collar. His face was inscrutable.

"You look wonderful, Jigger," she teased. "Are you getting married?"

"Begging your pardon, ma'am." He pulled a new black derby hat off of his head and turned it around and around in his hands. "I think there's something you'd better come have a look at."

Begging your pardon, ma'am? She had never heard that phrase come out of Jigger's mouth during the entire seven months she had worked beside him.

Her day began its slow collapse as he led her toward the small crowd of townspeople down at the bay. When they began to open up a path for her, she knew she was about to see something terrible.

Yes. Someone had drowned. She stared at the soles of the man's boots. She didn't want to look any higher, but her eyes crept upward against her will. The pants were a water-darkened gray. The long coat was decorated with a double row of brass buttons—an eagle was embossed on each one.

It was the uniform of a Confederate soldier.

And then her eyes caught the face and blond hair of the man who had made her life a living nightmare for so long. A long wound across his neck explained the reason for his death.

Slowly, slowly, with Jigger loyally standing beside her, his good arm around her waist to help support her, she realized that Harlan Calloway was no longer a threat to her or anyone. A great, yawning emptiness filled her heart where sorrow should have been.

"Who've we got here?" The sheriff pushed his way through the crowd. "Anyone know this fellow?"

"It's my husband, Harlan Calloway," Katie said. "He's been missing for several months."

The sheriff looked her up and down. "Robert Foster came to talk to me back in January about the husband of his camp cook. Wanted me to be on the lookout for the man. Are you her?"

"Yes."

"When was the last time you saw him?"

"The day after Christmas, when he left the camp."

"Did he have any money on him?"

"A small sack of silver coins."

He gingerly searched Harlan's pockets and came up empty. "Looks like it was a robbery." The sheriff, who was known more for his affection for his luxurious handlebar mustache than his enthusiasm for fighting crime, sounded relieved to have an easy answer for Harlan's death. "Bay City is attracting some seedy characters since the railroad came in. With the water so cold, I can't even guess how long he's been dead, but the man who did this is probably long gone by now. What do you want me to do with him, Mrs. Calloway?"

━⟨ഗ⟩━

Those members of Robert's crew who were still in town swore to the sheriff that no one had left the camp that night except Harlan. They also swore that none of them had murdered the man, although some admitted that they would have liked to—what with him threatening their little cook and all.

The sheriff, with no eyewitness or any evidence, was relieved to chalk this up to yet another mysterious killing. There was a lot of that going around. Especially when the shanty boys came to town. Unclaimed bodies showed up in the bay on an almost regular basis—usually near the mouth of the tunnels beneath the building known as the Catacombs.

The death of a Confederate soldier was not something the sheriff had any intention of seriously investigating. Feelings about the war were still too raw. There were at least a hundred veterans in the county who could conceivably be considered suspects.

The sheriff was the kind of man who didn't like to rock the boat. He kept law and order as much as possible—without actually upsetting anyone in power—and he left the shanty boys alone when they came into town. A man could get himself killed

294

getting in the way of a wild-eyed logger fresh from the woods bent on having a good time.

He made certain the death certificate was filled out as "unknown causes."

───◦◦◦───

If there was one thing Katie knew, it was how to do her duty.

Right now her duty was to take her husband's body back to his home in Georgia. Regardless of his actions toward her, taking him to lie in the cemetery alongside four generations of Calloways was the right thing to do.

It occurred to her, as she sat with Ned on the train, looking out at the bustling town of Bay City, that this was where her adventure had begun seven months ago as she had crawled off the train, ragged, fearful, and desperate.

Today, thanks to Robert Foster and his men—and in no small measure thanks to the tender mercies of God—she had money in the bank, new clothes on her back, and a shiny new valise with everything she needed to make the train trip all the way back to Georgia.

Still, she was disappointed that Robert had left, reportedly checking out the stand of pine that the timber-looker had found. It would have been helpful to discuss Harlan's mysterious death with him and see if he could help her figure out how this had happened.

It bothered her that the sheriff had not investigated more thoroughly. It could have been anyone—even someone she cared about. The only person she knew absolutely for certain had not killed Harlan was herself.

───◦◦◦───

"Hey, Foster!" The sound of a woman's raucous voice behind him made him jump. "You're letting her leave without you?"

It was Delia, looking older and more ravaged than ever.

"What are you talking about?" He had just arrived back in town after checking out Charlie's discovery and was dirty, hungry, and bone-tired. All he wanted to do was go home, eat a good meal, take a bath, and see his kids. Then he wanted to find Katie and . . . well, he didn't know what he wanted to do about Katie. He just wanted to see her. That's all. He missed her friendship, if nothing else.

"She's taking her husband's body back to Georgia," Delia said.

"What?" he exploded. "What are you talking about, woman?"

"They found him in the bay. Our overpaid sheriff listed it as death by unknown causes, but I think a knife might have had just a leetle something to do with it." She held two fingers a quarter-inch apart.

Robert couldn't believe what he was hearing. Was Delia lying? She enjoyed playing with people. He'd seen her do it before.

"Is Katie coming back?"

Delia pouted prettily, which was grotesque on a woman her age. "How should I know?"

"Who did it?"

"You mean you don't know?"

"Of course I don't know! I've been gone for days!"

Delia snorted. "Let me buy a stake in that new pinery I hear you just checked out—and I'll tell you all kinds of things you need to know."

"I don't have time for games, Delia."

"Neither do I." She sobered. "That was a serious offer. I want to get out of the business, Foster, and you're the only camp owner I trust."

"No."

"I'm a good businesswoman." She touched her mouth where a front tooth was newly missing, and he saw that beneath the heavy makeup was the yellowing skin of healing bruises. "But I'm in the wrong business. I have been for a long time."

There was something about the tone of her voice, the regret he heard there, that surprised him.

As she continued to list reasons it would be to his advantage to take her on as his business partner, her voice faded away, and the strangest thought came over him—how Rahab the harlot had been included in Jesus's lineage.

He was not a man given to seeing religious signs—but he felt strongly as though God was nudging him to give this broken, sinful woman a chance.

From a business perspective, Delia had one thing going for her—she definitely knew shanty boys and could be quite the judge of character. And the woman was shrewd, even if he had no respect for the occupation she had chosen.

"All right."

Delia stopped in mid-sentence. "What do you mean—all right?"

"I could use someone in town who could order quality supplies for me while keeping the costs down. I could take care of the logging camp operation and you could keep an eye on things here in town."

He saw hope dawning in her eyes.

"I'd be good at that," she said eagerly.

There was something in the ragged hope he saw in the woman's face that made him think she was truly serious about wanting to change her life—and actually, he really *did* need someone watching after his business here in town. Could he trust her? He had no idea—but his instincts told him that he could. He lowered his voice. "That pinery Charlie found is really something, Delia."

"How much?"

"More than I made on this year's crop. I'd like to buy all of it, but I can only swing a couple sections."

"I've been saving up." The eagerness in her voice was genuine. "I been praying for something I could do to get out of the business."

Praying? Who would have guessed? Not him. The thought shook him. How many other people had he dismissed as being too far gone to even think about God?

"I'm meeting with Charlie in a couple hours. You're welcome to come along if you want."

"Oh, I'd like that."

He noticed that she stood a little straighter than when they had first begun their conversation, and her voice had lost its perpetual wheedling sound.

"But first, I have some information you're going to need." Delia pulled a piece of paper out of her purse. "That redheaded cook of yours had the decency to treat me like a regular person back in October. I ran into her at the embalmer's yesterday and she told me what had happened to her husband. I figured you might be interested in where she was going, so I wrote her address down. You're a fool if you don't go to Georgia and bring her back."

Robert gratefully took the slip of paper. "Why do you care so much?"

Delia drew herself up. "If I'm going to become a respectable businesswoman, I'll need a good friend like Katie Calloway in town."

30

With grub hoes, pries, and axes
we loosed the roots and stumps
and we filled up all the hollows
as we leveled down the lumps.

"Johnny Carroll's Camp"
—1800s shanty song

April 24, 1868

The one-room church building the Calloways had built on their property felt close and suffocating. Katie had almost forgotten how humid and hot Georgia could be, even in the spring. As the preacher droned on and on about Harlan's virtues, she kept her eyes straight ahead.

It was not an easy thing to do when she knew that every eye was focused on her. Not the casket, not the preacher, just her. It felt as though the back of her head was in danger of catching fire from the stares she knew were aimed at her—the Northern woman who had the arrogance to abandon a Calloway. She was the woman who had not had the decency to stay and rebuild the plantation that her husband's family had labored upon for generations.

Oh yes, she was an evil one, she was.

There was nothing she could do about it. If she kept silent, they despised her. If she opened her mouth and tried to explain the kind of person Harlan was, they would despise her even more. The genteel, lost culture of the South, exemplified in the well-manicured plantations, had rested on the shoulders of men like Harlan—boys raised to believe that their needs, their desires, their wants, had more weight than those of other mortals. It was a myth that was perpetuated from parent to son, until most believed it without question—except for the slaves who had labored beneath the misbegotten myth and some of the mistreated wives who had silently endured.

Now destitute, the people of Harlan's county still clung to the memory of a chivalrous South and sweet abundance, all the things that Harlan Calloway had once represented. There were so few young men left. So few to start over again and rebuild. So few who could bring back a semblance of the vision that had once been Georgia aristocracy.

It was all bunk, of course. Harlan was no one to hang one's hopes on. She had, to her own detriment, done exactly that at one time. The only thing she could do *now* was endure the stares. And then, her duty done, she could go home.

Funny, when she thought of home, it was no longer Pennsylvania where she was born and raised. Instead, it was the wild, windswept wilderness of Michigan with its lakes and scent of pine and the raw exuberance and heroism of those rough-and-tumble shanty boys.

And Robert. If she went back, would he want her?

The service finally ended. A procession of mourners walked to the private cemetery where generations of Calloways resided. Most of the people in the procession were women. After living in the all-male lumber camp, there seemed to be an astonishing lack of men here.

She and Ned were at the head of the black-clad assembly, directly behind the preacher. The preacher was yet another soldier—one who walked up the small rise with much effort and a pronounced limp. She knew him. He had fought on the side of slavery—a dedicated Christian man who had felt justified in shooting at other dedicated Christian men—like her father.

That was the part she would never, ever understand . . . how Christians had believed it to be appropriate to go to war against other Christians—ripping apart the fabric of the nation, destroying entire families and cutting down the leadership of too many fine churches.

The service at the graveside was interminable. Many women, their grief still fresh over their own sons and husbands, openly sobbed. Katie felt tears fill her own eyes—both for the terrible waste of her husband's life and the pain and devastation she saw in the ravaged land and in the haunted eyes of the women.

When she thought she couldn't bear one more minute, the last amen was said and the mourners began to disperse slowly, almost reluctantly. She guessed that there weren't many social activities anymore. The days of large parties were over for now.

She felt almost embarrassed that she was wearing new widow's weeds purchased back in Michigan. Women who had once been noted for the extravagance of their wardrobe now donned worn and discreetly patched clothing. They watched her with narrowed eyes.

She had never had a close friend while she lived here. She had not been allowed to leave the plantation alone. Harlan had informed her that women of her standing did not go about the countryside by themselves.

She soon found out that most plantation wives were as trapped as the slaves who served them. Her only friend while she had lived here was her maid, Violet.

The quiet animosity with which she was being treated now made her long for a friendly face. She wondered where Mose and Violet were now. Had they moved to Canada as Mose had mentioned? Wherever they were, she wished them well.

One bright spot was Carrie Sherwood and her fiancé. She and Carrie had never been close, but she liked the woman and was happy she had dodged a lifetime with Harlan—even if she was unaware that had ever been his intent.

A man she vaguely remembered to be Harlan's solicitor approached her after the others had left. She stiffened, fearful that there would be something else she was expected to do.

"My name is Elias Jones." He bowed with gentlemanly courtliness. "May we talk in private, Mrs. Calloway?"

At least he spoke to her civilly. The first one so far today who had not had thinly veiled contempt in his voice. She supposed, as an attorney, he was used to hiding his feelings. Still, her heart fell at the seriousness of his voice.

"Of course." She glanced at her brother. This sounded like talk intended only for her ears. "Ned, why don't you go down and play by the creek for a bit."

Mr. Jones took her by the elbow and led her to a small bench. It was one that Harlan's mother had had built so she could be comfortable while visiting her husband's grave. Katie was certain she would never again need it.

Sitting down beside her, Mr. Jones extricated an official-looking envelope from his suit coat pocket.

"I hope you haven't brought me bad news," she said.

"I suppose that's up to you to decide. Were you aware that your husband had a will?"

"No."

"Did you know that he left Fallen Oaks to you in that will?"

Katie blinked in surprise. "That's not possible."

"Actually, it is quite possible."

"Harlan said the plantation would go to his oldest male relative, Fenton Calloway. Isn't that what usually happens to family property around here?"

"Usually."

"Why would Harlan leave it to me?"

"The will was dated a few days before he left for war. I was the one who drew it up. I remember specifically that when he came into my office, he was incensed over something Fenton had done—or not done. Your husband could sometimes be quite . . . volatile. But at the time, he had decided he would rather you have it than his cousin."

Katie had never expected nor wanted the responsibility of the land that Harlan and his family had worshipped.

"Fenton will surely contest this will. I certainly won't object if he does."

"Fenton fell at Gettysburg, Mrs. Calloway."

"Oh."

She thought that over.

"But what am I to do with an overgrown plantation? I'm no farmer."

"One thing you cannot do is sell it. He insisted that I write the will in such a way that you cannot sell it during your lifetime. Upon your death, assuming you have not left a will of your own, it will revert to one of the blood relatives."

"Can I give it to one of them?"

A strange expression passed over the solicitor's face. "Forgive me, madam, but do you mind if I ask you why you ran away from your husband?"

"You can ask, but after the glowing eulogy the preacher gave, you won't believe it."

"Try me."

"Harlan was a cruel man." Katie took a deep breath. "He hid it well, but those of us who were his victims knew the truth."

Elias Jones tapped the will against his knee. "I always suspected. As you said, he learned to cover it well, but that cruelty was in his eyes when he made that will disinheriting Fenton, a much better man than himself. Fortunately, at that moment, he was angrier with his cousin than with you."

"Why didn't he change it after I left?"

"Harlan didn't come to town often after that, and frankly, I deliberately avoided him. His behavior became very erratic after the war and he seemed to fall into a steady decline. I'm surprised he sobered up long enough to follow you north."

"Won't the other Calloway cousins contest the will?"

"Probably, but I'm a very good lawyer. I made absolutely certain it was ironclad. Fallen Oaks belongs to you. Except you cannot sell it or give it away."

"Can I leave and let it grow into brush and brambles?"

"I suppose you could. Or you could stay there. The cabin where Harlan lived is habitable after a fashion. You might consider renting it out. There are quite a few sharecroppers now, former slaves who work the land as they did before, giving their former masters a portion of their earnings as rent."

"How many acres are left?" she asked. "Did Harlan sell any more than the section by the river?"

"As far as I know, there are approximately eight hundred acres. It seems a shame to let the soil go to waste when there is such a need for food in this country—and so few able-bodied enough to raise it."

"Are you suggesting I take up the plow, sir?" she asked.

"No. I'm suggesting you find someone willing to do so." He handed the will to her. "Or you can let it grow into brush and brambles and forget all about it. Of course, you realize you will be expected to pay taxes. Fortunately, as far as taxes go, the land is now valued at less than half its prewar value."

"I can't sell it. I can't work it. I don't care if I ever see it again. But I'm responsible for it." Katie creased and re-creased the stiff paper. "It appears that I will have this albatross around my neck for the rest of my life."

"There are many people who would not consider the ownership of eight hundred rich, bottomland acres an albatross."

Her fit of annoyance left her. He was right. Even though it was Calloway land and held too many bad memories to count, would the Lord want her to allow it to lay fallow when so many people were trying to survive on so little?

She knew what hunger felt like and she hated the idea of innocent people having to endure it—especially the elderly and children.

"You have given me a great deal to think about, Mr. Jones, and I thank you for your kindness."

"There is one more thing, Mrs. Calloway."

"Oh?" She wasn't certain she wanted any more surprises.

"Very little gets past me in this county. I know that the reason your husband was able to find you was through your connection to Violet."

"That's true."

"Did you know that Mose and Violet have married and are living at Mrs. Hammond's?"

"I wasn't certain they were still there. I would love to see them again."

"I believe that could be arranged. Mrs. Hammond passed away three weeks ago. Unfortunately, even though Violet nursed her faithfully during her last illness, Mrs. Hammond's son is planning on turning Mose and Violet out soon."

"I hate to hear that."

"It is especially unfair since Mose has already finished the plowing and planting of Mrs. Hammond's farm this spring."

"Are you trying to suggest something, Mr. Jones?"

For the first time since they had begun their conversation, Mr. Jones smiled, and it was a smile worth seeing. His heart and soul was in that smile, and she saw for the first time that the elderly solicitor was an exceptionally kind man.

"Very few people know this, Mrs. Calloway, and I would appreciate it if you kept this between the two of us, but I have been an abolitionist at heart my entire life. There was little I could do about it before the war, and I was too old when it broke out to enlist. But in many small quiet ways I have done what I could." His eyes twinkled. "I have to admit, as I sat through the eulogy, it occurred to me that there would be an ironic justice to a freed slave making a living off land his master once owned."

The idea he proposed shimmered before her, silvery with justice. Mose and Violet would have the skill and the heart to turn the humble foreman's cottage into a haven. They had all the knowledge it would take to farm the rich soil.

She did not want rent. She didn't want to sharecrop. It would be her gift to Violet and Mose—her friends and fellow sufferers, to see what they could do with the place.

And yet . . .

"Wouldn't an arrangement like you're suggesting cause problems for Mose and Violet?" she asked. "I don't believe the white community would accept such a thing."

"Oh, Mrs. Calloway," Mr. Jones said with a chuckle. "Of course most of the white community wouldn't accept it. But as your solicitor, and the extremely respectable representative of the Calloway family, I would be most happy to oversee your . . . employees. I don't see how the financial arrangements you and I choose to work out for Mose and Violet are anyone else's business."

Katie felt a warmth and joy spreading through her body at the brilliant simplicity and rightness of this good man's plan.

"Mr. Jones, would you care to accompany me, as my solicitor and representative, to visit the Hammond place? I believe it would be quite useful to have you along when I go check on my future . . . sharecroppers."

"Mrs. Calloway, it would be my honor and delight."

⸺◌◌⸺

Even after his conversation with Delia, it was not easy for Robert to extricate himself from Bay City. He had books to balance, business to attend to, and children to reassure. He had to ease Charlie over the hump of accepting the idea of Delia as his business partner—as well as getting through the unenviable task of breaking it to his sister.

He also needed to get Skypilot settled and make certain Moon Song had temporary food and shelter beneath his roof. He had begged his sister to take care of his menagerie of people for yet a while longer. Fortunately, she seemed to be so pleased with her new husband, the butcher, that there was a softness and happiness about her that he had never seen before. He even liked the butcher, a smallish man with worried eyes—not at all the red-faced oaf he had envisioned.

Going to Georgia was not an easy excursion. He might be gone for weeks or months, time he really should be using to build a new lumber camp—farther to the west—a stand of pine so glorious that if they got a nice, cold winter, and if there was a good thaw in the spring, and if he managed to find a good camp cook, and if there were no major accidents along the way—it might just make him rich enough in a few years that he wouldn't have to keep lumbering forever. Some men loved the work. He did not.

Frustrated beyond endurance by the delay, he took a leap of faith, dropped a load of business details into Delia's lap, and hopped the southbound train from Bay City. He had no idea where Katie would go after the funeral, and he was afraid he would lose his chance to find her again if she and Ned left the area before he got there.

If he lost them, it would be more than he could endure. His dreams and thoughts had been consumed by Katie ever since he learned that she was finally, truly free.

307

—⟨◊⟩—

Violet was one of the loveliest women Katie had ever known. Two years older, she had become more like a big sister than a servant. They had giggled together, tried different hairstyles together, and when Katie had begun teaching Violet how to read and write it had been almost a form of play to her. Katie, being from the North, had not fully realized the ramifications of what she was doing.

When Harlan had discovered her teaching Violet, he had forbidden her to do so. But she had very cautiously, and discreetly, disobeyed him.

Now, after all she had been through, after all they had been through together, she was almost overwhelmed by the joy of seeing her friend once again.

Mose was hoeing a small vegetable garden and Violet was drawing water from a well. Neither of them saw her at first as she walked up the long lane of the Hammond farm.

She had asked Mr. Jones and Ned to stay in the buggy for a few minutes so that she could greet her friends alone. It was a selfish act on her part, but she wanted the freedom to hug Violet and weep if she wanted—without any audience except Mose, who would understand.

Mose and Violet, from whom so much had been taken, were going to be given a chance at a better life, a secure life, a life where they could fully enjoy the fruits of their own labor. She couldn't wait to see what they could accomplish together.

31

While round a good campfire at night
we'll sing while wild winds blow,
and we'll range the wild woods over,
and once more a-lumbering go.
    "Once More A-Lumbering Go"
        —1800s shanty song

April 30, 1868

At the train station, Robert hired a horse from the livery and asked directions to Fallen Oaks. He assumed Katie would be living there, or at least staying there temporarily. It was his best hope of finding her.

His need to see her increased even more as he flew over the road, going as fast as he dared on the unfamiliar horse.

The lane to the plantation was deeply rutted and weeds grew over acres that he could tell had once been ripe with promise. A huge, burned-out shell of what appeared to have once been a handsome house sat atop a small rise.

So this was Sherman country. He had seen other examples of the General's handiwork as the train had wound its way through Georgia over repaired tracks that had been twisted into knots by Union troops.

In the distance he saw four figures following behind a great gray gelding pulling a plow. As he drew nearer, he saw that it was Katie, Ned, Mose, and a woman he didn't know. They stopped and watched him approach.

Even though there were other people around her, his eyes were only for her as he dismounted. Her hair had once again come undone from its bun. He vividly remembered the sight of it coming loose in straggles as she wound her way through each hard day—always with a triumphant smile on her lips as she brought a feast to the table.

She was dressed in a common work dress, the hem soiled from the red earth, her bare feet digging into the freshly turned soil. She had a bag slung around her neck filled with seed, and her face was damp with perspiration.

Robert had never seen a more beautiful woman.

She registered surprise when she saw him, then puzzlement. Ned started to run to him, but she stopped her brother with one hand.

"Are you lost, Mr. Foster?" she asked.

"No."

"You've traveled all this long way just to find me?"

"Yes, ma'am."

"You must surely be in dire need of a cook for this October."

"I am most definitely in need of a cook this October. Do you know of any who might be willing to come to Michigan?"

He was so close to her now that he could almost count the lashes fringing her beautiful blue eyes. The fact that there were three other people listening to every word didn't bother him in the slightest.

"I would have to think on it a while," she said.

"Don't think too long. I am in desperate need," he said. "Unfortunately, it has come to my attention that it isn't seemly for a woman to work in a lumber camp without a husband on hand. Shanty boys tend to fall in love with good cooks."

"They do, do they?" She put her hands on her hips and smiled.

"You need to know, as camp boss I've made a new rule at my camp." It wasn't the smooth proposal he had intended, but it was all he could think of at the moment. "I insist that anyone who cooks in my camp has to marry me."

"Oh, Robert, I'm so sorry." The regret in her voice made his heart plummet. Then she smiled mischievously. "But I'm not at all sure that Jigger will accept that proposal."

___ගෆ___

It was the oddest feeling having Robert beside her on Calloway property. They sat near the campfire Mose had built before he and Violet went to bed. This was where her old life had played itself out. Robert was part of the new life she had created up in Michigan. It seemed strange to have the two come together.

Until Mose could repair another cabin, she and Ned had been staying in two old army tents Elias Jones had found. She had insisted on Mose and Violet having Harlan's cabin. She never wanted to sleep in that place again. Every night so far, they had all enjoyed a campfire together after the day's planting was done.

The other slave cabin Mose had repaired housed the old house slave, Hannah, and her four-year-old grandson. They had taken Hannah in when they found her wandering around disoriented, trying to find her old cabin. It was the only home she had ever known. Once she got her bearings and some food, she became more lucid. As poor as it was, Hannah had never had any other home than the cabin where she now slept. Mose said he suspected there might be others wanting to come back too, now that Harlan was gone.

"Ned's asleep." Katie stroked the little boy's hair as he lay curled up beside her. "Now will you tell me what you know about who killed Harlan, and why you wouldn't tell me in front of Ned?"

"It was one of Delia's girls."

"You're not serious!"

"I'm dead serious. There was one who had red hair, looked a bit like you, and after what had happened in camp, Harlan was angry."

"Oh, that poor little thing!"

"Not so little. She was quite a lot bigger than you, according to Delia, and she had no patience with a man like Harlan. Evidently he finally met his match."

"Where is she now?"

"Delia said the girl headed out West carrying Harlan's money pouch."

Katie stared into the fire, absorbing the information. "So now we know."

"Yes, now we know."

"Harlan had everything a person could want." She threw a stick into the fire. "And yet he threw it all away."

"True, but I don't want to talk any more about Harlan right now if you don't mind." He cleared his throat and fidgeted with his collar. "Katie, I'm not a rich man. I'm not even comfortably off. Lumbering is always a gamble. I might make a lot this winter off the new section, or things could go haywire and I'll lose my shirt. There's enough left over right now to get me and my family through the summer, and just about enough left over to start another camp in another location. I don't have a whole lot to offer a woman."

"I don't care about that."

"A lot of women would."

"A lot of women don't realize how rare it is to find a good man."

"I'm not sure about good, but I can promise to love you until the day I die."

Katie went silent. There was one more secret that Robert didn't know, and she dreaded telling him.

She stared at the ground, not willing to look directly at him as she revealed the greatest wound of all. "I'm barren, Robert."

"How do you know?"

"Eight years of marriage. It was one of the many things Harlan grew to hate about me. Each month, when he found out that I wasn't with child—well, it was bad."

"He hurt you? For something you had no control over?"

"That was Harlan."

He stared into the fire, absorbing that information. She glanced at his profile as she waited, wondering if he would still want her in spite of her inability to give him children. The muscles in his jaw clenched as though in anger, and her heart sank. She stared down at the earth again, steeling herself for his rejection—now that he knew everything about her.

His silence seemed to go on for an eternity. She died a little, waiting for him to speak. Then he turned and with one finger lifted her chin.

"Look at me," he said.

She forced herself to look straight into his eyes.

"I'm sorry for your pain, Katie-girl," he said. "The fact that Harlan hurt you rips my heart apart."

He started to say more, stopped, and then abruptly stood and pulled her to her feet. "Take a walk with me."

"What about Ned?"

In answer, he lifted her little brother and carried him to the tent. She lifted the flap and watched as he tenderly tucked Ned beneath a light blanket, still sound asleep.

"*Now* take a walk with me."

He entwined his fingers with hers and led her to a more private spot beneath one of the giant magnolia trees that grew beside the barn. Its limbs spread above the split-rail fence surrounding the nearest pasture, where Rebel's Pride stood munching the rich grass.

It was the first time they had held hands, and she felt self-conscious about it as they walked toward the tree, but a bubble of pleasure rose within her at the intimate touch. She could feel her heartbeat throbbing against his palm.

Robert stopped when they were out of sight. She leaned against the rough bark of the tree as he gently bracketed her face with his hands.

At first, she thought he was going to kiss her and she was more than willing, but he stopped just inches from her nose. The moon was full and its light poured over his face. The love for her that she saw in his eyes nearly took her breath away.

"The way I see it, Katie-girl"—his voice was thick with emotion—"is that God has already seen fit to bless us with three little souls to raise. That's a whole lot more than some people ever get."

"You mean you don't mind?"

"I mind that it is a sorrow to you. But I'm proposing marriage because I need you by my side more than you can know. I want to laugh with you and talk with you and have you fuss at me for tracking mud across your kitchen."

He leaned closer. "I want to watch as you show Betsy how to make a pie, and I want to walk into church with you and our—yes, *our*, three children trailing along behind us. I want to wake every morning knowing that I'm going to sit at the kitchen table across from the most beautiful woman in the world while we plan our day." Robert's voice dropped to a whisper. "I love you more than my own life and I always will."

"You realize . . ." Katie felt a lump rising to her throat, but she had to get this out. "You realize that I will never again put up with bearing the brunt of a man's anger. If you ever raise a hand to me, I'll—I'll leave you. I will."

"Oh, Katie-girl." He sighed. "I could never hurt you."

"You say that now—but you have a temper, Robert Foster. I've seen it."

"I have a temper when someone I love is being abused." He tucked a stray curl behind her ear. "I have a temper when someone strong is picking on someone weaker. I can guarantee I'll get very upset if anyone ever tries to hurt you or one of the children. But hit you? Katie, I'd rather cut off my arm."

"Then we'll be all right."

For so many months, she had dreamt of running her fingers through his hair. She did so now, tentatively, smoothing her fingertips over silky hair. The lump in her throat grew and an enormous peace settled over her as she saw a future with this man blossoming into reality.

"It's finally going to be all right."

Robert took hold of her hand and slowly kissed each finger. "I've waited a long time for this moment, Katie Calloway." He smiled, and that smile warmed her all the way down to her toes. "If you don't have any more secrets you want to get off your chest or ultimatums you want to make—do you suppose a man could finally get a kiss?"

"I thought you would never ask."

His lips had barely touched hers when she heard a sound like a twig breaking. Startled, both of them turned to see what had made the noise.

Ned, barefoot and clad only in his nightshirt, stood near, rubbing the sleep out of his eyes.

"What are you doing?" the little boy asked.

"I'm trying to kiss your sister," Robert said solemnly.

"Does that mean you're going to marry her?"

"Just as soon as I possibly can."

Ned thought that over. "Does that mean Betsy and Thomas and me will be brothers and sister?"

"Kind of." Robert nodded.

Ned's voice got all shy. "And maybe—that means you'd kind of be like—my father?"

"Absolutely, and I'll do my best to be a good one—if you'll let me," Robert said. "I'd be proud to call a boy brave enough to take on a bully with nothing more than a pocketknife my son."

Ned broke into a run toward them. At first she thought he was headed toward her, but then she realized he was running straight to Robert, who stooped and swept the little boy up into his arms.

The moonlight glinted off tears on Ned's cheeks, and—were those tears on Robert's as well? Then she realized her own cheeks were wet, and she wiped them off with her sleeve as Ned clung to Robert's neck.

There would be time for kisses later. A lifetime of them. It was not every day that a person got to witness God putting so many broken pieces back together again. Betsy and Thomas needed a mother. Ned needed a father. She and Robert needed each other. By the grace of God, no matter what might come, they would make a safe harbor for the three children—and for each other.

Author's Note

Many years ago, while visiting a museum in Michigan, I saw an old photo of loggers gathered in front of a cook shanty. In the midst of these tough-looking men stood the camp cook— a sweet-faced young woman with her hands folded inside her apron. As my family wandered off, I stood mesmerized by the photo, wondering about the girl, wishing I knew her story, trying to imagine her life. That photo began my love affair with the history of Michigan lumbering and was the kernel from which this story grew.

As much as I personally grieve the destruction of the vast, ancient pine forests of Michigan, those brave old-time loggers, working with primitive tools, put their lives on the line to bring out the lumber with which our crippled country was rebuilt after the Civil War. I believe it's nearly impossible for most of us to fully comprehend the hardships they endured.

Acknowledgments

Much gratitude to Gary Leftwich for introducing our family to Hartwick Pines, the last remaining stand of virgin white pine in lower Michigan. Rob Burg, historian, for sharing his in-depth knowledge of lumbering. John Berry, magistrate, for unearthing an 1867 divorce transcript of an abused Georgia plantation wife. Dr. Aaron Ellis for medical information—any mistakes made are entirely mine. Sandra Bishop, literary agent, for being so good at opening doors. Most of all—eternal thanks to all who prayed my family through a difficult year. I am humbled by your love, tenacity, and faith. To God be all the glory, forever.

Serena Miller is the author of *Love Finds You in Sugarcreek, Ohio*, as well as numerous articles for periodicals such as *Woman's World*, *Guideposts*, *Reader's Digest*, *Focus on the Family*, *Christian Woman*, and more. She lives on a farm in southern Ohio.

Meet *Serena Miller* at
www.SerenaBMiller.com

Learn fun facts, read her journal,
and connect with Serena!

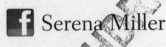 Serena Miller

Oct. - 2011